★ "Readers will appreciate the wide representation of
the African diaspora and will also take note of the multiplicities of
lived experiences, cultures, and gendered and sexual expression.
That the stories center Black girlhood creates layers of depth in these
racialized and gendered experiences alongside the joys and trivialities
of stories often missing from the mainstream. Luminous reading."

—*BOOKLIST*, starred review

★ "Absolutely stunning science fiction and fantasy in this collection
of short stories . . . The talented authors paint a vibrant visual album with
their words . . . Proud, resilient, loving and hopeful, this book gives
nuance and voice to a spectrum of truly wondrous Black experiences."

—*SHELF AWARENESS*, starred review

★ "Demonstrates the power, resiliency, and determination of the lead
female character . . . Each story is satisfying to read by itself, yet
more powerful when read together as there is an evenness in the narratives
which is not frequently found in most short story collections. Like the best
short stories, each jumps right into the action and character growth is
demonstrated quickly. There are twists and turns aplenty to be found between
the covers of this book. This is an outstanding collection, with an
evenness to its stories, unique characters, and a wide range of tales."

—*SLC*, starred review

A PHOENIX
FIRST MUST BURN

A PHOENIX FIRST MUST BURN

SIXTEEN STORIES OF BLACK GIRL MAGIC, RESISTANCE, AND HOPE

EDITED BY PATRICE CALDWELL

PENGUIN BOOKS

PENGUIN BOOKS
An imprint of Penguin Random House LLC, New York

First published in the United States of America by Viking,
an imprint of Penguin Random House LLC, 2020
Published by Penguin Books, an imprint of Penguin Random House LLC, 2021

TO OCTAVIA & TONI.
THANK YOU.

TABLE OF CONTENTS

INTRODUCTION

Patrice Caldwell

When I was fourteen, a family friend gifted me a copy of Octavia Butler's *Wild Seed*. I still remember that moment. The Black woman on the front cover. The used-paperback smell. The way I held it close like it carried within it the secrets of many universes.

I devoured it and all of her others. I found myself in her words. And I'm not the only one.

It seems only fitting that the title of this anthology comes from Butler's *Parable of the Talents*, a novel that is ever relevant.

The full quote is *"In order to rise from its own ashes, a phoenix first must burn."*

Storytelling is the backbone of my community. It is in my blood.

My parents raised me on stories of real-life legends like Queen Nzinga of Angola, Harriet Tubman, Phillis Wheatley, and Angela Davis. Growing up in the American South, my world was full of stories, of traditions and superstitions— like eating black-eyed peas on New Year's Day for luck or "jumping the broom" on your wedding day. Raised on a diet of *Twilight Zone*, *Star Trek*, and *Star Wars*, I preferred creating and exploring fictional universes to living in my real one.

But whenever I went to the children's section of the library to discover more tales, the novels featuring characters who looked like me were, more often than not, rooted in pain set amid slavery, sharecropping, or segregation. Those narratives are important, yes. But because they were the only ones offered, I started to wonder, *Where is my fantasy, my future? Why don't Black people exist in speculative worlds?*

Too often media focuses on our suffering. Too often we are portrayed as victims. But in reality, we advocate for and save ourselves long before anyone else does, from heroes my parents taught me of to recent ones like Alicia Garza, Patrisse Cullors, and Opal Tometi, the Black women who founded Black Lives Matter.

Malcolm X said, "The most neglected person in America is the Black Woman." I believe this is even more true for my fellow queer siblings, and especially for those identifying as trans and as gender nonconforming. We are constantly under attack.

And yet still we rise from our own ashes.

We never accept no.

With each rebirth comes a new strength.

+ + +

Black women are phoenixes.

We are given lemons and make lemonade.

So are the characters featured in this collection of stories.

These sixteen stories highlight Black culture, folktales, strength, beauty, bravery, resistance, magic, and hope. They will take you from a ship carrying teens who are Earth's final hope for salvation to the rugged wilderness of New Mexico's frontier. They will introduce you to a revenge-seeking hairstylist, a sorcerer's apprentice, and a girl whose heart is turning to ash. And they will transport you to a future where all outcomes can be predicted by the newest tech, even matters of the heart.

Though some of these stories contain sorrow, they ultimately are full of hope. Sometimes you have to shed who you were to become who you are.

As my parents used to remind me, Black people have our pain, but our futures are limitless.

Let us, together, embrace our power.

Let us create our own worlds.

Let us thrive.

And so our story begins . . .

WHEN LIFE HANDS YOU A LEMON FRUITBOMB

By Amerie

When I was ten, the orcs dropped out of a clear summer-blue sky and landed in the middle of Central Park. They were in something that looked like one of our ships, only a lot bigger with a lot less attention to aesthetic. I was at home in Brooklyn, sitting at the kitchen table playing cards with my uncle Junior and Cynthia IV. She wasn't playing because that capability was broken, and I was just reintroducing myself for the third time in twenty minutes, thanks to her facial recognition being shot. Yet another concession my uncle had to deal with, her being noncertified preowned AI and whatnot.

Anyway, on the wall we watched as more of these ships came down all over the world, looking like the latest publicity stunt for some rapper's album, only they were shooting people with laser guns and their victims didn't look like extras. They were cabbies and women with shopping bags and kids with hover soles and shawarma-eating pedestrians and police officers and foreign tourists with old-school point-and-shoot camera phones and not one of them was getting up.

Afterward, Uncle June covered the windows with foil, baked me his famous miniature sweet potato pies, and spent the rest of the day holding me under one arm, as if I were a package he'd sworn to keep safe, which, really, I sort of was.

After half a week, Uncle June ventured outside every day, patrolling the neighborhood in his Cadillac, riding farther and farther out, searching for anyone who might need help. *You can't keep doing that*, I'd say, but we both knew what I was really saying: *Keep this up, and one day you won't come back.* But he'd shake his head. *Lil Bit, you know I can't stay up in here while people out there need food, water, a ride, a shoulder.* One time I blocked the door. *You can't save the world, Uncle June!* And he paused long enough for me to think that maybe I'd gotten through. But then he shrugged. *You do what you can, Lil Bit.* He grabbed his homemade first aid kit and the plastic containers he'd filled with tap water and nudged me out of the way and didn't come back all day.

Not long after that, we got a call from Uncle June's aunt's best friend, Judith. She and her prayer circle were having a hard time. They were a handful of old ladies who didn't have any family (read: protection), and Judith begged Uncle June to come down to Baltimore and help. The orcs hadn't brought their killing spree down there yet, but there'd been several break-ins. It took him a while, but seeing as there weren't as many living people to help around the neighborhood, he agreed. I think leaving New York had a lot to do with me, with the promise he made my dad. Dad never would've expected me to be in the latest sneakers or have the latest neuralnet upgrade, but Uncle June and I both knew that at the very least, Dad would've expected his brother to keep me alive.

What I do way out here in the boonies of space means the difference between life and death for my uncle. *I'll get something, Uncle June, I promise.*

I've just thirty minutes ago finished patrolling the perimeter of Savior One. I sped around in a gleaming pod, blending in as much as a white washing machine amongst a heap of ashes as I swiveled my head to peer through the domed glass of the two-seater, eyes going 360 while my hands itched for my rifle. We've been here twenty-six days (more like one and a half Earth months), and forget finding a metropolis or orc city—we haven't found a single campsite. But we know they're burrowed somewhere in this watery ghost planet.

Now I'm sitting in the orc prison, the dim light of a distant red giant seeping through the tiny cell window. I'm glad to have finished my patrol before dark; I much prefer being indoors over being outside, where a swamp the size of an ocean is interrupted only by patches of blood-red grass and black, prickly trees and islands of bushes that look nightmarish under the reddish light of the sun and worse under the bloodlight of the double moons.

We sit silently at a metal table, Orc #176 cuffed to a chair, watching me as I wait for my neuralnet translation program to load. As usual, the speaker that plays our translations sits between us. Once the program sends a signal from my implant to my cerebral cortex, the light on the speaker turns green and I clear my throat. Fourteen other translators have managed to squeeze out at least a name from their orcs, though nothing else of importance. Yet.

"Your name?" I say.

A pause, and from the speaker comes a voice that isn't my own: "Yan mayun."

I think the orc is young. Though it sits, I can tell it stands about six foot five—a bit smaller than the others—and there are no greys threaded through its long, braided hair, but its shoulders are impressively broad; the whites of its red eyes shine a brilliant blue-white instead of yellow, and its grey, folded skin is smooth and supple. A hint of moisture—its viscosity somewhere between snail slime and nutri-gel—shines from a few of its folds. Seeing the aliens off-screen and, like now, in person . . . there's something a little less orc-ish about them. Something about their eyes.

Disconcertingly human.

I ask it another standard question, arguably the most important: "*Where* are the others?" Wayun go zi?

Every orc in our custody was captured on Earth and brought with us to this creepy place, and if we've learned anything, it's that their favorite—and usually only—reply is silence. I've always had a feeling it knows we're being watched, studied: it's observing me, I'm observing it, and the interrogator, via the grain-sized camera on the ceiling, observes the both of us from another room.

"What is your specialization? . . . Have you or any others worked covertly with any Earth government in the past?"

It won't answer and I want to throw my boot into its chest. Instead, I swallow. Take a breath. Gotta stay calm, despite my brain conjuring the image of Uncle June lying dead in the street. "How large is your fleet?"

Back on Earth, we captured a few of their ships, and it didn't take long for our engineers to figure out their systems. According to all the alien vessels, their origin was this here planet, six hundred light-years away. Now we're the ones who've dropped in on them, but . . .

"Where are the others?"

I run through the list of questions the brass wants us to ask, but question after question, the orc gives me nothing. I continue down the list even as my body shakes and I resist the urge to cry. I feel my chance to save Uncle June slipping through my fingers.

I set down my tray and take a seat beside Santos.

Santos and I joined the United Defense League—the international military created in response to the alien crisis—when we were sixteen, but our paths didn't cross until a year later, when we signed up for Mission Savior. Nearly a third of the soldiers that make up the UDL are teens like us. Child soldiers. No one could decide whether or not that was a good thing. But the way I saw it, tailgates and prom and grad caps in the air weren't going to be part of my generation's future anyway.

Not that Santos ever had any of that in her future; she's one of those super-smart girls who skipped high school and went straight to MIT.

I haven't seen her for a couple of days and she's got dark circles under her soft, hazel-flecked eyes. Her canned peaches and peanut butter crackers are untouched, but there are about ten Fruitbomb wrappers littering her tray. She's been hoarding Fruitbombs since the week the orcs touched down on Earth, and up to now has maintained a one-every-few-days rule.

"OK," I say, "what's up?"

Santos unwraps a pink Fruitbomb and bites into it with all the joy of hurling in a space suit. She whispers, "I don't want to torture people."

"You mean *the orcs*."

"They have nothing in common with the orcs in those ridiculous movies."

"First," I say, "flawed though they may be, those films are classic—"

"You never even read the books."

"That's beside the point."

Santos huffs and looks away, and I try to figure out what's wrong. It could be the predicament we're in: communication with Earth unexpectedly ceased the millisecond we went through the wormhole. Twenty-six days later, no one on Earth knows what's happening here, and no one this side of the hole knows what's going on there.

But then Santos yawns and I guess her problem's something closer to home.

"I told you you shouldn't have taken that prison detail," I say, digging into my bowl of UDL Protein Medley 2.

Between patrol duty and translating *and* prison detail, she can't be sleeping much. Plus, she's always volunteering to help the technicians and coders with the Earth transmissions, which is how I know about the comms problem in the first place. Santos is doing all she can to increase her chances of getting her mom, sister, and baby cousin into Sanctum.

"Don't worry," I say, "your orc will start talking soon."

Santos tosses a furtive glance about the mess hall. "I've spoken to a few of them, actually. During prison detail."

"One of those things just struck up a conversation?"

"No. I— The point is, they're not what you think. They have a rich history, and—"

"Are you serious?"

Santos sighs exaggeratedly and slides a slice of peach into her mouth. She's got full lips and that smooth, dark-brown skin that can make a girl forget herself. *A teasin' sip*, what my uncle would call it. Back on Earth when he'd see a woman in a park, one who *got no time for nobody, sashayin' through the city heat like a mirage to a man dyin' o' thirst.*

There'd be only the slightest hint of sadness in Uncle June's voice.

Thirst is right, I'd say to him before rolling my eyes, because Thirsty June is what my dad used to call him, and my uncle would chuckle and say, *Girl, please,* and knock his knuckles against my head while continuing to watch the lady walk down the street.

That was before, when there were NYC streets to walk on.

"Santos," I say, "if they felt for us half as much as you do for them, we wouldn't have needed to cross the galaxy in the first place. Let's just stick to our objective. The interrogators torture. We translate."

There are translation programs for every single language and dialect on Earth, and though I didn't expect them to figure out how to translate the orcs' language overnight, it didn't occur to me that no existing program would work. Turns out only a few of us in the UDL have the brain chemistry that can pair with a program to decode the orc language at all. We watched news feeds, paying close attention to the words the orcs shouted to one another; we watched their mouths move; we observed their body language. All this information was surveyed, diced up into 1s and 0s, and before long a relatively crude translation program was developed.

Santos says, "We're complicit."

"Nothing in the UDL Code of Conduct about torturing orcs from space." Santos looks tortured herself, so I soften my tone. "Look, you don't want to call them *orcs*, fine. But in case you missed it, the only conversation they've ever tried to have with any of us is one that comes out the laser end of their guns."

"You willing to sell your soul?"

"To save my uncle Junior?" I lean back. "In a heartbeat."

◆ ◆ ◆

In my second year in UDL, when I was stationed in Atlanta, I got a call from Uncle June. He sounded beaten down and slow and I knew before he told me it must be really, really bad. And it was: the orcs had made it down to Baltimore and laid waste to the whole area. He'd been traveling with Judith, the last surviving member of the elderly prayer circle; they had just the clothes on their backs, but she'd been injured and didn't make it. But he was still trying to help anyone he could as he made his way over the crumbled I-95 highway, sometimes pulling burnt bodies out of cars to sleep. He had nowhere to go, and we both knew that him roaming the countryside meant it was just a matter of time before he was killed—by orcs or by the humans who'd turned to anarchy now that the battle seemed to be a losing one.

Then there was news about a mission that was going to save us all. They'd found the orcs' home planet, and were going to bring the fight to their backyard. They needed fighters, doctors, pilots . . .

And translators, I told Uncle June the next time he managed to get a call through to base. *Anyone who volunteers for Mission Savior has a chance to win themselves and their families a spot in Sanctum. We don't do hardcore interrogation. Just translating.*

But Uncle June sucked his teeth. *I can't sit in that place knowing everyone else is left out in the cold.*

Only people like politicians, top scientists, and their families had refuge in Sanctum, an underground facility in the Rockies, but now I had a chance to secure a place for Uncle June and me. That's how it is for most people on this mission. Almost all of us have people at home, loved-one-shaped reasons why we signed up for what could be a one-way trip through a wormhole to an orc planet.

I told Uncle June I was doing it, and after a few moments he told me, *You do what you gotta do*, and that he loved me, but his disappointment was clear. And then he added, *But I'm not steppin' foot in that place*, like it was hell and not the haven it was.

And then his voice sort of drifted and he asked me, *You think those aliens sing?* and *Do they make music? Dance? Create art?* I was like, *Why does that even matter?* Uncle June was silent for a few seconds. *Because*, he said, *if they take the time to translate their world into sound and color, that means they know love. That means we have a chance.*

I said, *Whatever*, and didn't mention Sanctum again, figuring I'd convince him another time, after I secured him the spot.

It was our last conversation.

I am my uncle's niece, so I don't quit easily.

Since Orc #176 has yet to respond to standard questions, I've decided to try a less orthodox approach.

All right, Uncle June. I've got nothing to lose. "You know how to sing?" Sonari goan yan owla?

It isn't really a direct translation because we don't know their word for *sing* or *singing*, so the closest I get is something like *You know how to make good noise with mouth?*

A slight movement in that slimy neck. It's a curveball, no

doubt, and I've got its attention, despite the terrible translation.

"You draw? Paint?"

Still blank-faced.

"You like music? You like dancing?" I do a slight shimmy with my shoulders because the translation is more like I'm asking if it likes noise in the air and moving to the sound.

At first I'm thinking all that may have gone over its head but then it sits up a little.

Still, it doesn't speak. We stare at each other for what must be ten minutes.

"Sonari ahn anya."

I jump, and I realize I never expected it to answer. Its voice is so much gentler than what I thought would come from something so muscular. The translation program's speech-to-speech voice imitates but can't quite manage the orc's tone.

When I recover, I say, "OK, you don't sing. That makes two of us."

"Your questions are wasted on me," it says.

"We're just getting started."

"You do not seek conversation. You want only information. You are all alike."

"So you like music?" I force a subject change because this thing has wasted enough of my time. "You dance?"

"I enjoy music."

"So you have music down there."

A pause. "Down there?"

"We already figured your cities are underground. We've seen the state of this planet. It's dying."

A low grunt is its only response.

"Your lot went to Earth, laser guns blazing, in search of a new home, isn't that right?"

"And if we did not arrive wielding weapons?" Its voice is controlled but tight. "Would you share your planet with us?"

I stare at its eyes. It's almost as if they don't belong. They're too . . . full. "A friend of mine thinks you all are basically the same as people. Santos is soft like that."

It tilts its head sharply. If Santos had spoken to my orc, she would've mentioned it, but it's clear her name has sparked recognition, and I get a bad feeling. Not only did I give up information it didn't need to know, it also seems to know yet another thing I don't.

A red light begins to pulse in the left field of my vision. My alarm. Time's up.

I pick up the speaker and head for the door, but before I leave, I glance back, wondering if maybe I imagined the look in its eye when I said Santos' name.

I don't mention it to Santos the next morning. No need to unsettle her.

Not that she's paying me the slightest attention.

"Santos," I say, taking a break from making my bed to knock against the metal frame of hers. "Where are you?"

"Sorry, I'm . . . I'm fine." But she looks shaken. Plus she's shoving into her mouth the second Fruitbomb in three minutes.

"Tell me."

Santos motions for us to leave, and doesn't speak again until we're just outside the barracks, alone. "They've figured it out. Why we lost contact with Earth."

"So they've regained contact?" Maybe I can get a message to Uncle June.

Santos shakes her head, her eyes reddening. "And they're not going to."

She takes several seconds to eat another piece of candy, swallow, and breathe. Whatever it is, she really, really doesn't want to say it.

"They're not going to because . . ." She stares down at the scarlet grass. "Because there's no one there."

"What do you mean there's no one there? The transmission center's been abandoned? Did they set up somewhere else? Was it attacked?"

"There's no one *there*. On Earth."

Now I'm the one who needs to breathe. Uncle June, Santos' family . . . the whole damned planet? "They're . . ." It isn't possible that they've killed billions of people. Is it? "They're dead?"

"No." Santos wraps her arms around herself. "No one's on Earth because no one's been born yet."

I frown in my attempt to understand.

"No one's been born. Not a single human being. No homo sapien, anyway."

I laugh, my voice shrill and brimming with hysteria. "The hell are you saying?"

"We traveled through time, Mitchell. The wormhole was

some kind of rip in space-time. Or maybe it caused the rip. Either way, Earth is thousands of years in the past."

"But . . . no . . . Wait." I shake my head. "If Earth is thousands of years in the past and these monsters invaded us, then where—I mean when—are we?"

"They don't know."

Just over twenty-four hours later, I'm staring at the orc. It looks at me differently than before; something else has replaced its previous simmering hostility.

It studies me, but all I can think about is Uncle June. Part of me feels like my uncle is dead. The other part thinks of him as being alive but extremely far away, as if Present Day isn't a time but a location, like the Hawaiian Isles of China.

Finally, I manage to speak. "Santos. You've heard the name before."

"You're young," it replies.

"So what?"

"I am young, too."

"How old are you?"

"I have eleven years."

Damn. What're they feeding these things?

But the incredulity lasts only a few seconds and then I'm lost again in what Santos said about Earth, about humanity not existing because Earth is so far back in the past; meanwhile, we're on this alien planet, a mission of four hundred fifty UDL soldiers and two hundred prisoner orcs and a handful of weapons of mass destruction.

I feel alone.

"Santos," I say again. "You recognized the name."

"I will speak of it. But first, whom do you call upon? From whom do you request favor? Guidance?"

"Like God?" I shake my head. It's difficult to believe in something I can't see. Besides, nobody's Good Book mentioned a thing about orcs in space. Who spiked God's sweet tea on the day He created them?

"You are," it says, "certain your friend is *Santos*?"

"Of course I'm sure."

It clasps its grey hands and begins to cry, and I can't tell if it's happy or sad or both.

"What is it?" I say, the hairs at the nape of my neck rising.

"It is true," it whispers to itself. "It was written."

"What was written?"

It looks at me. "We do not return."

Santos and I have shared double-shift perimeter duty the last couple of days, but all I've been able to think about is getting the orc to talk. After the last session, the interrogator, his expression hard and unforgiving, asked me, *Where are you going with your line of questioning? Names, chain of command, coordinates—that's what we require. If you want your ticket to Sanctum, you'd best focus on that.* But the orc's opening up, and I know it won't be long before it gives up the important stuff.

When I finally return, just after dark, it sits with less tension, almost like I came for tea instead of answers.

I set up the speaker, but before I ask it anything, it speaks. "I was a weapons maker. Before."

I glance upward at the camera on the ceiling, knowing the interrogator's watching. *Eat it.*

I don't say anything, sensing it might go on.

"I did not want to make weapons, but I excelled and my family was compensated well and my people needed them."

"To attack us. To kill us all." I can't help it.

"We don't want to kill you all."

"Just enough of us."

"Just enough of you for peace."

"Because murdering us will bring peace."

"Does it not? From war comes peace. After peace comes war. And so on."

"Maybe that's how it works around here." But when I actually think about the cycle of wars throughout humanity, the orc's worldview—*worlds*view—isn't so far off.

"Learning to share a planet," it says, "will prove difficult."

"Humans aren't always the best at sharing." I can't say much about the orcs, but the fact that they crossed the galaxy to not play nice doesn't speak well for them, either.

"The Great Leaping," the orc says, "was foretold when Goddess descended from the Dreaming Place with her retinue."

Now it's gone off track, talking about the first tribes and queendoms and kingdoms and I'm only half listening because I keep thinking, *Just give me the good stuff*, but I'm also surprised at how human it sounds. Not human like me . . . or maybe human like me. I'm getting confused and I think of Uncle June and all the movies I've seen about time travel and I wish I and Uncle June and Santos and her family and everyone on Earth could just leap into a different universe, a different timeline, one in which we weren't invaded by orcs.

"I have a sister," it says, and then it stops talking, like it wants me to say something.

"That's . . . nice."

"You belong to a family?"

"My parents passed away in a mining accident. Asteroid mining. My uncle Junior is . . ." The orc's shoulders slump a little, and when I see its eyes I jump up because it doesn't deserve to be sad. "You orcs should've left us alone. Do you know how many lives you've snuffed? How many you've ruined? Why couldn't you just stay here? Or find some other planet? Why Earth?"

"We are all part of a greater whole, of the Vast Story. The Great Leaping was foretold many ages past, from the Time of the Beginning."

In the dimness of the cell, the orc looks just like Uncle June, and he kind of talks like him, too, the day he told me about Mom and Dad. The day he lost his little brother. Uncle June rasped about things being meant to be and part of something bigger. I stormed to my room and kicked a hole in the closet door.

I realize it now:

The orc . . . he feels alone, too.

"What's your name?" I ask.

"I am Kaizahn."

I take a breath and say, "I'm Mae Mitchell," and he gives a short nod.

There's a reason they use certain words in the military, words like *eliminate* and *target* instead of *kill* and *person*. It's so you gain distance. It's so you don't waver. It's so you don't see your enemy close enough to see yourself.

I whisper, "What *are* you?"

"We are the Nokira," he says. "The first companions of Goddess Santosa."

The next morning, everyone's called to muster at what would be Earth eleven hundred hours. As most of our fellow UDLs crack jokes in the main hall, Santos and I sit in uneasy silence. Probably because we know about the time-travel issue with Earth and they don't.

"At exactly nineteen hundred hours tomorrow," says the commander, "all personnel will leave this base via transport ship. You will report to the transport at eighteen hundred hours. If you do not report, no one will come looking for you. No one will wait."

Are we returning to Earth? Have they found the solution to the time issue? I know what the others are wondering. We're supposed to be here for another five, six months, so they're surprised we're heading out already, and the whole thing about no one waiting is against code, which makes the withdrawal sound like an evacuation under duress.

A senior officer takes over, briefing us about the withdrawal, but all I can think is: if they *have* figured a way to get back to our own time, where does this leave me? I'm finally making progress with Kaizahn, but I need more time. Will our objectives be considered met? Can Uncle June make it to Sanctum after all?

As I raise a hand, someone asks that very question.

"That would be affirmative," the senior officer says, but I don't feel better. Something about his voice. Like it's not going to matter.

"What about the orcs?" someone blurts.

"They return to Earth with us." To remain imprisoned and interrogated.

I tell myself there's no difference. That here or on Earth, their fate remains the same.

But I'm unconvinced.

Afterward, I pull Santos aside. "Why the rush?"

"The wormhole is closing. They'd leave tonight if they could do it safely."

"And the fact that the only person on Earth to talk to right now is covered in fur and hanging ten from a tree branch?"

"They . . . they think going back through the wormhole might return us to our own time."

"Might." I cock a brow.

"I don't trust it any more than you do, but what other option is there?"

She's right. "Let's just hope we don't come out the other end to discover the continents are fused together and we've got meat-loving dinosaurs waiting, mouths open."

I turn to leave but Santos grabs my arm. "The Nokira."

"What about them?" But already guilt tugs at me from beneath my ribs. "Well, what are we supposed to do? Let them escape so they can find the others?"

Santos shakes her head. "There are no others to find."

"What do you mean—"

"We can't let them go back to Earth. You know they'll be killed. And it'll be on us. The right thing is to let them go. Tonight." I start to say *no* but Santos closes her hand around mine. "Help me."

"But I don't want to help you to a death sentence, Santos. Myself, either." Because that's what we'd earn in a court-martial. "And it probably won't work."

"We can only try."

A familiar sentiment. I think of Uncle June heading out to save the world one person at a time.

"Mitchell."

It's obvious she's made up her mind. "Fine. But only because you'll definitely get caught if I let you do it alone."

But this is a half-truth. The other half is that after all that talking, it's gotten harder to see the orc—see Kaizahn—as a target.

As an it.

We don't make our move until hours into Santos' shift.

"Like I said, I've been talking to them," Santos says as we creep through the main corridor of the prison. "The Nokira. For a couple of weeks, I've been learning about their people, their history, their various cultures." She glances off to the corner of her eye, and I know she's reading the time from her feed. "The guards will be waking in an hour. Maybe forty-five minutes."

They'll be real pleased to discover that the so-called UDL .Reg3.3 regulatory neuralnet feed update that Santos claimed was from the guys in the comms department was, in fact, a sleep-enhancement virus.

Now we're running through the prison, unlocking the doors so that the Nokira can make their way to the south wing to escape. According to Kaizahn, they don't need pods or anything: *We need only the water.*

As we open the doors and the Nokira rush out, I read their expressions. Some look as if they want to kill me despite the rescue, but most just look tired. And sad, a heavy sorrow that jars against the relief I'd expect from them in this moment.

When we get to Kaizahn's cell, I hesitate before unlocking the door. Maybe because it's probably the last time we'll ever see one another, maybe because I'll be labeled a traitor to the human race if anyone finds out.

When Kaizahn does step out, he gives me a brief look of gratitude before nodding to Santos, and then the three of us unlock the other cell doors before sprinting down the corridor, dozens of Nokira prisoners behind us as we head for the south side of the prison.

When we step outside the facility, I'm hit with the moss-scent of humid air. My eyes adjust to this planet's strange predawn light, and in a few seconds I'm able to see through the light mist that hovers over the grounds. When I'm certain all is clear, the Nokira rush to the black waters of the swamp, their prison-garbed bodies submerging quickly and quietly. They can breathe underwater. Part of me wants to follow them, to discover the secret they've kept so successfully.

Kaizahn steps forward, but turns back to face Santos. Some communication—something closer to reverence than gratefulness—passes between them. Then he turns to me.

"Salquay."

The translation program isn't turned on, but I don't need it to know what he's saying: *Thank you.*

Hoping he understands everything I put into the gesture, I nod: *You're welcome. I'm humbled. I'm ashamed. I'm sorry.*

There's something else in Kaizahn's expression, in those too-human eyes of his.

But before I can interpret it, he's off, and then he's gone beneath the murky deep.

Needless to say, this morning, all hell broke loose.

The base commander was beside himself. "The damned orcs!"

But there were no altercations, no throats slit in the middle of the night. The orcs, thanks to us, disappeared without a trace.

Still, while everyone prepares to head out, some of us have been ordered to patrol one last time beyond the perimeter in hopes of securing at least a few of the Nokira.

Santos and I have been riding in the pod the last two hours, and we finally park near the edge of an especially large expanse of swamp water.

"What do you think is down there?" I ask.

"Nothing," Santos says.

I turn to her. "What do you mean?"

"There is nothing and no one, Mitchell. The Nokira are all they have. Each other and the clothes on their backs."

"There's got to be something . . . Santos?" But she just keeps her gaze fixed on the water. "A couple of minutes and we head back."

Santos turns to me. "I'm not going."

"We've got to get back to base right now or we'll be stuck here."

Santos dives forward and frees the navigation cell from the dash. In half a second she's wrapped her jacket around it, and before I can stop her, she drops it out the window, at the roots of a black tree with winding, leafless branches.

I glare at her. "Is this some kind of tantrum?"

Theoretically, the pod could travel even through space back to Earth, though without the navi cell, only on manual mode. But we know our way back to base, so I don't understand the point of throwing the navi cell from the window.

"Santos."

She stares me down.

"You want to stay here?" I throw up my hands and panic shears the edges of my voice. The transport ship will be leaving in just over an hour. "This planet is dead. There's nothing here."

"But there will be."

"Why did you throw out the navi cell?"

Silence.

When I ask again and she doesn't answer, I bang my fist against the tempered glass. Beneath my consciousness something stirs . . . "Santos!"

"I drop you off at the base, and I keep the pod." She means it with every blood cell in her body but her voice is also strangely practiced, like she's reciting a line.

"You're seriously trying to stay? Alone? Why?" But I don't wait for an answer because the question was just a distraction.

I lunge for my door in an attempt to get out and grab the navi cell, but Santos has secured the doors. We end up staring at one another, chests heaving, limbs trembling.

"We're going to need the navi cell," Santos says. "Much later."

"*We?*"

The navi cell is virtually indestructible. Meant to stand the test of time. A long time. I feel like I'm going to be sick.

Because I realize.

I see everything Santos must've known for days, now. I understand the sadness of the Nokira as they escaped: they, too, are separated from their families by time. And I understand the look Kaizahn gave me a couple of hours ago: solemn expectation.

I whisper, "This navi cell . . ."

They need it. Thousands of years from now, the Nokira will need it to find their way to Earth. Because thousands of years from now, they'll have developed an entire civilization. And they'll have built spaceships.

I swallow. "They have to find Earth to find us so that we can come out here and . . ."

"And they can exist in the first place," Santos finishes quietly. "We're their ancestors."

My knees weaken and my head pounds at the paradox but there it is.

She whispers, "You don't have to stay."

"You don't either."

"I do. The reason they even have a chance on Earth is because they are part human, too. It's a small part, but it's in their genetic makeup."

Their eyes.

That strange sensation of encountering someone foreign but familiar. I recognized it in Kaizahn, in all the Nokira. I recognized myself. Their bodies are stitched with human DNA, are fueled with whispers of human blood. Whispers of Santos.

"But just you alone?" I say. "You're enough to influence genetics so far down the line?"

"There will be others. Five UDLs are staying behind."

We're their ancestors, Santos said. *We*. Goddess Santosa and her retinue, and the Nokira.

"If you stay," Santos says, "it will make all the difference. Genetically speaking."

I don't want to stay. I want to see Uncle June. I have to make sure he's all right.

But I will see him. Not me, but a different version of me. Uncle June and I have been thrown into separate timelines and there is nothing I can do about that now.

I can make a difference here, though, for the Nokira. I can stay here with Santos so Kaizahn and the Nokira can exist.

You do what you can, Lil Bit, Uncle June said.

I laugh to myself and sniff. My eyes burn. Because we will return thousands of years from now. Only it won't be exactly us, will it?

"How many times has this happened?"

I don't realize I've said it aloud until Santos responds. "An infinite number of times, I think."

The Great Leaping, Kaizahn called it. Leaping and simultaneously creating new timelines.

Finally, I look up at Santos and nod. She hands me a lemon Fruitbomb. I unwrap it and pop it into my mouth as I lean back into my seat, kick my feet up onto the dash, and take in the fiery sunset. Santos leans back, too. This certainly wasn't what I signed up for, being left behind on a swampy alien planet and helping to birth a new species. Plus I'm pretty sure there's nothing on this rock that tastes this good. Maybe in a few thousand years. I tuck the candy wrapper into my pocket. As a reminder.

A few tears slide down my cheeks, and I don't bother wiping or sniffing them away, not even when the huge transport flies up through the burning sky and we are left behind.

This is the end.

But it's also another beginning.

GILDED

By Elizabeth Acevedo

THE INGENIO OF THE ADMIRAL DIEGO COLÓN
LA HISPANIOLA, 1521

Tía Aurelia, the healer who raised me, says my mother was a stoic woman, evidenced by the fact that she did not cry out, not even once, as I pummeled myself from her body. She simply squatted in Tía's leaf-thatched bohío, and pushed me forth. She caught me with her own two hands, hands still covered with mineral dust from the gold she'd been panning for in Río Ozama. Tía Aurelia says the metal on my mother's palms mingled with the slick that covered my body and turned me into a gilded, black being.

She says I was god touched, gold touched, from that moment forward.

The other ladinos stood outside our bohío, listening to sounds they never thought they'd hear again. I was the first babe born breathing to a negra. To the ladinos, I was proof that survival here was possible. But I was also a troubling omen: the first of a future generation born on this island and domesticated, declawed by their own lack of memories. The blood that puddled down Mamá's legs would not stop, and although Tía Aurelia packed her body with herbs and prayed, calling on the true names of God, and stretched out a hammock for Mamá to rest in, Mamá's strength exited her body in much the same way I had: one hard breath after another until she was emptied of life.

Her gift to me? The gleaming palm print that could not be scrubbed off my back, and the magic that came with it. Tía Aurelia, who has seen more than she can recount, and has story upon story of unbelievable marvels, said she'd never seen anything like it, flesh transferring to flesh a miracle of metal. Even as an infant when I would cry, the tin spoon would rattle in the trencher. If I was having a nightmare Tía would have to put down her sewing, since the needles might fly out of her hand without warning.

There are rumors that some of the Tainos have the ability to disappear into thin air. Other stories whispered late at night assert that there are dragons to the west that crawl out of a lake on hind legs and speak with the voice of a man. Some even say they have seen a negra, blue as a moonless night, wandering through the mountains with backward-facing feet, in her throat a song that lures soldiers deeper and deeper into the woods until they are never seen again.

But I have never heard of someone quite like me, born with the ability to bend copper and bronze to my will.

My gift looms over me like the fifteen-foot cane we harvest at the ingenio, as dark as the molasses I stir all day.
Metal sings to me. Sometimes when the admiral is coming
to watch us work, I can hear the copper buckles on his shoes
even though he is still several miles away; I usually warn the
others to put a bit more strength into their swinging arms.
It's the same when I'm at the ingenio working with molasses. I stand at the large bronze vats, and as I get tired the big
metal spoon makes itself lighter, helps make the stirring easier. When a ladino gets injured, they come to our bohío. Tía
numbs them using a tonic of rum spiced with anise, cinnamon, and cloves. As long as the injury is not in a visible place, I
bend scraps of metal to graft a broken bone, or seal a bleeding
wound. Every single ladino at the ingenio has had my touch
on their body, and they pray over my hands, and they help
keep my abilities secret.

If the admiral knew, or any of the friars, they would burn
me alive—for only a bruja can manipulate the elements, and a
witch is considered a blight on the world.

When I was a babe, the ladinos kept me hidden from the
admiral. Children, like women, are rare here. They are not
brought to work the land, or considered valuable stock, and
although I have heard of other babes born after I was, I was
not raised near other children. But when I turned three the
admiral was made aware of my presence, and he put me to
work. Tía Aurelia says it was a trap. The moment I proved useless the admiral would have me killed or would force me into
the forests, but my ability to metal-whisper was helpful; back

then we were working in the mines. Every week when we had to lay ore at the admiral's feet, it was my pile that stacked up the highest. I knew exactly where all the largest deposits of precious metal were.

I was branded lucky, but not magical, and the difference was enough to spare my life.

I was ten when the admiral and I negotiated my coartación, or manumission. The opportunity to buy one's freedom was not something that had ever been offered on the admiral's ingenio, although we had all heard of ladinos elsewhere who were given the chance. Tía says it is a way to keep the slaves hoping. Pick one slave to make the others believe that if they work hard enough maybe they, too, will be presented a chance at liberty. And how better to inspire—and strike jealousy— than to offer freedom to the youngest at the ingenio? At least, that is how Tía believes it to be, and from her night work she knows the intention of men like the admiral better than their own wives do, which means she is probably correct.

And so as a child with freshly washed hair and dirty-soled feet, I stood in front of the admiral and an appraiser, who determined I was worth the purchase price of seven hundred pesos, to be paid in seven years. An almost impossible amount if I was not attuned to metallics. But these men did not know I was a girl formed by impossibilities.

When the rivers of gold dried up at the Río Ozama, the admiral moved us four leagues west and transformed his estate into this ingenio, a massive sugar mill. And so we, his ladinos, laid brick for his dungeon, set the doors for his armory, and raised his entire mill: an altar to sugar. Despite his grand palace in the center of the city, he had us build a new house with ballroom and bedrooms. For ourselves we built a tight circle of bohíos bordering the fields we would work. And we prayed to be useful enough to live another day, for the admiral was known to have the guillotine ready for any slave who was considered lazy, or worse, rebellious.

Tía Aurelia says I am a fool for believing the admiral will honor his word regarding my freedom. And she is right; the admiral is a man with small, soft hands and a hard, cruel heart, and no court or contract will change either. But regardless of how she feels, Tía gives me salves for my palms, and ointments for my feet, and if she gets an extra peseta for her healing, or the men she offers comfort, she gives me that toward my coartación. My manumission date is in a month's time—I have five pesos left to pay. From sunup until the stars are twinkling I slash, and carry, and peel, and boil, and churn, turn my arm around the molasses vat, and heal the broken, and dream and dream and dream of belonging to no one but myself.

The boy was never a factor in those dreams.

For the last few months, we've heard rumors from other ingenios that new enslaved people have been brought over by the hundreds. Black like us, who unlike us do not speak Castilian, are not Christian, have never set foot on the Iberian Peninsula. Since the first, the admiral's ingenio has been toiled over by the ladinos—those who lived in Sevilla and served the admiral's father before being brought here—and me. But today a group of five men show up. I hear the metal when they are still half a league away; it rings louder than the admiral's gold rings, louder than the horses' shoes. This metal is not from here, and I almost drop my stirring spoon into the boiling molasses.

The men appear at the ingenio in a straight line, all of them with ankle shackles hindering their steps; thick chains around their waists connect them to one another, and their garb is unlike any I've seen before. Of the five men, it is a young man my age, a boy with a proud forehead and fearless eyes, a brass collar around his neck, it is he who for a second stops my arm from stirring, and perhaps my heart from beating.

I drop my head, and the metal in my hand pulls slowly through the thick, dark sugar. Yet from the corner of my eye I see the admiral address the young man, and then motion with his bejeweled hand for him to explain to the others. I cannot make out the boy's words, but his voice is lower than I would have imagined for such a young man, and I know he is someone who is used to giving orders. The admiral yanks the chain that binds the men together and pulls them like a pack of dogs behind him. His treatment is not unusual, but it makes me want to snarl with my teeth. Just before they leave, the boy looks over his shoulder, and his eyes find mine.

Tío Prieto and Nana Silvia are gathering leftover bits of cane to dry in the sun, and they begin whispering like a chorus of crickets; soon the other ladinos join in. The same word erupts from their mouths: *Bozales. Bozales.* The muzzled ones are here.

+ + +

A week after the bozales arrive, I exit Tía's bohío to see the five men in the fields. Every morning since the day they arrived, I find them like this: kneeling and genuflecting and rising, and doing this time and again as they chant. I stand at the edge of the field with a hand shading my brow so I can watch them. When they have finished, the youngest stands up, and his head swivels toward me as it has done whenever we are in the same vicinity. But today he does not move deeper into the field and instead walks my way. I do not smooth the linseed cloth of my skirt, although my hand itches to do so. I am glad Tía ran her fingers through my hair last night, and rubbed the part neatly with coconut oil before plaiting a tight coronet around my head and saying, "You will be your own woman soon, Eula. But I can mother you for a little bit longer."

She greased my scalp, and I nuzzled into her hand. Outside our bohíos, the ingenio is a place of fear and shadows, stone and sweat, blood and raised voices. But in the circle we've built, and in Tía's bohío, love is the fixed sunrise.

"Eula, I've heard whispers that one of the new men keeps finding his eyes on you. You've always been something to look at, but I have a sense this one will be different."

I groaned when Tía said that. But maybe she wasn't wrong.

The boy's long strides shake me out of my reverie. He soon stands before me and dips his head into a slight bow. I do not return it. Instead I scan the sky, I read the colors cast by the sun. If we are not at the cutting site in ten minutes the admiral will be told we were tardy. He will not take kindly to stolen minutes. I take a step from Tía's bohío, and the boy walks beside me.

"What are you called?" he asks me, and I jerk back when I hear the passable Castilian come from his mouth.

He must see my astonishment. "I was translator for my father. He was ruler of our village. For the past five years I have spoken to the pale men on our behalf and convinced them to look elsewhere for what they sought." His accent is boiling sugar, sweet and thick, but his next statement is burned bitter. "These last men who came used their swords in place of their tongues."

I do not know why he is telling me this. Perhaps because he has taken stock of the ingenio and seen I am the only person near his age. Or perhaps because he sees I hold a place outside the ladinos. Even though we have not been introduced by any elders, I decide we do not have to stand on formality.

"What happened?" I ask.

"My father, he was on the same water vessel as me, but he did not survive. None of my kin did. The four other men here with me are all that is left of my village." He runs his fingers against the calluses on his palms.

"Eulalia." I answer what he first asked, to avoid any more discomfort being brought on by my ignorance. "Before she passed my mother named me, but she is the only one to ever utter my full name. I am simply called Eula. Your name?"

He shakes his head as if shooing away a thought. "The

pale men had us stand at the shore, and a bald man in a frock sprinkled us with water and told us we are to have a new name and a new god. But I renounce neither of mine. My god is still yàlla. And my name is still Khadim."

I have never heard this name before, or anything like it, but my body responds like a well-strung lute; this name is a song, and I love to raise my voice in melody.

Khadim works side by side with me. I show him how to hold the machete, which is shorter than any sword he would have been familiar with, but also heavier. I move slower than usual to ensure he can copy my moves and that he swings his machete in such a way as to fell the stalk without injuring his wrist. As we work, I fill the silence. I tell him how I was born here, how my mother died before I was a full day old, but it is when I say this next bit that his head swoops up: "I am almost done paying for my freedom. In a fortnight, at the Christmas Day celebration, I will receive my manumission papers."

A frown wrinkles Khadim's forehead. "How can you pay for a thing that you should not owe? It is . . ." He waves his hand in the air, a mosquito trying to land on the right word. "Nonsensical."

I use my sleeve to wipe the sweat that covers my forehead. The front of my chemise is soaked and sticks to my chest, but Khadim keeps his eyes on mine, unlike the admiral when he speaks at me.

"It is how it is done," I say. "I am lucky to have been offered such a contract. Not everyone has the chance."

Khadim drops his arm to his side, his machete loose in his fingers. "Lucky to be complicit in laying the rabbit trap that snares your own foot?"

Unlike him I don't stop moving. "Pick up your machete," I say between clenched teeth. "The admiral punishes idleness."

We thwack at the cane in silence. The machete in my hand hums, and I have to calm down my breathing or I might hurt myself.

"You don't know the life I've lived. What would you have me do? Work these fields forever? And when I am too old, clean and cook and scuttle in the admiral's house? And when I am too old for that—led out into the fields like a lame donkey and shot with an arrow between the eyes? Would you have me run into the trees, where the admiral will send a pack of hunting dogs to eat me alive?"

This time when Khadim shakes his head, there is sadness in the gesture. "I would have you do none of those things, as I will not be doing them. This is not a life I will submit to. All I know is that if they keep putting this machete in my hand it is not their cane I will cut down."

I believe him when he says it. The metal in his hands murmurs, *blood blood blood.*

We do not speak for the rest of the day, but when the sun dips behind the hills, I stoop to shoulder the long canes and gesture for him to follow me to the mill. I am strongest when at the vats, but when cane must be cut none of us can shirk our duty, especially not the one who catches the admiral's eye. Khadim looks at me intently as if he would shoulder my cane for me, but I shake my head: he would be doing me no courtesies. There is something brewing in his eyes, and Tía Aurelia would say there is something brewing between the two of us, too.

Five nights later, a soft tapping on the wood of our hut wakes me from my slumber. Tía Aurelia is not in the bohío, and whomever she is with must not be a nice man, since I see she has brewed herself a tisane, something she only does to help calm her spirit.

Tap. Tap. Tap. I raise myself from bed and shuffle to the opening.

"Tía?" I ask quietly.

"It is Khadim."

I hesitate for a second and ensure my sleep shift covers me wholly. I pull back the cover of the entryway. And sure enough, Khadim stands before me, half his face cast into light by the candle in his hand. My heart thumps wildly in my chest.

"Will you walk with me, Eula?" He offers me his hand, but I turn and pull down the opening, working a complicated knot that keeps animals from wandering inside. When I turn again, Khadim has dropped his hand, and I am glad for it; the only time I have ever held a man's hand is when I am using my ability to heal him. I would not know how to hold his hand for the simple sake of touching.

"Khadim, if word reaches the admiral of us taking a midnight walk, we will be punished, or my coartación might be docked."

I keep to the shadows as we walk.

"Eula, I come to your door with ulterior reasons than to walk beside you." He takes a deep breath. "My men and I are planning an uprising."

My feet stutter at his words. I have never heard of an uprising happening at any of the ingenios. People run away. And sometimes the admiral's dogs catch them. Rumors abound that sometimes they make it far, far west to safety in the Bahoruco Mountains. But no one has ever attempted to overtake an ingenio. I tell Khadim this.

"No other ingenio has had me. And no other ingenio has had you." He takes my hand in his and turns it so my palm faces the sky. I am glad we are in the fields, where the tall cane shades us from prying eyes, where no one can see me shiver on a warm night.

"I have been watching you. At first I thought it was because you are lovely. But, there is something uncanny about you."

I do not flinch at either the compliment or the insinuation that followed. He continues before I can unravel the meaning of his words.

"And then I realized your machete never slows down, it never stops, and you never have to clean the stickiness from it or sharpen its edge. Even back there, at your hut, the hook that held your doorway closed twisted in ways that were unnatural. And when that old man cut his hand a few days ago, everyone else turned to you, although I have been assured you are not a healer."

I pull my hand from his. If he accuses me of witchcraft out loud it could cost me my life.

Khadim leans in until his breath is by my ear. "You know more than we do about this area, about finding help at the other mills nearby. I think you are highly favored. I think we will only succeed if you help us. And convince the others to help us, too."

An ache spreads in my chest. I cannot do this thing he asks of me. "Khadim, I have not known you long. I will tell you about the area and wish you well. But I cannot convince the only family I've known to join you in this ill-conceived dream. And I cannot be a part of this. I have worked relentlessly to earn my freedom, and if your uprising were to fail, even if they do not slaughter us all, I could not live knowing I had a chance at manumission and I cast it away."

Khadim makes a sound low in his throat. "Could you live knowing you had a chance to free many more than yourself, but you refused?"

I want to swat away his words like the pest they are, but they bite me nonetheless. If I could build a world of metal to protect me and my kin, I would do it without question or regard to my own safety. But here we labor until we die. They rely on me to buy my freedom and then help make the settlement better for those who remain. I *am* giving the people of the ingenio a better chance at some small freedoms. How could he possibly understand? I wish I could explain to him that there are nights when Tía's breathing is slow and steady that I let myself imagine walking into the woods of my own accord, living off low-hanging fruit with the hummingbirds as my only companions. That there are days when my arm feels like it might fall out from overwork, and the only thing that keeps me from dropping my face into the boiling molasses is the belief that soon I will ask no one for permission to eat the grains I harvest, or to rest when I am sick with fever. I want to explain that I have seen mules walking alongside the roadway who know freedom in ways I have never known.

But I do not have the language to explain this. So instead I ask, "Have you ever tasted sugarcane, Khadim?"

I cannot see his brow but I imagine it is furrowed. "I have not. We do not grow this where I am from, and here the admiral's men are always watching."

I reach into my head wrap and pull out the slim knife I always keep tucked under there. I curved it to fit like a half circlet beneath my hair. I slice a chunk of cane, easily skinning the bark from the flesh. It is a reckless thing to do, and if I were caught I cannot even fathom the punishment for enjoying the admiral's crop without his permission, but it seems suddenly as urgent as taking in breath to teach Khadim this lesson.

"Here," I say, and press the cane to his lips. "Suckle the juice."

He follows my directions, and I am close enough I can make out the wonder in his eyes as the sweetness covers his tongue.

"Do you know what it is like to covet such a honeyed thing your whole life, and to have tasted just enough to have the memory plague you, but also to know that you would be cut down if you ever tried to claim it as your own? You at least have walked before, knowing you were your own person. Perhaps with obligations, but not destined to slavery simply due to your birth. I just want to remove this yoke from around my neck, Khadim. I just want to possess something sweet, even if it is only my own life."

I stomp the remaining cane into the ground.

Khadim takes a step back from me. "I will leave you out of this. If we are successful, I hope to see you in freedom. If we are not, I hope yàlla continues to watch over you."

I nod. "I will tell you what I know, but I refuse to be involved." I explain that the admiral and the viceroys of nearby mills get roaring drunk on Christmas Eve and the days that follow. I point to the mountains and tell him the rumors I have heard, that the Tainos have built a settlement there and welcome runaways into their folds. I tell him of the armory that holds weapons, and the stables where he can find the mill horses to take them swiftly away once the deed is done.

When I fall silent, we stand still for a long while, gazing at the sky. I wonder if the stars are configured the same where he is from. I wonder if anything feels familiar. I wonder what it must be like to have memories of a place that loved you; to have somewhere to return.

Khadim walks me back to Tía's bohío, and it feels like we are saying goodbye. Because either he will die on Christmas

Eve trying to cut down the admiral, or he will be caught and killed. And either way, I will keep my head down and hope to be free the day after.

For the next few days, in the fields and around the bohío circle, Khadim avoids me. I try not to feel bereft, but I am always aware of him, and always waiting for him to speak. Perhaps that is why I think it is him knocking impatiently on the bohío door three nights before Christmas Eve. I unlock the door to find it is one of his men. The tall and lanky one with a perfect row of teeth.

He speaks to me with unstrung Castilian words, using his hands where language fails. "They came for Khadim." He mimes the admiral's uniform. "They take him away. He stole machetes. And was caught."

I take in his words and the gestures. The admiral will not allow even a hint of insurgency, and there would be no reason but that for a man to collect more than his own blade.

"And why are you at my door?" I ask. There is a knot in my stomach that is more vast than hunger, more painful than a blow.

"Khadim said if anything happened, to come to you. He said you are the key to all of the locks."

And for a second I hate Khadim. I hate all the bozales. They who came here with their feral hearts and unbent spines. And as if the thought tightens my mother's palm print on my own back, I straighten up. If I choose to help Khadim, I have three days to make preparations.

✦ ✦ ✦

On Christmas Eve, the night before I am to receive my manumission papers as a gift, I fold my knife into my hair and with Tía's blessing slip into the darkness.

The dungeons are quiet, and I run my hands against the slick brick so as not to fall. I know Khadim is unguarded. I watched as the admiral's men entered the house; they think lock and key is enough to keep Khadim restrained. Above me the admiral and his guests dance and sing and laugh, and the walls shake from their good cheer. I pray Tía Aurelia's spiced wine is as potent and drowsiness-inducing as she promised.

"Khadim?" I raise my voice as much as I dare as I walk down the stone stairwell. "Khadim." I can only hope they have not attempted to make a spectacle of him at the festivities.

The sound that reaches my ears is not his voice, but I follow it anyway to bars that have him encaged. It is the collar around his throat that has called to me, loud as a clarion. Although I do not have a key, the thick lock that keeps him barred warms under my hand. *Come now*, I coax the lock. *Unhinge yourself.* The lock gives way with a soft whistle that sounds akin to relief.

Khadim is slumped against a big stone wall, and he doesn't move when I call his name. When I go to lift his head he flinches; the admiral has sharpened the collar placed around his neck and chained it to the wall. There is little slack, and blood is encrusted around the area where the metal has bit into his flesh; any pushing or pulling merely digs the metal deeper into him. I'm afraid that if I try to saw into the collar I might cause him to bleed out.

"Khadim, can you hear me?" I crouch so we are eye to eye and grasp his face in my hands. His left eye is swollen, and there are knots the size of eggs under his skin. Tears prickle my eyes at the sight, but I grit my teeth and do not let them fall.

"Eula." Khadim's throat sounds parched, and I wish I had a gift for water instead of metal, if only to relieve him of this one simple thirst.

I clear my throat and keep my voice firm, the way I've seen Tía do when someone comes to her with an incurable illness. "I'm here."

Khadim opens his eyelids as much as he can through the swelling, and there is something in them I have not seen before and I can't quite place. He slowly turns his face and places a kiss onto my palm. "You are here."

Instead of answering, I guide my fingers to the chain in the wall and I coax the links open; when the collar is separated from the wall chain Khadim's head slumps into my hands and he moves his fingers upward, trying to get them beneath the collar. Despite cuts that immediately appear on his hands, he tries again and again to pry the sharpened metal off his neck. His breathing grows labored, and I know it is despair building up beneath his skin. I move his hands away and run my fingers softly around the collar, avoiding the sharp edges that curve into his skin. I search for a clasp or opening, but it's almost as if Khadim was born with the monstrous thing on. I grow still at the groan of the door that leads down the stairs. Khadim trembles but I keep my hands as steady as if I were sewing closed a wound. *Come now, Eula. The metal wants to cooperate. Just teach it how.*

A hollow sound makes the hairs on my arms stand. A Castilian is coming; they are the only ones with wood soles on their shoes. And only wood soles make this sound.

I take a deep breath and move my hands even slower. I squeeze and pray and coax until I can feel all the coils that have been melted to make this collar.

"Khadim. I don't think I can take this off without it causing too much bleeding. I have an idea, but it's going to hurt at first. Just breathe."

He nods in my hands, and I am scared he is going to faint. I place my fingers on the collar again and use my gift to warm the sharp edges. When it is malleable I bend it inward toward Khadim so that it melds into his skin. Under my breath I utter Tía's charms, but Khadim's gasp of pain still fills the cell.

I run my fingers around the metal circumference, welding it into his skin. He has stopped moaning, but I know he must be faint with pain. If he appeared born with the collar before, now he appears even more so; what metal has not been folded into his skin is like a ribbon of brightness against his throat.

I grab his hands and help him to his feet; he stumbles, but I pull him behind me as I run into the darkened halls of the underground keep, the halls that lead away from the door I came through.

If I am not careful I will get us lost, or worse, captured. Khadim swallows sobs as he runs behind me, but I feel him picking up his pace as the pain lessens.

I strain my ears to hear past my loudly thumping heart, bypassing doors until I get to the one we need. The armory. I can hear the song of a thousand metal weapons call to me.

"You don't have to do this, Eula. My men and I can take it from here. I do not want you hurt." Khadim's eyes are full of pain, his voice full of sincerity.

"I made my choice the moment I came for you, Khadim. We deserve more."

I push the door open. The room is filled with lances, spears, bows and arrows, swords, short steel knives, and barrels of oil. The lone window in the room lets in enough light for me to see there are enough weapons to outfit an entire garrison. I gesture Khadim to the spears, and we slide several through the barred window. Next, we each grab a machete, and I maneuver with care to get them through the slats of metal.

I press my palms into the bars and will them to bend the metal. Sweat breaks out on my forehead, but the iron softens and stretches and creates a large enough hole for us to jump and crawl through. I pull myself up into a patch of dirt not covered with steel. I push my hand down to give Khadim assistance, but before he grabs it I hear a familiar scratching sound. He jumps and scrambles onto the field.

"What did you do?" I ask, grabbing a machete while Khadim cradles three spears in one arm.

"I lit the base of the barrel on fire." A blast of heat behind us almost sends us to our knees.

The ingenio is burning.

We run as far as we can, until we make it to the circle of

bohíos. There, Khadim's men stand with the ladinos who raised me: Prieto, Tía, Nana, Rosalinda, Samuel. These folks who suffered through years of service in Sevilla, and then years at the Río Ozama and then years here at the ingenio, are ready to follow the youngest amongst them. Not all. Some shake their heads, afraid to follow. But my closest kin are here. Khadim and I pass out spears to the handful of men and women who do not have their own machetes. Then in unison we all turn back to the mill. The clouds above us clear, and in the moonlight I can make out the peaks of the hills, and if we keep walking, behind them are the Bahoruco Mountains.

A place to hide, to build, to create a new life.

The admiral is expecting me to come calling for my freedom, but he is not expecting me to lead everyone else to theirs. I slash the humid air with my machete, and it is feather light in my hand, whispering, *onward onward onward*.

From the open windows of the admiral's house, I can hear a harpsichord being struck. The occupants have not yet realized they are on fire. We march forward, and I hum along to a brand-new song.

WHEREIN ABIGAIL FIELDS RECALLS HER FIRST DEATH AND, SUBSEQUENTLY, HER BEST LIFE

By Rebecca Roanhorse

NEW MEXICO TERRITORY. 1880s. WINTER.

Abigail Fields was dying. Slowly, terribly, the gunshot wound in her stomach leaking, her lagging heart stretching too long between beats.

The man who had shot her was named Barton Smalls. He was a coward of a white man, and he had abandoned her in the ice-crusted dirt road outside the all-Black settlement of Pueblo Libre to die, no doubt believing that she would expire in the course of time and worry him no more.

Abby hated to admit he might have the right of it.

Breath was getting harder to come by, the space between inhale and exhale as wide as the Rio Grande valley where it cut through the high desert just below town and the far shore could barely be seen. But Abby kept on breathing anyway, hoping that Mo would come. That anyone would come. But Mo, especially, as she'd like it to be her lovely brown face she saw last in this world.

She imagined there weren't too many folks like her and Mo in heaven. Nothing in the Bible they'd made her read at the old nun house said much about Black girls making it to the right hand of the Lord, at least to hear those old white spinsters at the nunnery tell it. If Abigail was honest with herself, the life she'd led so far was just as likely to land her somewhere a bit hotter anyway. Good, then. Hell suited her just fine. Just fine, indeed.

A distant howl broke her from her reverie, followed by a mob of high-pitched yips. A shiver of fear rolled through her body, but all she could do was blink up at the grey winter sky above her. Catch the snowcapped tops of the distant mountain range out of the corner of her eye. Feel the rough touch of dirt and the wet of melting ice beneath her back. And try to keep breathing.

Snowflakes fell, soft and silent. Too silent.

Silent meant everyone else in town was dead. Jolene at the schoolhouse and Francis and Lucy who ran the post. Mr. Henderson and Rose and Rose's sisters. Oh, and their little ones, too.

Even Mo? No, not Mo. She'd been out hunting this morning, shooting grouse to fill their table. She was miles away. Should have been, at least. But she was expected back by now, wasn't she? Oh Lord, not Mo. It would be too much.

Another howl, closer now. Coyotes, out there in the distance. Scavengers, tricksters. Likely coming to this little township that was now only a buffet of fresh death. Perhaps it would be the scavengers and not Smalls's gunshot that took her life. Just like what had happened to her great-aunt Mary, only Mary had survived a wolf attack and lived to tell the tale. But then, Aunt Mary was a legend, and what was Abby but a sixteen-year-old girl, shot in the belly by a coward of a white man, waiting to die?

Part of her thought maybe she'd drawn Barton Smalls to her. Of all the settlements in all the places west of the Mississippi, she'd never thought to see him again. He had looked right at her when he pulled that trigger, and then looked away, her face unrecognized, unremembered. But she remembered him. There was a penny in her pocket to make sure she always remembered.

"Let me live, Lord," Abby whispered through cracked and bloody lips. "If you let me live, I will murder Barton Smalls. I will forsake love and match him hate for hate. Save me, and I will become an instrument of your vengeance. I swear it!"

It was a bold prayer, and who was Abby to make it? She was not particularly brave. Not a gunslinger. Just a girl and not quite a woman, at that. But she was determined, and she meant it with all her heart, and sometimes, and in some places, that's enough.

It went without saying that hate and vengeance were not sentiments she'd learned from the nuns at the convent, so their God did not hear her. But there were other things in the desert, listening. They did not mind hate; they held no fault with vengeance. They found her offering pleasing and struck the deal.

Abigail knew the moment it happened. She felt the covenant take root in her bones. Her breathing eased, the wound in her side knit closed, her heartbeat became strong and steady.

She thought to cry out, and perhaps she did, with only the scavengers and tricksters and the dead to hear her.

And that, too, was enough.

The sun crawled across the sky, and Abby faded in and out of consciousness. After a while, she felt something heavy and warm fall across her body. The smell of wool and smoke filled her nose, strong arms wrapped around her and lifted her up. They pressed her against warm skin, a wide chest. Her eyelids fluttered open. Deep brown eyes met hers, concern and relief battling in a lopsided grin. Mo's face was blood-spattered. Her own? Or someone else's?

"Now, aren't you a blessed sight," Abby murmured.

"Shhh," Mo said, her voice as warm and soft as the blanket she had wrapped her in. "I came as fast as I could. I'm so sorry, Abby. I should have never left you." Mo was breathing hard, fear etched in her face. Her hand hovered over the blood-soaked place on the front of Abby's dress. "Are you hurt?"

"Nothing bad," she lied. "Only grazed."

"I better check the wound . . ."

"No!"

Abby calmed her voice. Mo's hand hadn't even moved. She wouldn't touch her without her say-so. Such manners.

WHEREIN ABIGAIL FIELDS RECALLS HER FIRST DEATH

"It's not necessary for you to fuss," Abby said lightly. She knew even if Mo looked, she'd find no trace of the bullet that had rent Abby earlier. The wound was gone; that was a fact.

"I'm shook up, Mo, but I'm fine. Just take me home."

"Of course," Mo said, abashed at her delay.

Abby slipped her arm around Mo's neck to pull close to her. "Is anyone else alive? Jolene? Francis? Rose and her sisters?"

Mo's face was as bleak as the Rocky Mountains behind them. "They're all dead."

"Oh."

"I'm sorry, Abby." Her voice hitched. "It's too lawless out here. We'll have to move on. To somewhere with a lawman, a real town with a sheriff to protect us."

"No. Lawmen won't fix this. They cause more trouble than they cure, and you know that's true. We've got to do this ourselves."

Mo fell silent, as she always did when Abby got it in her head about the evils of white men. But Mo hadn't seen that kind of ugliness firsthand like Abby had, hadn't watched what a mob could do. Of course, there was more to it, this time.

There was Barton Smalls . . . and there was a promise.

She didn't tell Mo of the pact she'd made with the desert. She knew Mo would disapprove of any truck with spirits. The nuns had done more of a brainwash on Mo than she cared to admit. Plus, any scheme that put Abby in danger would worry her. That was one of the things Abby liked best about Mo: her worry. And once Mo knew what she had planned for Barton Smalls, Mo would be worried plenty.

"Take it," Great-Aunt Mary had insisted the day Abby left the nun house where her auntie worked. "Take it and use it. This gun don't miss."

"All guns miss," Abby scoffed.

"This one won't," Aunt Mary said, her voice made rough from whiskey and homemade cigars. "It's special. Kept me alive against a pack of wolves."

Abby laughed and adjusted her ladies' hat. It was a fine piece, made all of lace and silk, and no other girl in the convent had anything like it. Certainly not her aunt, whom she loved dearly but whom Abby found a bit plain and uncouth. "Ladies don't carry guns."

"Take it, Abigail." She thrust the revolver into her hands. "And when the wolves come for you, you'll know what to do."

Abby had taken it to be polite. After all, they were family. And perhaps she could sell the thing once she and Mo arrived in Pueblo Libre.

She'd put the gun in a box and put the box in her steamer trunk and forgotten about it, mostly. So when the predators did come for her, she hadn't been ready.

"Wake up, Abby," Mo's voice called excitedly from the other room.

The command was followed by a series of booms and

bangs and a mild swear as something heavy struck the old pine floor. The dining room chair. Mo had a habit of knocking it over when she was excited.

"What in the world . . . ?" Abby murmured, sitting up in bed. It had been a month since Barton Smalls had razed the settlement of Pueblo Libre, killing all but two of its residents. In that month, Mo had begged her a dozen times to leave. To move north to Trinidad or all the way up to Denver, where the mines were bustling and there was work to be had in the laundries and saloons. But Abby had refused.

"How do you think they'll treat us there?" Abby had asked. "Two young Black women on their own, and no proper male guardian? And not a dress in sight for you. They'll figure us out lickety-split, and then what?"

"It's safer there . . ."

"Safer for whom?" Abby asked, unrelenting, even though Mo was beginning to droop. "Not us, Mo."

"But if we keep our heads down, don't cause trouble."

"No place is safer than right here," she lied, thinking only of her covenant and the blood she owed the desert, "so we're staying."

"Abby, be reasonable."

"You don't like it, then you're free to go!"

The words were an angry snarl, and Abby didn't mean them. Lord, she'd like to die if Mo left her. But she had made promises that couldn't be broken, and the reckoning was coming. She could feel it in the soles of her feet when she walked the open desert, in the cries of birds that circled the small graveyard where they had buried the dead, in the rush of wind through the door that Mo had left open in her haste. And when her palm cupped around her penny.

"Abby!" Mo called again as she burst into the bedroom. She had an envelope in her hand. Not too large, but not small either. Whatever was in there was making Mo dance with excitement like she had bees in her bonnet. Abby chuckled to herself. Mo in a bonnet? That would be a sight.

"What is it?"

"I got you a present. Well, us. I got us a present." The girl was practically bouncing in place as she presented the packet to Abby. Abby grinned.

"What is it?"

"Open it!"

Abby kept a small knife in her pocket, and she slid it out now to slice open the envelope. Mo's joy was infectious, and Abby couldn't help but grin along . . . until she saw what was inside.

"A ticket to Los Angeles?"

"Two tickets. One for me, and one for you."

"Mo—"

"Now, don't say no yet," Mo rushed on. "I know you're not keen on Colorado, but Los Angeles was founded by Black folks just like us. It's a place we could be welcomed. And it's right near the ocean. You told me you always wanted to see the ocean."

"I do," Abby admitted.

"See? And the new train tracks that the Santa Fe Railway built go right there. And it took some doing, but I got us tickets. We leave tomorrow. We can start over. Live how we want to live." She grasped Abby by the arms. "Come with me, Abby. Say yes!"

Abby wanted to. So much her heart hurt just thinking about saying no. But "no" is what she had to say.

"Why not!?" Mo cried, throwing her hands up in frustration. "What is so special about staying here? What hold does this place have on you?"

Abby opened her mouth, but she didn't have to answer. The desert answered for her, with a gale of hot wind on a winter's day, the chorus of coyote song, a low rumble of thunder across the mountains.

Mo rubbed her arms, chilled despite the gust of heat, and looked out the window. "Is someone coming?" she whispered.

Abby didn't have to answer that, either.

"A gun, Abby?" Mo cried.

"Not just any gun," Abby countered, lifting the box that held the revolver from her steamer trunk, where it had lain since they'd come to Pueblo Libre. "A special gun."

"All guns are the same."

"This was a gift from my great-aunt Mary. She told me it couldn't miss."

"All guns miss."

Abby grinned. "That's what I told her, too."

"Barton Smalls is an outlaw, and a sharpshooter by reputation. Plus, he won't come alone, Abby. To face him and his men down with one gun? It's suicide."

"I'm not afraid of a little death."

"There is a perfectly good train ticket to somewhere green and beautiful and safe lying on the kitchen table. Pick it up and claim it and come with me!"

Abby opened the chamber of the .38 revolver. "You know they call this gun the Lemon Squeezer," she told Mo. "On account of the way you must squeeze the grip to pull the trigger."

Mo stared at her. "Are you even listening to me?"

"I already told you—"

"I know. Your great-aunt Mary. She would have stayed and fought. But she ain't here. And, besides, that's a maybe. You don't know. She might have gone to Los Angeles, too."

Abby smiled, sadness warring with resignation.

The other girl deflated like somebody had let the air out of her. "Please come."

"Maybe in the spring. After I've taken care of things here."

"You can't stay here alone. Who's gonna keep you safe?"

Abby patted the box that held the revolver. "Aunt Mary."

The walk back from the train station was long and lonely. Tearful promises had been made. Not the kind a dying girl makes to the desert. The kind two girls in love make to each other. Hopeful, full of dreams.

I have forsaken love, Abby thought to herself, *for a chance at revenge.*

Soon, the desert whispered. And the desert never lied.

✦ ✦ ✦

Barton Smalls was in her dreams. Not looking as he had when he rode into Pueblo Libre, but as he had back in Texas, when Abby still lived with her mama and hadn't been sent to Aunt Mary's and the nuns yet. Young, light-haired and dark-eyed, a handsome man, at least in her child's eye.

He'd been one of the men who'd come for her daddy. Not screaming and ugly like the others, their voices screeching demands for blood, but he was there just the same, guilty just the same. Smalls had watched them take Daddy away, and when he'd seen her watching him, he'd flipped her a penny. A real copper penny. And laughed as it fell at her feet.

She'd never forgotten his face or that contemptuous penny . . . or the star he'd worn on his chest. And she'd never told Mo about any of it, how Smalls was the reason she knew lawmen couldn't be trusted, that you couldn't find safety in towns. That maybe there was no safety but the kind you made yourself, and even that had a way of failing sometimes. But then, maybe safety was overrated, and a girl had to embrace danger if she wanted to survive. And maybe survival itself was overrated, and a girl had not to fear death, and that's the best she could do sometimes.

Abby awoke with a start. Bolted straight out of bed like the devil was on her heels, and maybe he was.

Barton Smalls was coming.

She fumbled the covers away, dressed hurriedly in trousers and a long coat. The Lemon Squeezer rested in its box, and she claimed it and the single bullet, chambering it before she left the house.

The sun was barely a glow of white on the horizon when she came to the road. She stood resolute in the very place he had left her to die. The earth knew her, recognized her by blood and bone, and welcomed her back. To finish what had been started.

Mo was wrong.

Barton Smalls came alone. Riding an alabaster mare and wearing a white church suit, a pale rider on a white horse.

His hair was unkempt and his eyes were wild. There were places on his face where he had scratched the skin clean off and sores ran yellow with pus. He was skeleton thin, and his hands trembled around reins that threatened to fall from loose fingers.

Abby paused. This was the man who had almost ended her life? Who had haunted her nightmares and kept her from her love? This was the thing she had feared since she was a child?

"What's wrong with you?" she asked, her voice carrying across the emptiness between them.

Barton didn't answer, and at first she thought he didn't hear her. But his brow lifted, his eyes turned in her direction, and the corners of his mouth tilted up.

"Don't I know you?" he asked in a voice slurred from pain and drink and the business of dying.

Abby took a step back, horrified. Had he finally recognized her? The penny was hot in her pocket, next to the Lemon Squeezer.

Barton's head rolled on his neck. "Don't I know this place?"

"You have a sickness," Abby shouted, raising the revolver. "The plague . . ." But even as she said it, she knew that wasn't it. The desert stripped a man of his pretenses. Barton Smalls had always been rotten underneath, only now it showed through.

"They're all dead," Barton said, his gaze falling earth-ward. "Old Charlie and Dewey and the other boys. All dead."

"Then why'd you come?"

"The desert's been calling my name."

Abby gasped. Could it be her? The covenant she made? Or even . . .

"Do you know who I am?" she asked. "Do you recognize my face?"

He peered at her, leaning precariously over his horse, and she held her breath, waiting. After a moment, he shook his head. "I can't say I do."

In a way it was a relief, she supposed. It meant he hadn't come to Pueblo Libre because of her. This was just another Black settlement to terrorize for him, her friends here just nameless lives stolen.

She still held the gun, but she was unsure now what to do. Now that the moment had come, it didn't tempt like it had before. Smalls was wretched, inside and out, and she need not end his life to prove that.

Her free hand went to the penny in her pocket. She thought about giving it back. Throwing it in his face. Screaming that he might not remember her, but she sure as hell remembered him. And then pulling the trigger on the Lemon Squeezer to make it bark lead until Barton Smalls was dead.

But she also thought of Mo's eyes when she'd boarded that train. The way her entire face had flushed hot when she leaned in to kiss her. Even though it was chaste, a brush of lips against her cheek, it was enough to make Abby warm.

Mo, who had believed in a future. Mo, who even now was somewhere far from the desert. Mo, who would not want this man's death to stain her hands.

Abby lowered the gun.

"I'm too good for you, Barton Smalls. You stay right here and rot away and die. Let the desert keep calling your name until it swallows you whole. I'm done with it."

And she turned her back on Barton Smalls.

The desert pulled at her feet, whispered words of covenant, dark promises, stolen life that she had bartered for but had not yet earned. Distant coyote howls broke across the Rio Grande in the valley below town.

You owe us, it said. *A life for a life. You promised!*

The rumble started far off and closed in fast. It took Barton by surprise, knocking him from his horse. He lay unmoving on the ground, on the road where he'd once left her. She watched in horror as he seemed to deflate, the life draining out of him. And then his skin bubbled and split and filled again, but not with Barton Smalls. Something else inhabited his body now, and it rose up on coltish legs and reached out overlong arms and blew hot breath across her face. Colorless eyes caught her gaze, and a gaping hole of a mouth spoke.

You promised!

"You have your life," she said. "Take Smalls and be done with me."

Still hungry, and you promisssssssed!

The creature was greedy, and Abby was not impressed. She raised the Lemon Squeezer, the gun Aunt Mary said never missed. Pointed it at the thing that had been Barton Smalls.

"I changed my mind."

She pulled the trigger.

"Good morning, ma'am," the conductor greeted her as she stepped on the train. He motioned for the younger man next to him to take her steamer, and he dutifully complied. Abby handed him her ticket for inspection. "You heading to Los Angeles?"

Abby nodded.

"You have friends there?"

"Someone special who I hope will be my family someday."

"A sweetheart," he said with a knowing wink. "Well, they'll be mighty happy to see you." He gestured down the aisle, indicating the seat assigned to her. "Get comfortable, and I'll let you know when supper is served."

"How long is the trip?" she asked, taking her seat.

"Not too long. And the scenery is quite something. We'll pass right by the Grand Canyon."

Abby dug into her pocket and flipped the young man who

took her steamer a penny. He grabbed it out of the air and bobbed his head, grateful for the tip. Abby pulled down the window shade.

"I don't much care for the desert scenery," she said, "but I'm quite looking forward to the ocean."

THE RULES OF THE LAND

By Alaya Dawn Johnson

Years later now, when I look out over the mangroves at dusk and hear the gray waves whispering in my mother's tongue to return, to return, I think of my father, who took from the sea and was taken in his turn, and whose failures haunt me as much as his love.

My mother has turned her back on the sea. My father sleeps among the mangroves. I stand watch at the midline, my voice muted and my feet clumsy. It was not always this way. I'm sure it won't always be. There is a war on, after all, and war changes things. I am bound to Yemaya now, and one day I will step into the white-capped waves and never rise again. What was my parents' debt is mine; I took it willingly, I don't complain. Yet it is a tight vise around the free heart of a young girl who knows that her parents cannot bear the weight of how she came into the world. They could not bear the fire of my voice. I had to fight for that for myself.

In those days before the steel ships of the Tanger blockade sat with cannons ready to rain fire just beyond the horizon at the mouth of the Egun Bay, Laarin fishermen like my father made good livings going a few days out to the sea mouth in their brightly painted one-sail skiffs and returning with holds so full of catch the boats waddled low in the water like black ducks. Rumor held that my father had caught a sea maid in his nets, huddled among the bass and the ladyfish, and brought her back to Laarin to be his wife. It was a good story, an expected and understood story, and Daddy never tried to correct it.

The truth was that my mother found him passed out from too much palm wine, about to drown at the breakwater. She saved his life.

I don't regret my birth. Mami sure could have picked a better father—but then, who am I, if not my daddy's child? I'm no drunk, but I have my vices: dancing past reason, dancing till dawn, dancing with my feet or in my little skiff as I dare those soldiers secure in their slow metal ships to stop me. I can hear his laughter when I slip by them, smell the yeasty ferment of his palm wine as he congratulates me on another successful run. It isn't so bad, keeping a bit of him close.

He gave Yemaya's daughter a kiss in return for saving his life, even though she had come to him as a sea cow. But when he entered the water it was a pair of human arms that wrapped around his bare torso, and it was human lips, soft as clay, that touched his.

"Don't you look at me, fisherman." That was Daddy's voice, imitating my mother. "Don't you dare look." And so he didn't, not the whole while they spent in the warm water. But when they finished, he opened his eyes, just a slit, for just a peek—

All he saw was a sea cow's sleek brown back as it dove for deeper water.

Eight months later, a woman walked out of the ocean. A woman with hair the color of a whitecap at the break-water and a belly as shiny and round as an onyx cabochon. At that point in the story, Daddy always got quiet and soft. Not precisely remorseful, but his mouth full of a devastating awareness of what he had done.

"I had the advantage, Nena," Mami told me once, in that singing tongue that belonged only to us and to the sea. "I knew his face in the moonlight, and he had loved me without ever knowing mine."

"He knew one of your faces, Mami."

At that her nose crinkled, a little joke between the two of us. "Nena, your father is a fisherman. He does not see the face of a fish any more than he can see the face of the mangrove."

"The mangrove has a face?"

She sighed like a wind across the open sea. "Child, you cannot imagine how beautiful."

Mami lived with us and cooked for us like a good Laarin fisherman's wife. She and I took baskets of salted herring south every ten days to the great market on the nearby Ofu border. We stayed until sundown, when only a layer or two of fish sweated at the bottom of our great baskets, and the red canvas stalls lay in their deconstructed geometry on the packed earth of the international fairground. Mami would ask, "Is there anyone left to give us their money, Nena?" And I would reply, even when I could spy a few hearthwomen hurrying from last stall to last stall like panicked vultures, "No, I don't see anyone, Mami." The last few fish were for the beggars. I knew that, just as I knew we were never to tell Daddy. After the market guards were off drinking the day's pay at the tavern boats docked in the placid north edge of the Egun River, we gave one herring each to anyone who approached us until we had no more left.

When we returned, Daddy would count the money, look at Mami, and mutter something about selling the stock too cheaply. Mami would pretend that she hadn't heard, if it was a good day. If it was a bad day, he'd go on and on about shoddy business practices and make wild conjectures about how Mami spent the extra money. Food, wine, prostitutes of all genders, trinkets for me. I would try to intervene: "Daddy, don't you want to hear a song I learned at market?" or "Daddy, why don't we go to Uncle Uche's tavern together?" When he'd really gotten going, even this last wasn't enough to move him. He'd look at me as though I were a runt of a fish left straggling at the bottom of his boat. He'd take Mami's hand and drag her into the bedroom and lock the door. Sometimes he'd hit me, sharp, between the ribs, and I would sit, gasping just like that fish. For years I sat watch outside that door, as though I could do something about whatever was happening inside. Their screams. Their silences.

One day, Mami shattered his wine jug against the wall.

She pulled open the door so fast that I fell backward, staring up at her face, still as a mangrove's. She stepped around me and walked out to the sea. She waded up to her waist in the waves, and no further, the white of her hip-cloth billowing around her. "Yemaya, Mami Wata, Mother," she called, over and over, in that susurrating tongue, while I watched with my heart in my throat.

Daddy stumbled out of our two-room cottage and down to the shore, telling her to come back, begging her forgiveness, swearing his love. She ignored him until he gave up and went back inside. I stayed; I was always the stronger of the two of us. After the moon had risen high in the sky, she left the water. She climbed up that hill on legs that did not tremble, and paused like a ghost in the doorway, limned by the moonlight behind her. I crouched between them, forgotten, afraid I might not exist, afraid I was no one's child.

"I went to find a locksmith," she said, in a careful, clipped tone I would not hear again for years.

Daddy gasped as though she'd shot him with a Tanger cannon. He looked up at her and then down, disbelieving, at the wound: the iron key strung on a double cord of twisted rhinoceros leather that had never left his chest since I had known the world.

"I-it's been charmed," he said.

Mami's lips curled up. He lurched to his feet and ran to the other room, where he kept the strongbox. I had never seen him open it, and he didn't now. He just cursed in smugglers' pidgin and squatted in front. He was so scared. I wanted to ask Mami what she'd done, but she stayed staring at the hollow space he had left, and I knew she could not see me. I cried for her, instead. I cried for the child they had never let me be.

Daddy got sober for a few years after that. Got sober and found religion, old Ofu style: he was baptized for Olokun, the god and goddess of the deep, the progenitor and partner of Laarin's own Yemaya. He went out as a sailor and shrine-keeper on Ofu-sponsored deep-sea voyages to other islands and the Tanger coast, trips that lasted months and gave me and Mami plenty of time alone. No more night smuggling raids for Daddy's drinking money. He was a respectable Laarin trader now. She remembered me, with Daddy gone. She smiled more, but not as wide. Daddy had moved us to a better house in a better part of town. It was also farther from the water. We stayed in our familiar hut until the days when the ship was due back, when we'd break out the fancy cloth and head scarves and cowrie ankle bands that he had bought for us, and clean the dust from the floor and the eaves of the two-story house in eastern Laarin, with real windows of thick, opaque glass.

When Daddy left, there was the mother tongue, the waves, and the deep. There was the water, which ran through me as it did my mother, though it had been transmuted by humanity.

"I'm weaker than you, Mami," I told her.

"I cannot even put my head beneath the waves, Nena. It is you who are powerful."

"You would be a goddess if he had not kept you here. I'm half human. I'm weak, like he is."

"You think your human side makes you weak? Your father became weak, Nena, but he did not start that way."

I could hold the lightning in my hands when I was thirteen. I could drink a rain cloud like a pint of palm wine, and the next morning my piss was orange as fire. But when I hovered in secret over a noontime pool of still water, the haunted eyes of a little girl stared back at me; her face faded into the scenery, like a ghost in her own life, barely there.

When I was fourteen, and the Tanger trade partnership turned into something quietly ominous, Daddy skipped the dry season's trading expeditions. Mami and I worried that he'd go back to the taverns, but he stayed with us. He took me out among the mangroves and then to the breakwater so I could learn how to throw the nets and haul in a catch. He taught me how to knock a red-beaked parakeet from a tree with a slingshot and how to smoke out a wasps' nest so that we could feast on the honey-soaked paper within. I felt some new, spiky thing growing within me over those long, hot afternoons, with their easy words and loamy silences. I was not just the daughter of a sailor and the granddaughter of a goddess: I was a girl whose eyes looked past the shoreline, and whose face was just coming into color. I don't know if he saw it, but it wasn't for him anymore, in any case. "Do you want to dance, child?" he would ask me some evenings, as he rowed us back along the mangrove coast. I always said yes. When we got back at sundown, he brought us to the town square.

Mami was a terrible dancer. She balanced on those banyan legs like a newborn giraffe, and even her years on land, it seemed, couldn't change that muscle-deep distrust of open air and hard ground. Laarin is famous for its feast days and dances—at least, it was, before the Tanger blockade stopped the flow of foreign ships and the musicians who lined our circular plaza and played until sunrise. But she sang like a summer storm, and Laarin opened its heart to her in those blessed days. That's what we call them now, the last free trading season before the Tanger invasion of the southern Ofu territories and the blockade of the Egun Bay. The last time we had our music. Not the gods' chants of Ofu priests and priestesses or the rolling drums of the Highat tribes to the east, but a Laarin beat: polyglot, inventive, wild, and irreverent. To us, this was Yemaya's music, no matter what the official Ofu liturgy held. And my mother was one of ours, though Laarin had watched her with careful eyes since the day she rose from the shallows, clad in a simple shift of white. She had never tried to appear human, which angered and embarrassed me and made me love her even more fiercely. She was a child of the sea, a daughter of Yemaya, a goddess stripped of her skin and locked behind one uncanny face.

When Mami whipped us with her song, Daddy and I went dancing. We did Omozgo two-step, and the broom jumpers of the people he had traded with farther up the northeastern coast, and the jerk-motion hat tricks he had learned right here as a Laarin smuggler's boy. Daddy might be a sailor, but he was at home on steady ground. He tried to ask Mami to dance when she sat silently on the border wall, but his tongue was as clumsy as his feet were fluent. He stuttered his way through: "Would you do me—the honor?—of da—"

Mami took pity on him and held her long fingers against his full lips. "Of course not, but I am honored by your asking."

Daddy liked to claim he lost his speech around Mami because he could never forget he was talking to a "princess" of the kingdom below water. Right around the time he died, I realized that her status had never intimidated him. It was his guilt. He wielded his water wife as though she were the talking tortoise of the tale: to get better work, a better house, better wine. But he always knew Yemaya would have her due.

A year after those blessed days, when the Tanger blockade had set the full force of its cannons and steel against us, my divine grandmother made her displeasure known. It started with heavy rains, far too late in the season. Then the rain stopped, and the fish stocks of the bay plummeted. Even the seaweed beds died of a mysterious disease that left them inedible, stinking of eggs. I would go with the neighborhood girls to collect larvae beds of water flies from the shallows and bake them into cakes. Daddy was dismissive: "Poor-man's food," he said, and went out again to pray at Olokun's rites. He came back with millet cake and red beans from the offering and we ate in secret, before anyone could see our prosperity. He told us that Olokun wouldn't let these light-skinned foreigners track their bloody boot prints across the Egun Peninsula. The great kingdom of Ofu would stop them. But the Tanger with their steel and cannon and deity of gunpoint benevolence ran across the southern plains as though they were in a feast day footrace. They stopped at the southern mouth of the Egun River. They squatted down in the mud and watched. Daddy prayed and offered to Olokun. But he returned from his fishing night after night with a net full of empty crab shells and old fishhooks. Everyone's catch was bad, but his could have glowed from the bad mojo. All of Laarin kept clear of us, as though Yemaya's punishment would touch them if they lingered.

One day, the fishermen returned to harbor even more long-faced than usual. An armada had been spotted just on the horizon: Tanger steel ships, cannons bristling like teeth from the hulls. The mandible of the Tanger. With the land army encamped a few days' ride south in Ofu, we were now trapped in their jaws. It would be easy work for the armada.

The whole city gathered for our war rites, which had not been invoked in nearly a century. We sang to Yemaya, sacrificed our best livestock, and threw garlands of white flowers into the water. For a week, Laarin begged our own Yemaya for her help, but the sea kept her counsel, quiet and sterile as a puddle. Mami stayed home, her lips pursed, her back to the sea.

"Mami," I asked her, fear so hot on my skin that it made me brave, "why is Mami Wata so angry with us? Why won't she defend us?"

She gave me a cool stare. I swallowed back the terror I always felt at these moments when her alien remoteness took her too far for me to follow.

When she finally spoke, it was in smugglers' pidgin. "You don't take from Yemaya," she said, "if you'd still like to sleep." The phrase was common among Laarin smugglers. I had heard it whispered in reference to my father. But I had refused to understand until that moment.

"But how could he have *taken* you? Didn't you come to him?"

Her eyes came back to me and crinkled at the edges, as though she really were human. "I did. And he made sure I had to stay. He never gave me the chance to choose."

Daddy had started drinking again. He never did handle responsibility well, and guilt is the heaviest kind. He hoarded bootleg palm liquor instead.

I knew what she meant, though I had struggled to avoid thinking of it most of my life. I had known since the day they fought and she threatened him with the locksmith: the charmed iron key and the strongbox that he checked every night but never opened. He was terrified of her leaving him. So he made sure that she never could.

I said to my mother in the language just the two of us shared, "You've slept next to him insensible for a thousand nights. Why not take the key from his neck?"

"It burns my skin. It has a charm."

"Why not ask me to do it?"

"Would I ask my own daughter to betray her own father? Have I been such a poor mother to you?"

I squeezed my eyes shut. "Go back! Go back now! Can't you see she's killing us? If he's too weak, then do it yourself." We were sitting at the shore. She twisted herself to look at the water, as though it repelled her but drew her just the same.

"I will return there eventually. I am Yemaya's daughter. But not yet. He needs me, Nena. He will die without me."

I knew my father, knew how he looked at her, how he drank when she went to the water, how his gaze followed her like a moth follows the moon whenever she was in his sight. I knew Mami only told the truth.

I felt it again, as though I were losing myself, drowning in the storm that raged between them, as though I were not their daughter but a bit of seaweed, a tossed spar splintered from a wrecked ship. I filled my lungs with air and dug my nails into the soft skin of my wrist. "If you don't go, we might all die."

My mother, she did not even answer me. The waves heard me, though. They said, "Come, daughter, come. Make it right, if they will not."

Mami grimaced and hurled a stone into the shallows with the force of a boulder.

The armada held off for a week, but when none of the prophesied waves and storms arrived, they made their cautious way forward. Laarin's reputation could protect it for a while, but reputation would never match Tanger's ambitions. Only a show of force would turn them back. And our force, our most reliable ally, Yemaya of the kingdom below, had abandoned us.

Daddy did not pass a moment sober. He kept to the new house, and not the taverns, where the sailors and fishermen and smugglers waited in icy silence for him to order his wine and depart. They knew. We all knew. This was Laarin, after all, and we had always been Yemaya's. He began to vomit, and there was no one but me to clean it. So I did; I had practice. I was my father's daughter and I loved him, as much as Mami loved him, as much as he loved the both of us.

"I wish we were dancing again, like last year," I said.

His eyes rolled bloodshot past me, steadied, and came back. "Your mother would never dance."

"You never gave her a chance."

"I asked!"

I heard my mother's voice in my head as though it were my own. A calm certainty steadied my racing pulse and cooled my disgust. "You cannot ask for that which you have already compelled."

He closed his eyes. I left him there. It was not a long walk to the ocean. It never is, in Laarin City. We are Yemaya's, first and forever. But I walked out along the mangrove coast and then slipped myself into the muddy water. I felt Yemaya around me, buoying me up, lighting my path with a swirling tail of phosphorescence. I was her granddaughter, but now, for the first time, I entered her domain alone. As I swam, the water and the moon and the clouds came together in a solitary baptism. I was fifteen, that night I became a woman. The moon had moved a thumb in the sky by the time I reached that tiny mangrove island that marked the limit of the bay. I climbed their thickly tangled roots and sat with my back against a trunk. A crocodile peeled its eyelid back and we exchanged a long look before it slid into the water and away from me. I laughed softly. I was so afraid. From here I could barely make out the breakwater and the masts of the nearest ships of the Tanger armada. They would be here within a day.

The air was as still and thick as soup, faintly but unmistakably spiced by the sulfur of foreign gunpowder. We would not survive. Ofu might stave off the Tanger battalion on their southern border, but not if Laarin was overrun in the north.

"Yemaya!" I called, though not precisely that, because in her language her name is the sound of water itself, a rushing accretion of force that rips through the vocal cords and plummets like an arrow into the ocean.

She appeared to me in a blink, in the heart of the mangrove. I fell back into the water, all terror and wonder.

"He will pay for what he took!" Her voice through the mangrove crackled like burning tinder and ripped at my ears.

"But we will all die in the morning, when those ships come."

"He will pay!"

I dipped my head below water; the pain was too much. "And if I promise myself in his stead?" I said. My words wrapped themselves around the thousand legs of the mangrove island. They held them tight.

A solitary sea cow with skin as white as a pearl swam out

from their protective shadow. Her face was my mother's, her face was my mother's. She kissed my forehead and swam away.

I barely made it back to shore before the storm did. I found Mami sitting alone in our old straw-thatch hut, Daddy's iron chest at her feet. The rain lashed the mud walls like the drumming fingers of an angry god.

"We have to get to higher ground," I said.

"Your father will come for this." Her voice was shorn and clipped again, that remembered spear of disquiet from a childhood I hadn't understood. She did not look at me. Of course she didn't. But it mattered less, now.

"Let's go, Mami," I said. "Leave the damn box."

"I loved him, Nena. You can't imagine how much . . ." Lightning hit the sea with two fists. Her head jerked up. Her eyes were wild, the whites had disappeared. They'd gone black as pebbles. Like those of the sea cow who had claimed me by the mangrove. "What did you give her, Nena?"

"The only thing I had."

We ran from that place with just the clothes on our backs. We ran with hundreds of others whose homes were too close to the shore, who knew as well as my mother did that Yemaya had, at last, sent us her storm and that her aid would not be without price. We passed Daddy, shocked halfway sober. He was running in the wrong direction. I begged him to come away with us, but he ignored me like he always had when she filled his vision.

"I'll get it back," he told Mami. "Don't you leave me now."

Mami's eyes still hadn't gotten their irises back. I wondered if Daddy even noticed. "Stay with us," she said. Just that, but it was a plea as fervent as the rain that stung our cheeks.

He shook his head. "Take care of your mother," he told me absently. Dismissed, like that runty fish left over from the catch, like a child gasping and forgotten.

He started running back down the road. That spiky thing inside me snapped and flowered. I sprinted to catch up, grabbed his wrist, and hauled him around. He had a wild look, lips pulled back from his teeth, chest heaving. I wondered if he would hit me. But I raised my own hand, pulled a thread of lightning from the rioting sky, and told him, simply, "Try."

He froze, staring at the crackling light sparking against my fingertips and palm. I could kill him right there if I wanted. The joy at being powerful, being more, being *seen at last* was so intense that I felt the spark of Yemaya's flame leap from my outstretched fingers to his wet curls. I pulled it back, the acrid stink of scorched hair thick in my nostrils. Daddy stammered my name.

"Just leave it," I told him.

"Your mother—she won't—you don't understand, I *have* to—"

"Let her go, then!" I yelled. "Stay for me!"

I might as well have asked him to stay for the seaweed, to stay for the sand. He stared at me, confused, searching. For a moment, I hoped—but his gaze grew distant again. He hugged me, though my hand still glowed with lightning and my whole body buzzed with friction. Then he was gone, running down the road as the floodwaters came up.

That was the last time I saw him alive.

The storm sank every ship of the Tanger armada right at the breakwater. Lined them up like hens in a market stall. And our divers have been making good use of whatever we can scavenge for the last three years.

After Daddy drowned, I took the key from the tangled hide cord that had strangled him to death in the confusion of the flooding. Together, Mami and I opened the chest.

There was a shift inside, so small and plain. It did not fit her anymore. We burned it with Daddy's things.

"The rules of the sea," Mami said that night, when we shared a pint of palm wine in his memory, "are harsh, but fair. When you go to her, you must remember that. They are not like we are here."

"We were beautiful here."

"Yes."

She still lives in that tall house with its thick windows where you can't hear the whispering of the sea. I've made my way all up and down this mangrove coast, into Ofu and the Highat territories and beyond, smuggling goods past the Tanger armies that are still trying to choke us to death. She will not return to Yemaya, who killed her love. She cannot, I think, forgive herself for loving him. One day I will have to go to Yemaya in her stead. But not yet. Not until my grandmother calls me.

And when I go down to that place, no matter how much the rules of the sea differ from the rules of the land, I will bring my fire with me, and the air in my lungs, and though I may not be free, I will be seen.

A HAGIOGRAPHY OF STARLIGHT

By Somaiya Daud

Betimes I wonder, if I had not been so secure in my own power, if I had thought beyond my own abilities and my own desires, whether I would have seen it. If I had listened more and learned to worry, if I would have marked the slow decay, the discord in song, the apocalyptic tune that led my world to the point of no return. But such is the power of hindsight.

I was born in the city of Baal, or so I assume, for I have no memory of the people who bore me and abandoned me in its alleys. Baal was an ancient city with buildings that had stood thousands of years. The song of their age ricocheted against the newer boulevards and pleasure gardens, and rose up in the great sandstorms that assailed the city from time to time. It was the capital of the Baal Empire and therefore its center, just as it was the center of my world.

My world was filled with song, and in Baal's cradle I learned the difference between the flower song of the gardens and the songs of flowers that grew freely and without human control. It was in Baal I learned the wood song of newer buildings and the stone songs of the ancient. And it was in Baal that I began to understand what people meant when they said kazerach and to whom it was they referred. For it was from the kazerach twining its way around and through our world that all song flowed. It was from the kazerach that we were given life, and it was on the back of his spirit that we flourished.

As a child, shameless and without guile, I sang, and in song, I caught glimpses of him and his glory. Never anything I could hold on to, never a song note I could replicate, but always I came away from such song certain that I had glimpsed a little more of his majesty, of his beauty. And it was in such song when I was eight, as the morning sun rose, that the priestesses of the kazerach—the kazervaaj—made note of me and took me in off the street.

Until then, mine had been a miserable existence, filled with hunger and cold and fear. A girl with no family and no pack of orphans to watch her back was seldom safe in a city like ours. Joy and safety were seldom and fleeting. But the morning the kazervaaj discovered me, I felt joy rise in me as a tidal wave. As the sun touched my face I felt the flush of divinity, like a rising tide of pure light churning inside me, pushing at the edges of my soul. The world was louder and quieter all at once—song rising over the clamor. The air warmed, my breath stalled. It filled me up until it couldn't, until I could feel it pressing against the barriers of my skin, and then it robbed me of it all at once.

And in my retrieval I finally learned the kazerach's name: Bayyur.

The House of Bayyur was unlike anything I'd ever known. The kazerach of Baal had many aspects, but key was his love of love. He gave and took life, burned and warmed, starved and nourished. Bayyur sought to illuminate the beautiful in the ugly, and he reveled in pleasure. And the longer I lived in the Baal monastery, the more intimately I learned these things. I had been denied them when I lived scurrying from alley to alley, but now I knew them all in abundance. It took longer for me to understand what it was the kazervaaj wanted from me—that my voice was a prized and holy thing, that it rendered my flesh and the sight of my face sacrosanct.

In the monastic structure of the kazerach there were three orders: the kazervaaj, the hagaad, and the saagkazaar. The kazervaaj were priestesses. Almost all members of the temple were kazervaaj. The hagaad were the warrior order, and resided primarily in the Temple of the Great Mother Serpent. They left only when a saagkazaar was found.

Saagkazaar was an old word with no equivalent in the Baal tongue, but it meant "the state of being prior to bridehood." Those who left that state were either dead or turned kazerkai—the bride of the serpent.

There were no kazerkai in Baal. There had been none for over a thousand years. The learning of the dance that turned one from saagkazaar to kazerkai had been outlawed, for a bride of the kazerach held untold power over the fates of men. Her word was that of an oracle, and her allegiances determined the results of battles.

I was not named saagkazaar, for the kazervaaj knew they trod dangerous ground even bringing me into the monastery. You could not leash song and dance—you might make the singer and dancer afraid, or you might choose their death. What is one soul in the face of empire? I did not understand this when I was young—I understood only that I was lucky and that I was blessed and that they trained me in what I loved best: song and dance.

Even as I loved the House of Bayyur, I chafed at my restrictions. I could no longer go out, could not enjoy the marketplace. And I was the only child, my companions the hagaad—bodyguards—who protected me.

The head of the kazervaaj understood that my world of palm fronds and still ponds was not enough. She would not give me free run of the city—she would not risk its pollution poisoning me. But we began to take leave of the temple, to travel out of the city environs, and it was in this way I came to know a little more of the empire.

When I was thirteen we went to the imperial palace, which was called the Temple of Kings. It was nestled against a great cliffside, and framed by six waterfalls, three on each side. Spanning north, west, and east was a great jungle with a single, paved road all the way through. By then I had been to the grasslands, the sea, and the great northern mountains. And at last, it seemed, the king had heard of me and requested my presence.

I heard whispers of the saagkazaar, dancers and singers of the kazerach. I wanted so desperately to be one, to be so connected to the kazerach, to pour all my heart into song for him. And I believed the king's summons—the *king*, who was the vessel of the kazerach in the mortal world—was a sign of what I was. But as our caravan made its way along the road, my mind turned with unease. I sat in a litter as we made our way from the palace, each side hung with linen, dark enough that no one could see within, but light enough to allow in a breeze.

There is a concept in dance called *ukun*: discord. It is the missed heartbeat, the skipped step, the hitched breath. Sometimes, it is good. A kazerach's appearance often produced ukun. Their touch, their gaze, would disrupt the saagkazaar, no matter how well trained. Sometimes, however, ukun was deadly. It was the world misstepping. A saagkazaar's song was the song of the world; the enchantment of the kazerach relied on our ability to work in concert with it. But if the world was out of step, if something was wrong, ukun was unavoidable in song.

I was neither priest nor scholar, and I was young besides—only thirteen. But I knew the cadence of Bayyur's song intimately, the notes as it issued from all lives, both human and not, and I could recognize where it faltered, where there was good ukun and bad. In the most holy among us, his song wreathed us the way fire wreathed logs in a hearth. It was not so with King Kegaad—the song and his spirit seemed to be constantly at war, as if he might beat it into submission, as if it might feed him with no price or offering in return. And as it flowed from the king I detected discord, unease, fear. It was discord I was familiar with—the cacophony of Baal, the unrest of the sick and poor shoved into alleyways, starving. When I knelt before the king I had to remind myself that he was as I was—his flesh was sacrosanct and therefore he had the right to look upon my face as few others outside the monasteries did. But it sat ill with me, and took away from the joy of my journey, that I'd found such song inside the king. And the bitterness of our meeting only amplified when our eyes met.

I said little as we left the palace that morning, and less when we stopped to make camp that night. No longer was I the rambunctious girl who ran from her baths and struggled when younger priestesses undressed her. I sat through the rituals silently, my eye turned inward, playing over and over the meeting with the king. Even the Temple of Kings, ancient and beautiful and laden with history, had sounded sorrowful. Despite my difficult younger years, I knew little of sorrow now. I could not stomach it, could not sit with it as most people might.

The priestess who'd found me when I lived in alleys entered the tent. She was called Keda, and her face was thin and severe. Though Bayyur venerated all things beautiful and abundant, Keda seemed to live an ascetic life. Her gown was black, her hair bound into many thin braids and lashed at the back of her head. She abjured gold and gems, and wore neither perfume nor cosmetics. When she'd found me, I thought she despised me. I had such a hunger in me for everything, and she found it distasteful, but I'd grown on her as a barnacle grows on a ship's hull.

Keda stared at me kindly and dismissed the priestesses.

"I told you we should not go."

I nodded, glum and on the verge of tears. "Why was it so bad?"

"None of us knows," she said.

I blinked up at her, her old and grave face cast in shadow by the lanterns. I did not burn incense in the tents when we traveled, for it troubled her lungs, and it was an easy thing to give up.

"I wish to dance," I said at last, and she nodded.

The kazerach were not gods.

Many foreign to Baal believed this—or at least, believed that we believed this. In the tongue of outsiders the kazerach would be called world-serpents. For it was their spirit that coiled around worlds and stars, that drove life in galaxies, that connected us all through song. They had loved mortalkind once, long ago. Their spirit drove us into creation. And they so loved our dance and song and our reverence. But kazerach were not mortal, and our lives were fleeting, and the grief of loss, and the grievousness of the mistakes we made, drove them away.

They were—are—divine in their way. But true gods do not care or rely on us. And the kazerach were bound to us as we were to them. Our health was theirs, our disease was theirs, and our disregard and corruption meant their ruin. Remember this, for I did not.

The women of the hagaad escorted me to a clearing in the jungle then stood a little way back. I was not yet old enough that any of the priestesses had chosen to teach me the dance of the saagkazaar. But I knew the lesser dances that priestesses performed regularly and many songs besides.

I spun as the song unspooled inside me, as I thought to fix all the discord that reverberated in my mind and chest. It felt like a physical thing, mold that grew on my arms, cobwebs that filled my lungs. The sadness and defeat sloshed around in my mind until the song began to take root in me and crowd everything out. I sang for the glory of Baal, the beauty of the city I'd left behind, the majesty of Bayyur's sun as it rose over ancient spires and heated yellow stone. I sang, thinking of the palm fronds that wafted in the breeze of his house, and the heavy brass lanterns that swayed and danced, twined with incense smoke. I danced, my mind filled with the glimpses of him I'd gotten, the purity innate in dance, untainted by the sorrow and grief of men.

I wished, in my most secret of hearts, that Bayyur would come down. No one who danced for him danced thinking they were separate. But all knew that Bayyur had not descended from the heavens, had not crossed the dimensional divide, in eons.

So when the sky split in two and cosmic thunder broke open the vault of heaven, I did not understand. I stopped, my face turned upward, my eyes wide as the black night sky turned white and then gold. It settled back into its velvet surface, and a column of silver poured down from above.

I understood, distantly, that the Bayyur I saw was but a sliver of his true self. That his spirit fed a world and replenished it, that he could not be anything like a man. But a man was what I saw, tall and broad-shouldered, his hips narrow, his skin dark as night. His shoulders were dusted with gold and silver, and his hair fell to his shoulders in many braids. From his left ear hung a gold chain from which in turn hung a gleaming emerald. He was beautiful and resplendent, and when he saw me his mouth ticked up into a smile.

"How wondrous," he said, and held out a hand.

I walked toward him as if through a dream. Every glimpse of glory suddenly made sense to me, every note I had ever gleaned from the world around me suddenly shone brighter. Discord and harmony lived together in him, for he encompassed all, and I thought little of how closely that discord echoed the king's. I thought even less of the quiver of fear in the grass, and the way animals seemed to shy away from the clearing. And I ignored the women of the hagaad who came closer, their spears in hand. I could think only of how he sank to one knee before me to be eye level with me, and how later, when I asked, he took the chain from his ear and gifted it to me.

The year I called down Bayyur, the mother priestess relocated me to a monastery well outside Baal. I did not mind it—Baal was loud, its air clouded, its song cacophonous. And in Baal I could not leave the monastery. In the grasslands I could see the stars, I could hear the song of the *world*, I could walk beyond the monastery's walls and sing without worry of violation. It was no hardship to leave, though many of the sisters who accompanied me resented the relocation. In the grasslands Bayyur came often when I danced. I was young still, and could not mark things that should have worried me. In love with love, with the joy of the dance, with the knowledge that he had come for me when he had not descended from the firmament for anyone in a millennia, it was easy to put my meeting with the king behind me. It was even easier to ignore the song of discord in the world, which each year seemed to grow louder and encompass more. Betimes it seemed that Bayyur's hair curled as mine did—and when I said this to him lines appeared at the corners of his eyes when he smiled. That too was dusted with gold.

In the monastery was a prayer bower, its floors swept clean, its ceiling open to the night sky. There, often, between sunset and true dark did I dance, and wait for him. And there, more often than not, did he come and recline and listen to me sing. And there, too, I was finally allowed to learn the dance of the saagkazaar.

Perhaps, if I had not been so secure in my own power, if I had thought beyond my own abilities and my own desires, I would have seen it. How often he reclined, the tired way he looked, how often he came when truly, he should not have come at all. I would have thought how strange it was that he appeared to me and never the king, his vessel in the realm of men. I would have listened—to the discord inside him, to the discord in the world. Perhaps if my teachers had trusted me, if I had been less in love with love, I could have been made to understand. What the king did, how Bayyur struggled to hold him back. How he came to me tired and left rejuvenated.

Whatever was happening in the empire, I knew little of it. But I understood my teachers' reluctance to name anyone saagkazaar, for in the hands of a saagkazaar lay the fate of nations. None but her might call the kazerach from the king's side, might unseat his power. And I was young—thirteen at first—and did not know what I had done.

But I cared nothing for the world outside—there was the song, and dekaad, and Bayyur himself. Nothing else mattered.

And perhaps it was because nothing else mattered that I made the choice that I did.

There were three parts to the dance of the saagkazaar: gatha, suku, and dekaad. Twilight, dusk, and dawn.

Gatha was not the dance—it was the ritual by which incense was lit, by which the place of offering was swept, and the steps a saagkazaar took to kneel before the heavens. It was the ritual of choosing what one wore, which jewelry to hang from and adorn your wrists. It was the oils pressed against your skin, and the ochre on your eyelids.

Suku were the opening notes. Some of the saagkazaar played instruments, or so I had been told. Those of us who did not still understood the importance of the link between twilight and dawn—the enchantment of the half-light. The will necessary to bring down a kazerach, to turn his ear and his mind—ancient and beyond our comprehension—for a few moments to our world.

And finally, dekaad. Dekaad was the dance itself, the revelry of love and desire, the moment the flesh met the divine. It is said that in the golden age when the kazerach came regularly that dekaad was a deadly dance—that the kazerach enjoyed it too much and that we mortals had not the strength to bear their love or attention. That many saagkazaar died before ever attempting to become kazerkai.

It was dekaad that I loved—I had little patience for gatha, and the inherent talent at song that I paid too little attention to suku. But in dekaad I reveled, and it was in dekaad that my instructors found the most fault. For I loved too much and too clearly, and showed none of the humility necessary before the kazerach. And I was so eager to finally learn, filled as I was with the thrumming energy of desire in adolescence, that I did not pause to think why I learned at all. The power of the dance and my love of Bayyur were so heady a thing that I forgot fear and sense both and threw myself into the lessons.

If I had remembered . . . if I had paused to think . . .

But such is the way of things.

✦ ✦ ✦

I rose every morning before dawn to join the sisters in their prayers. I did not know if Bayyur watched me and so knew this, or if the cosmos conspired so that I might be where I was needed at the proper time. I dressed for prayers every morning as if I were in gatha, perfumed and oiled, my many braids coiled at the back of my head and wound in gold, ochre on my bottom lip, and the corners of my eyelids. I had lit the first of nine incense bowers in my room when a sound, as if thunder had struck in my room, split the air in two.

The lit reed in my hand dropped from my fingers and for long moments I could not move at all. As if the world had shifted and forgotten me, or death had come and my mind had not yet found it. When at last I could move, I spun around.

I was sixteen by then and as I was, as I have told you, had never had reason to fear anything in my life. For a single moment he appeared as I knew him, bare-chested, dusted in gold, his eyes shining in the darkness of my bedchamber.

"Khefa—" My name tore itself from his mouth, warped with pain and sorrow. I had never heard him thus. Had never heard him as anything but detached, amused. He was a kazer-ach, the spirit of all life on this planet.

But before my eyes the form I knew, the form I loved, tore itself apart. He came back together as skeins of darkness weaving themselves into something whole, and he turned into something I did not know. A man, still, with his night-dark skin and glowing eyes. A man, with his curled, coarse hair and his chest dusted in gold. A man, and yet he glis-

tened and his hands were tipped with claws, and there was
something—

Something. Ukun.

Here it was in the heart, in the soul, of our world.

I felt it—discord, misstep—in my heart as Bayyur pulled
away from my bed and stumbled toward me. Felt my heart
miss a beat as he fell at my feet and did not rise. Remembered
how easily I had ignored it and let it continue to take root.

"Khefa," he said again.

I could not breathe. Bayyur was kazerach—ancient and
undying, and though loved by me, beyond my ken. I had
thought him—

He remained on his knees even as he looked up at me, his
eyes black where they had always been gold. Had he hid this
aspect of himself from me? Could he no longer do it? I could
not move, could not *think*—what had happened to him?

He shuddered and I heard something spill from his mouth
and strike the ground. Heard several breaths dragged in and
out of his chest.

Ukun happened not only in dekaad, but in life itself. It
was death too early, summer too long, a rainy season that
drowned crops. It was the slow decay of the world. The slay-
ing of the spirit that gave it life.

I had never touched Bayyur. As my flesh was sacrosanct,
his was divine beyond imagining. His was not for me to touch,
ever, and yet I reached for him and held his shoulder. It was
a single touch, and yet it seemed to undo us both. I understood, at last, what my teachers meant when they said I lived

too much in the flesh. Divine desire unspooled through me, and I felt there were no words to express it. What does a single blade of grass say when the heavens unload a storm on her back? What does cosmic dust say when it is swept away by solar winds? How was I, a mortal girl, meant to contend with divine flesh, even as broken as it seemed?

I could not. And yet my grip held and I knelt beside him, and when he bowed his head over my shoulder, I raised a hand to cradle his head. He felt mortal then, though he shouldn't have. And I felt—not mortal, not divine. I felt as if I were dekaad and ukun incarnate in one moment, two cosmic forces churning in me as I held Bayyur. It felt as though my skin were too tight and not tight at all, as if a flower had taken seed inside my rib cage and at any moment would begin to blossom, winding its way around my bones, and burst through my skin.

"Do you remember," he began, his voice hoarse, "when I first came to you?"

"Yes," I replied softly.

"Besieged on all sides by corruption and rot," he continued. "And then a single light. A gleaming mote in the darkness."

He shuddered again.

"Help me," he whispered. "I beg of you."

I had never held lightning or thunder in my hands, but it felt as if thunder clapped and lightning struck to take him from me. My skin burned and sparked where he'd sat. And the ichor that spilled from his mouth had burned a hole in the stone floor.

I did not go to prayer. For long hours I sat where I'd held

him, immobile, unable to think. Or rather, able to think only one thing. For I knew what I must do, what it was, truly, that he was asking of me. And I knew too that it was forbidden— that the priestesses would never allow it, that the king, as many kings before him, had decreed it a crime. For the power of rulership of our world was to be held by the king alone, and a saagkazaar could not be seen to hold the influence of the kazerach. It would tip the power of nations.

Bayyur was dying, and he would take our world with him.

I was sixteen and it was easy to mistake my love for him as love for the world. But I think, if I had loved the world more and Bayyur less, I might have trod more carefully. I would have gone to the Temple of the Great Mother and asked for assistance. But I loved Bayyur and I believed he loved me, and I thought in doing this I might save him. Perhaps more arrogantly, I believed I would survive my wedding rites.

Two nights passed before I prepared a gatha unlike any other. I dyed the ochre paste I put on my eyelids and lower lip black, and I chose a simple linen gown dyed in saffron. I wore no gold—not in my hair nor at my wrists. From my neck hung a single pendant, the emerald stone that had hung from his ear on our first meeting, given to me by his own hand when I was a child.

The monastery was quiet as I swept the small prayer bower. The kazervaaj were used to my calling Bayyur, and none had guessed what I called him for now. But the leader of my hagaad, Vala, looked down into the prayer bower, her spear in hand, her eyes hard. I could not hold her gaze, for if she guessed my purpose she would drag me, screaming, back to my chamber, whether my skin was sacrosanct or not.

Songs of love had been forbidden to me, for—or so the mother priestess said—I did not understand their power. I did, or I thought I did, for the arrogance of what I'd accomplished at thirteen was a powerful drug. And I understood that to enchant Bayyur, to call him for this even as his essence decayed, I could not use joy or ecstasy. It had to be love.

And so I sang the suku softly, as if only to myself. I sang of love as I knew it—all-consuming, fractious, like thunder and lightning at once, roiling between my two palms. Love, for me, was Bayyur looking up at me in wonder, was his voice rasping for my help, was the moment—the single second—my skin had touched his.

How little I knew of love, and yet how much.

Suku flowed into dekaad, and so, too, did the bitterness of what I had to do. I had grown up loving Bayyur and being told that he could never love me in return. What use did a kazerach have for a mortal's love when it was fleeting, a brief moment in the shade of ages?

And I had been named such, hadn't I? Khefa—a mote, a speck. Named such because I was the mote irritating market sellers, and I remained such in hopes that I would be the blood mote in Bayyur's eye, as close to him as his own heart.

So here I was, my heart song lifting from my throat, my feet moving through the paces I'd learned since I was a girl. The dekaad of love, too, was different. It was not sultry or beckoning. It yearned and it pleaded and it desired. The dekaad of love was love unfulfilled, waiting for the kazerach to join and turn it to joy.

And so I danced and I danced and I danced until it seemed all stars had gone from the sky and all the lanterns went out. And when at last I stopped, my skin shining with sweat, the ochre at the corners of my eyes bleeding down the sides of my face, Bayyur stood before me. Gone was the gold dust from his skin and hair. He gleamed, instead, with blood.

But I felt hope, perhaps foolishly. Hanging from his left ear was the emerald stone I loved so, swinging from a delicate gold chain. He held out a clawed hand. I did not hesitate to take it, to let him draw me to him. The orange of my gown, soaked through with his blood, turned crimson and then black. His free hand swept over the curve of my cheek.

No one had ever touched me. No one had dared. I was meant for Bayyur and Bayyur alone, and I knew, too, that in all likelihood he would not have me. But now, in the circle of his arms, with his black eyes fixed on mine, I understood the yearning in love, the way flesh and the divine were inextricable from one another.

He did not warn me before he raised a clawed thumb to my bottom lip and split the skin. It was painless, and yet I felt my own blood drip down over my chin, taking the ochre dye with it.

"Do you take the step forward?" he asked.

Here was the Bayyur I knew, confident, assuming, without fear or doubt. I did not question the blood on his skin or the look in his eye. I knew only that the dance had worked, had brought him to rights. And the marriage was not yet done.

"Yes," I said.

His mouth came down on mine. Where I had felt thunder and lightning at the touch of his skin, this—

How I loved him, and how I loved this. The divine was fire and thunder, the implosion of suns, the horrible, cacophonous unmaking of worlds. It thundered through my blood, it stretched my mind to its limits. We mortals were not made for kazerach, not like this, and yet my body held and my mind, too, though I waited for both of them to disappear.

When he pulled away I knew what would be left on my mouth and chin; a black line splitting my bottom lip, and carving its way over my chin. The mark of the kazerach's bride. But I thought little of that as I looked at him. He had not changed, and yet some aspect of him was different. Something in his sight unsettled me. He caught my eye and smiled as he had long ago, and it did not ease my fear. He came forward and did not pause when I stepped back.

A hand, without claws, rested on the emerald hanging from my neck.

"Why do you balk at me?" he asked.

The saagkazaar knew song and dance beyond anyone and anything. And I understood suddenly, horribly, what had changed in the patterns of his voice.

He was become part mortal.

Not all. Not even most. Half of a sliver's sliver. And yet,

I knew, it was enough. The part mortal could not power the divine. Could not sustain our world.

"Bayyur—" I breathed, searching his face. A man stared back. Not a kazerach. "What have we done?"

I felt sick hearing the tones of my own voice, because I understood without his speaking. For the mortality that had seeped into his voice had been leached from mine. And in exchange he had given me a little of his divinity, a little of his cosmic fire.

"You will save me, Khefa," he murmured, pressing his forehead against mine. "You and your light will hold the corruption at bay. Long enough—"

"*Long enough?*" I gasped. "Long enough for what?"

"Long enough for an end to let flower a new beginning," he said. "When I pass, you will become Kumzala—the garden by which a new world will be born. A mote that will turn to fire and bring about rebirth."

MELIE

By Justina Ireland

I clambered over the rocks, nearly slicing my hand open on a jagged edge as I steadied myself. From far off, the jetty had seemed like the perfect place to find my quarry, but now that I was on the rocks I began to worry that maybe I should've picked another spot. There was no way I'd be able to get out any farther into the water, at least not this way.

Well, not without swimming.

Klydonia was a prosperous place of fertile farmland, rugged mountains, and a seaport that had allowed us to trade with most of our neighbors. But it was also a land brimming with beasts of all sorts and sizes. It was the kind of place where jumping into a dark current was a terrible idea. There were half a dozen sea creatures that would drown a human just for fun, and I wasn't the best swimmer even without a selkie dragging me toward the bottom of the sea.

I started to head back to the beach to find another spot when I saw them pulling themselves up onto the rocks:

mermaids. Gloriously fat, their rainbow hair knotted with bits of seashells as well as coral and kelp. Their skin was a blue-gray, and only their brightly colored tails stood out against the rocks.

For months I had been running errands for the High Sorcerer in hopes that he would see fit to take me as an apprentice. He had sent me on task after task, all with the promise of sharing his great wisdom. Anyone in Klydonia could learn magic, but it was incredibly dangerous to be self-taught. One never knew when a spell might backfire and turn an aspiring sorcerer into a lump of clay or a toad. So a teacher was a must.

And since the only teacher strong enough to help me learn the advanced spells that would let me help my village thrive was the High Sorcerer, I had to get to those mermaids. Otherwise, it was back to the stacks of the library, reading spells I was too inexperienced to try.

I redoubled my efforts, finding a couple of handholds, finally hopping across a particularly dangerous gap from one rock to the next. The water swirled with dangerous currents, and one false step would definitely mean my end.

But, mermaids! It would be worth it. Maybe.

"Halloo!" I called, once I was within shouting distance of the mermaids, giving them a jaunty wave. A few mermaids screamed and quickly dove back under the safety of the water, but those who had pulled themselves farther up the rocks stayed where they were, their bodies taut with aggression.

"Don't run, it isn't even armed," one said, the statement directed at me as much as the other mermaids. *It?* Ouch.

"Leave us be, landling! We'll never tell you the location of our castle or give you any jewels," called a mermaid with turquoise hair.

"Don't think we haven't seen your ships, docked out in the deep, waiting for an opportunity to strike," said another, her expression hard.

"And if you try to come any closer we'll pull you off the rocks and into the cold, dark water," said yet another, leaning back on her rock.

I didn't think that one was lying, so I looked around at my rock and carefully found a seat. The mermaids were near enough that I could talk to them without too much effort, and I had no intention of letting them make good on their threat to drown me.

"I'm not here for your jewels or to conquer your kingdom! I'm an apprentice to the High Sorcerer, and I've come to ask for a vial full of your tears. It's for a very important spell," I said, grinning with newfound confidence. I had no doubt they would help me. After all, if I were a mermaid I would've helped them. Helping was just a natural instinct. Right?

A few of the mermaids poked their heads up out of the water. "Mermaids don't cry," said one.

"What kind of spell?" another called.

"I believe it's to heal the sybaritic fever," I said. This was a lie. I didn't actually know what the tears were for. The sorcerer never told his lowest-level apprentices what they were fetching ingredients for, and even my translation of the old books was suspect, as the High Sorcerer constantly reminded me. Not that he deigned to talk to me. When he did speak in my general direction it was usually to call me the wrong name and then tell me my readings were incorrect. But never to offer the right translation.

"Also, why would we help you?" asked the turquoise-haired mermaid, interrupting my small pity party. I was beginning to think of her as the leader. "We hate the sorcerer. He sends his apprentices to hunt us for our scales."

"And they stare at us in a gross way," another mermaid said.

I made a face. "That was probably Ernst. He's icky. Look, I don't like the sorcerer very much, either, but he's kind of my boss, and if I want to be a great sorcerer then I have to do what he says."

"If you're an apprentice, where are your robes?" called another mermaid, one with lavender hair, who had pulled herself a little bit out of the water.

My face burned, and not from the afternoon sun. "Um, they didn't have the robes in my size." I couldn't help but remember the sorcerer's cool gaze as he'd told me, "You are too large for robes, so your regular clothes will have to do."

"I'm too fat," I said, the admission feeling like something shameful even though I wasn't sure why.

At this the mermaids cried out in dismay. "Too fat?"

"But you look positively malnourished!"

"She'd never survive in the water with so little blubber."

"Ugh, humans are the worst."

"I like her skin, though. It's so brown!"

"So," I said, seeing an opportunity in their outrage. "It would be a huge boon if you could give me some tears."

A few of the mermaids murmured agreement, but the turquoise-haired mermaid was unmoved. "We aren't going to give you them for nothing. It's very hard to cry. So what can you give us in return?"

I grinned, and leaned forward as much as I could while sitting very uncomfortably on a very jagged rock. "How about a story?"

By the time I got to the end of "The Dragon and the Moon Maiden," the mermaids were sobbing piteously. One of the younger ones swam over to claim a vial I held out, and another besides. When the mermaids returned the vials, their tears sparkled in the fading sun, strange and unusual. A deep sense of relief and satisfaction sank into my aching bones.

I had done something right. Now the sorcerer would have to take me seriously.

The mermaids slipped into the water, going on about their business, and the turquoise-haired mermaid swam over to me, handing me a couple of bright-yellow scales from her own tail. I took them with the reverence they deserved. Mermaid scales were among the rarest of ingredients for magic working.

"We really liked your story. If you want to come back and

tell us more, we'll let some of the others know. You could get a lot of scales and tears," she said.

"Thank you," I said, but the mermaid was already sinking beneath the waves, back to her underwater home.

It was a long walk back to the castle, up the steep and winding path along the cliffs that overlooked the bay. I turned to search over the water for the ships the mermaids had spoken of, but I saw nothing but evening mist. Perhaps they were confused? Still, it would bear mentioning to someone in the defense ministry after I got back.

I took my time, and when I finally got to the top I was breathing heavily, and my stomach grumbled. I'd missed lunch, and the eventide bells were already ringing, meaning that I'd missed dinner as well.

Still, there was work to be done. So I pushed my hunger and disappointment aside and headed straight for the sorcerer's tower.

The castle had once belonged to the monarchy, but when it had been overthrown the Council of Ministers decided to expand the original castle grounds into a sprawling complex of apartments and offices that merged nearly seamlessly with the nearby town. The sorcerer's apartments were in the old, original portion of the castle, and I had to wind through the more modern white-stone hallways in order to reach the staircase that would lead to the sorcerer's spell room.

I deftly navigated the various wards, nearly singeing my curly hair when I miscalculated the length of a fire ward, but eventually I was at the door to the sorcerer's potion shop. I pushed it open like I had a thousand times before, only this time I was met with the door slamming rudely in my face.

"Who is it?" an irate, masculine voice demanded.

"It's Melie. I have the mermaid tears," I said with some irritation, rubbing my nose. I recognized that voice, and knew nothing good could come of this interaction.

There was a scrabbling on the other side before the door opened a small crack. A single blue eye peered out at me. Ernst, the sorcerer's favorite apprentice.

"Hand it here, and I'll give it to Hansen when he gets back."

I snorted and put my hands on my hips. The tears and the scales were tucked away in my satchel, and there was no way I was going to give either of them to Ernst so that he could take credit for my hard work. I'd made that mistake too many times before.

"What is taking you so long finding that foxglove?" came the bellow from the other side of the door. Ernst looked back, and I took that opportunity to lean into the door, unsettling Ernst and making my way through. He fell back with an *oof* and I strode inside, head held high. On my way to the back of the potion shop I snatched a jar of foxglove off the shelf and upset a jar of singing bees, all without pausing in my route.

The sounds of breaking glass and Ernst's yelps of dismay from behind me were a dark source of pleasure. I even let myself smile.

At the back of the potion shop a cauldron bubbled over a banked fire, and Hansen murmured to himself in annoyance.

The first time I had met the sorcerer I'd been surprised at his age: he couldn't have been more than twenty-five summers. He had a shock of yellow hair and skin like unbaked pastry, a hallmark of his people. He'd come to Klydonia to learn the craft of sorcery from the previous master, and had taken over the position when the last sorcerer died.

There were voices within the court that didn't like having a foreigner, especially one so ready to bring on his own countrymen as apprentices, in such a high position of authority. But those voices were usually silenced. Not because he was any sort of well-loved personality, but because his critics always ran afoul of some sort of mischief. A wiser council would've considered that perhaps there was some intent behind Councilmember Guth being attacked by a basilisk right after accusing the High Sorcerer of murder, but the rest of the council were so enamored of the man that it never came up again. Once they'd managed to move the stone that had been Councilmember Guth into a courtyard, that is.

I didn't much care about court politics. I just hoped that at some point I would be able to stop fetching ingredients and do some actual spellwork. I didn't even like Hansen all that much, and I sincerely doubted he had translated some of his texts correctly, but without his approval there were several very powerful texts that were off-limits to me.

Mostly, I didn't understand why Hansen was so against teaching me the sorcerous arts. I could feel the possibilities simmering in my veins whenever I read a passage aloud, despite what Hansen had told me on several occasions: that my power was so low I'd never be much more than a hedge witch. There was nothing wrong with being a hedge witch, but I knew I wasn't one. I could feel the potential inside me. I just needed a way to direct it.

Where I came from, we didn't much believe in only certain people having magic. My village elders all had some measure of ability, learned through practice and study. It wasn't until Hansen came to our land that people began to speak of some folks being better than others, and it was one more curious thing that made me suspicious of the High Sorcerer.

I still really, really wanted him to teach me magic, though.

Hansen glanced up at my arrival. He stood over a mortar and pestle, grinding a basilisk tail into dust. "Molly. Where is Ernst?"

"It's Melie, still, and Ernst is cleaning up a jar he knocked over. Here is your foxglove," I said, just as Ernst ran up, huffing and humming some tune under his breath. There were several red welts on his face, and I grinned at him while he glared back in response. I'd been the one to gather those bees in the first place, so it was only just that they'd provided some measure of usefulness now.

Hansen took the foxglove without looking at me. "I see you've also brought me my mermaid tears? Yes, yes, hand it over," he said, cutting me off when I opened my mouth to tell him about my day.

I gave the sorcerer the mermaid tears but decided to keep the scales for myself as a memento. I had to have something for my troubles.

Hansen went back to muttering over his potion, and after a few seconds looked over at me as though surprised to see that I was still there.

"Oh, you are dismissed now."

"Oh," I said, my face heating at the abrupt dismissal. "I thought I might watch."

"Absolutely not. Observation is only for apprentices who have undergone elementary spellcasting and demonstrated some talent."

"But you told me I couldn't take elementary spellcasting until I was potion adept," I said, sinking once more into the trap of frustration. For an entire season I'd been trying to get some sort of training, any training, and every time I got even a little close I was given yet another reason why I wasn't ready. But I came to the high court precisely because I was ready. I'd reached the limits of the teachings of the local witch back home, and the sorcerer of the north had told me that with all of my power I needed a stronger teacher.

But now here I was, being turned away once more.

"You heard the master," Ernst said in a singsong. He wouldn't be able to talk without singing for some time, but even that small spite didn't bring me any measure of joy now. I deserved to be taught and to learn without constantly being turned away.

"Thank you for the ingredients, Malia," Hansen said, still not looking at me. And that final insult was enough to drive me from the room and down into the kitchens to scrounge up dinner and maybe a sweet to assuage the bereft feeling in my heart.

I woke the next morning to screams. At first I thought I was having a nightmare or that maybe there was a banshee in the castle complex, but when I opened my eyes I realized they were sobs of despair, and they were very near.

I didn't stay in the sorcerer's tower like most of the apprentices. Instead, Hansen had secured lodgings for me in the servants' quarters. In hindsight I should've known right then that I was never going to get anything more in the way of training than a lot of time in the library, studying and translating.

Poor Malia, Molly, Meredith, too weak and useless to even bother training.

But Melie, she was going to stop wasting her time. I'd decided last night that I'd look into going abroad to study. Klydonia was not the only land with a High Sorcerer, and perhaps I'd find someone more amenable to teaching me someplace else.

But for now, I had to see what sort of disaster was afoot in the palace.

I got up and dressed quickly and went out to find the source of the disturbance.

A trio of maids sobbed in the hallway. They each wore a different-colored dress to denote the part of the government complex where they worked, but their skin was all the same reddish brown usually found in people of the north. Their hair was in the single high braid of northern ladies as well, and their tears gave me momentary pause. Northerners were rumored to be reserved in their emotions, but apparently these girls hadn't gotten the memo. "What's the matter?"

"Oh, Melie, it's just terrible! The Minister of War's son has been cursed! The most handsome boy in all of the castle, and he's been turned to stone!" said one of the maids.

"The sorcerer said he's helpless to undo the spell without the heart of a dragon, and now everyone has taken to the mountains to find one!" said another.

"And everyone knows that bothering a dragon is the fastest way to die!" wailed the third, which set the trio off on another bout of tears.

"There, there," I said, quite awkwardly, patting one, then another, then the other of the maids. "I'm sure someone very brave will find the dragon's heart and save the, uh, minister's son." I tried to sound concerned, but the truth was that these petty nobles were always getting themselves cursed in some way or another. Especially those fellas in the war department. It was a side effect of kicking over stones in places one didn't belong.

Either way, the wannabe heroes in the castle could go adventuring for a dragon's heart. I was going to spend the day studying in the giant complex library. Hansen might not want to teach me anything, but there were still books. I would just teach myself.

But less than a turn of the hourglass later, as I sat in the library translating a book on dragon lore, since it seemed apropos, I realized that everyone was looking for the wrong thing.

Hansen had sent the castle's best warriors out to find a dragon's heart. But the translation said enchantments could be broken by a dragon's heat, which I took to mean its heated breath.

And I began to suspect that perhaps that terrible sorcerer had something else in mind. Because there was no way anyone with a basic understanding of magic theory would get a dragon's heart and a dragon's heat confused. There were plots afoot, but even though I didn't know what they were, I had a responsibility to see if I could discover how to stop them.

Because whatever woe befell Klydonia would impact my small village as well. "Crap," I muttered, closing the book.

I was going to have to find a dragon.

Three turns of the hourglass found me riding in the back of a hay wagon through the foothills outside the castle, across farmland, and up into the aptly named Dragon Kill Mountains. Not because it was where dragons killed people, but because it was the spot where the last great king, who hadn't been all that great in reality, had slain one of the last dragons before being slain himself. His death had prompted the people to cry "Enough!" and overthrow the crown, and declare a treaty with the mountain dragons, not just because the king had been stupid, selfish, and lazy, all very terrible traits to have in a leader, but because dragons were an endangered species and people were aghast to see a king spend his time hunting and killing such a majestic beast.

And yet, no one had seemed to remember that as they stormed out of the castle, up into the mountains, intent on returning with a heart. Fools.

On the way out I'd overheard a new piece of information. The Minister of War had offered some prize to the person who returned with a dragon's heart: gold, a daughter's hand in marriage, a firm handshake and whatnot, but I didn't really care about that. I was determined that not only would I find the dragon, but I would be the one to reverse the curse on the minister's son. An act of magic like that would prove that I should be taken seriously, that I wasn't just some farm girl from the edge of the country.

I would prove that I could be a sorcerer.

First, I had to find a dragon.

But as I traveled farther from the castle complex it seemed clearer to me just how very suspicious everything Hansen had done was, when taken in full measure. And during the wagon ride I wrote myself a little spell for clear eyes, clear heart, clear mind. I was somewhat suspicious that Hansen had managed to cast a spell that had infected everyone in the complex with some kind of strange admiration. Bumping along in the back of the wagon, it seemed incredible I would want to work with a man who couldn't even remember my name.

And the more I thought about the entire situation, the more convinced I became that I needed to find these dragons before anyone else did. Because they might not be enamored of Hansen this far from the castle, but greed was always an effective motivator.

The wagon dropped me in Grantham, a small town that was considered the last vestiges of civilization before one entered the rough part of the mountains. It was clear from the activity in the town that I would have some competition in my dragon hunt. Men and women in armor traipsed through the town, leading horses laden with provisions. I hefted my own bag, mostly filled with books, but also containing a few pastries and apples, and headed toward the winding road outside of town.

The trees grew closely together, tall pines with thick trunks, and the undergrowth was thick with ferns and waist-high ant-hills that I had no intention of disturbing. As I walked until the town was no longer visible through the trees, I wondered how all of those warriors had planned on finding a dragon.

Luckily, I had magic on my side. And the one thing I knew how to do was find something.

A seeking spell was simple enough that even a child could use it. I used a pocketknife to slice off a thick lock of my hair and wrapped it around a fallen pine branch. Then, with a prick of the knife, I bound the hair to the branch with a bit of blood, because magic always requires a sacrifice of some sort, and began to mutter the incantation.

> *"By my hair*
> *By my blood*
> *Take these offerings*

Search this land
For the thing I seek
And direct me
In my searching."

I was supposed say the incantation thrice, but on the second time through, the stick began to glow and pull me through the forest. Quickly.

I had to hop and skip to avoid rotten logs and fallen debris, and a near miss with one of the giant anthills had me squeaking and brushing at my trousers to rid myself of the small creatures. But it seemed like my spell was working.

Eventually the woods opened onto a beautifully clear lake, the water reflecting back the sunset. Nearby was a small cave, far too small for a dragon, and disappointment flooded me. I'd wanted a dragon, but what I'd gotten instead was a lovely place to spend the night.

I sighed, sat down on a rock, and began to eat one of my apples. Maybe Hansen was right. Maybe I wasn't cut out to be much more than a hedge witch.

Despair weighed me down, making me sleepy even though the sun was just beginning to dip toward the horizon. I walked into the cave, making sure that it wasn't occupied, and then bedded down for the night.

I would worry about finding the dragon on the morrow.

I woke with a start to the sound of someone singing, the sound low and musical and heartbreakingly beautiful. A boy. And it was coming from outside the cave.

I climbed to my feet and walked out into the cool night in search of the source of the melody. I kind of wished I'd thought to bring a coat, but my blanket did the trick well enough.

Just a few feet outside the cave sat a youth tending a small fire. He startled when he saw me, and I held my hands up so he would see I meant him no harm. "I'm sorry, I heard you singing. Mind if I join you?" The boy had a brace of fish roasting over the fire, and my stomach growled loud enough to silence the sound of the chirruping night creatures in the nearby woods.

"I only had an apple for dinner," I said by way of apology.

The boy smirked. "I have an extra fish if you're hungry."

I grinned, sheepishly. "That would be delightful. I have more apples I can share."

I went back into the cave and came back with two of my apples. The boy took one and bit into it with gusto.

"I'm Lyle, by the way," he said. His manners were definitely better than mine.

"Melie. Are you out here looking for the dragon as well?"

The boy stilled and tilted his head to the side, the motion so endearing that I felt warmth that could not be attributed to the fire. His face was very nice, from what I could tell in the firelight, and I tried to tell myself that my fluttery feelings were caused by hunger, not by him. "Dragon?" he asked.

"Ahh, I suppose you haven't heard." The boy had the same deep, dark skin of the southern clans, his hair in a pattern of tight braids. His eyes were strange, though, a golden color that seemed to glow in the firelight. I wanted to ask him where he was from, how he came by his strange coloring, but that would be rude, and I was so looking forward to his fish that I didn't want to offend lest he change his mind.

"You were speaking of a dragon?" Lyle prompted. I mentally shook myself and nodded.

"The Minister of War's son was turned to stone by a curse, and there is a horde of adventurers now looking for a dragon's heart to break the spell."

"What about you?" he asked, sliding a fish off a stick onto a wide green leaf and handing it to me. My fingers brushed his as I took the generous gift, and a shock of power flashed down my arm. Not magic, but the kind of power that made me wonder what it would be like to kiss this boy.

"Thank you," I said, embarrassed by the sudden thought, even though Lyle's smile had warmed considerably at the contact as well. "I'm trying to become a sorcerer. It's not going great. But about the dragon's heart? I think Hansen, that's the High Sorcerer, well, I think he's wrong. Or maybe plotting something, I'm not quite sure yet. See, I've read up on dragons, a lot, and one of the reasons they were hunted back in the old days is because they had the ability to break curses, and the old mages didn't like that."

Lyle stared at me, and I picked at my fish, feeling indescribably silly. "Anyway, I doubt I'll find a dragon anyway, since they've been hunted near to extinction, and my seeking spell led me here."

Lyle took a fish from the fire and bit into it, picking bones out of his mouth as he chewed. "What would you do if you found a dragon? Kill it?"

"What? No! Dragons are supposed to be intelligent and witty. I'd mostly want to talk to one. Well, assuming it didn't incinerate me first. Not that I could blame it for taking offensive action, especially given how awful humans have been in the past. Anyway, that's a lot about me. What brings you to these woods?"

He smiled, a flash of teeth that transformed him from handsome into something more, and I found my heart pounding in a way I didn't quite care for. "Oh, I'm out here because once a month our village sends someone to check the nets." He pointed to the lake, which now seemed to boil as fish thrashed in the silvery light of the moon. "The moon brings the krike to the surface, and we catch them. By morning there will be enough fish in the nets to feed my village for a month."

Something about what Lyle said rang false. There was something he was leaving out, something important, and my face tingled with the omission thanks to my clear eyes, clear heart, clear mind spell. I watched him carefully, waiting for the spell to show me that lie, but I got nothing beyond the tingle.

I really wasn't having much luck with my spellcasting.

I couldn't deny that there were indeed fish and nets, so I wasn't sure what he'd said that was untrue. I pushed the feeling to the side. "That's amazing. I wasn't aware there were any villages up this high in the mountains."

Lyle nodded. "You should come back with me. Our elders have many stories of the dragons that used to roam these mountains. Maybe they could help you?"

I grinned, and my suspicions evaporated like mist in the early morning sun. Perhaps the knowledge of dragons was what had triggered the spell. Either way, this was a turn for the better. "That would be delightful." There were few things I loved as much as stories, especially old ones told by village elders.

"Then it's settled. We leave at dawn," Lyle said, giving me a grin I liked far too much.

We finished eating and spent the rest of the evening talking about everything and nothing. I told Lyle about my village and how much I missed everyone there, and how my magic never seemed to work right even though I did everything I was supposed to. He told me about life in the mountains and how the trees looked like they were on fire in autumn. By the time I fell asleep, I felt as though I'd known Lyle my entire life.

But when I woke the next morning, cold and stiff, I almost wondered if I'd imagined the entire meeting. The remains of the fire were there, but there was no Lyle, and every single one of the nets was gone from the lake.

But then a crashing echoed through the underbrush, and I turned toward the woods. And there, coming through the trees, was a real-life dragon.

I froze with fear as the creature lumbered toward me, unsure whether to scream, run, or just fall to the ground and cry. The creature was black as onyx and had eyes of amber. It stopped a few feet away and peered at me, sulfurous smoke leaking from its nostrils.

I took a deep breath and let it out. If the dragon wanted to hurt me it already would have.

As I studied the creature I began to see that the dragon looked familiar, and the more I studied it the more certain I became that the dragon and I had met before. "Uh, Lyle?" I said, feeling beyond silly. But the dragon let out a *whoof* of air and bobbed its head, and I laughed.

"You're a dragon! Wait, that means my spell did work. Which means my translation is right," I said, pacing as I put the pieces of the puzzle together. "I knew Hansen lied. Which means my suspicions about him having the castle complex under some sort of enchantment are correct. Ugh, that snake!"

The dragon tilted his head and I began to pace, my mind working through the possibilities of the depths of Hansen's treachery. "What if he's been translating everything wrong all this time?" I could suddenly see the entirety of the sorcerer's plan, as though the universe had just laid it out for me. "He wanted all of the nation's best warriors to head inland, away from the bay. But this also means that the ships the mermaids were complaining about weren't ours. Oh no," I said, as I realized what was going on. "Lyle, I know dragons have absolutely no use for us, especially in light of our history, but I think Klydonia is about to be invaded. Do you think you could give me a hand?"

The dragon shifted and shimmered, and then Lyle stood there before me. "What do you mean? What's happening?"

"The spell the sorcerer was doing yesterday required

mermaid tears, which everyone knows are used for trans-formation, and I just didn't think about it until now . . . Ugh, then the Minister of War's son was turned to stone . . ." I slapped my forehead. "Hansen's spells had my brain all muddled, but now that I'm outside his influence I can see what he's truly about. He's planning on helping an invasion."

Lyle nodded. "Let's go back to my village and tell the elders what's going on. I think we can help. Besides, I think it's time the people of Klydonia remembered why the dragons were left alone in the first place."

I had a moment of worry. What if I was wrong? But then Lyle shifted into his massive form and gestured for me to climb aboard, and I put my doubts aside.

For once, I was going to believe in myself.

The dragon elders were more than happy to follow me down into the more populated part of Klydonia. It turned out that while they lived a very good life in the mountains, they were quite bored.

"We haven't had a single battle in at least fifty years," cried one of the older dragons, who looked like the kind of nice old lady who would bake cookies for everyone in the village. "I miss the crunch of bones."

I wondered if I was making a mistake bringing a pride of dragons into Klydonia, but there was nothing in the treaty that said they couldn't fly toward the bay.

And so, I scrambled up on Lyle's back and hoped that I

was right, even though it meant that my country was being invaded.

As the dragons came into sight of the bay, it quickly became clear that my hunch had been correct. Ships fired on the castle complex, the sounds of screams and fighting coming from inside the complex itself.

"We have to destroy those ships," I yelled at Lyle, and he let loose a low bellow that the rest of his pride echoed. An amethyst dragon with emerald eyes and two other smaller ones peeled off toward the ships, and as Lyle tilted toward the castle complex, flames were already engulfing the sails and masts of the invaders.

"Can you put me down in the center of the castle?" I wasn't sure what exactly I would do, but one of the books had told of a spell for repelling invaders. I was hoping it was still active, because I now had no doubt that Hansen was a part of this. I had to stop him before this invasion became an all-out war.

Lyle landed softly in the middle of the main court, which was eerily abandoned. It was usually the source of much activity, and the absence of people frightened me.

"Halt!" cried men in a livery I didn't recognize. Their pale skin marked them as not from Klydonia, and their speech was rough and harsh. They stormed the court and flashed swords that caught the sunlight. Lyle took a breath, but before he could unleash a fiery blast at the soldiers an incandescent blue light hit him, shifting him from his dragon form back to the boy I'd met in the moonlight.

"Lyle!" I cried out.

Hansen walked out from behind the soldiers, Ernst by his side, their faces smug. Hansen's usual vacant expression had been replaced by a sneer.

"Oh, Melie, it's too late. We control the castle, and there's nothing you can do." Well, at least he'd finally gotten my name right.

Lyle was on the ground next to me, and I fell to my knees beside him. "Are you okay?"

"Yes. It hurts to have the transformation reversed like that, but I'll be fine."

I took a deep breath. I was going to believe in myself, even if I just wanted to curl into a ball and sob. "Okay, I have a plan. I'm going to need you to run toward the gardens. Can you do that?"

The soldiers moved toward us, and Lyle nodded. Without warning he jumped to his feet and ran toward the flowering arch that was the entrance to the palace complex gardens.

The soldiers were stunned for a moment, but then chased after him, Hansen and Ernst on their tails. After all, Lyle was a dragon; I was just an apprentice with unremarkable abilities. Which one of us was the greater risk?

But I was also a girl who had read the entirety of the spell section in the royal library.

I ran toward the Liberation Fountain in the center of the court and away from the direction everyone else had gone. Perhaps Hansen's teacher had suspected what the sorcerer was about and hadn't told him about the true use of the fountain. Or maybe Hansen's translation had actually been wrong, not just wrong to protect the knowledge from aspiring sorcerers like me. Either way, I jumped into the fountain, sliced my palm on the sharp horn of the unicorn rampant in the middle of the sculpture, and said, "By my blood, by my heart, defend Klydonia from those who would tear her apart."

The book I'd read had said the spell was meant to be a last-ditch effort against invaders, triggered by the blood of the High Sorcerer of Klydonia. I'd banked on that part being an embellishment, and that any Klydonian would do. And I was right.

What it hadn't said was that the spell would unleash a herd of very angry, very murderous unicorns.

The unicorn rampant at the top of the fountain shook its head and charged off the marble pedestal, heading right for the gardens. A few others ran into the castle complex itself, and the sound of screaming and swords clattering to the ground echoed from every corner. I had, it seemed, unwittingly unleashed a bloodbath.

Whoops.

I sat in the courtyard and watched as the unicorns tore every last soldier to pieces, and tried to remember that if not for the enchantment, it would have been us.

It didn't much help.

Lyle came back from the gardens, covered in blood. He sat next to me on the edge of the fountain.

"Wow," he said, his eyes kind of wide.

"Yeah," I murmured. Klydonia would be safe, but I couldn't help but feel sorry for the soldiers being torn asunder by beautiful horned horses.

After about a turn of the hourglass the unicorns returned to where I sat. One by one they bowed their head in salute and retook their place on the fountain, some of them shrinking and twisting so that they were little more than hand-sized engravings. I closed my eyes, but every time I shut them I saw soldiers being run through by beautiful golden horns.

I was going to have nightmares for months.

People started to come out of the buildings, some badly injured, but most were okay. They saw me sitting on the marble bench, hand bloody, and began to murmur.

"Who set the protectors free?" came a reedy cry near the double doors. The crowd of people parted, and an old man with very dark skin wearing heavy robes limped toward me.

"Um, I did. Sorry?" I suddenly felt very, very bad about releasing the unicorns. Although I had been entirely correct about Hansen being awful.

The old man's eyes widened, and a smile split his face. "It's the sorcerer foretold by the prophecy!"

The crowd erupted into cheers, a few people even crying. I took a step back, and Lyle was right behind me. It had been a long day, and while I was ready to believe in myself, this was entirely too much.

"Hey, so, uh, I know a really cool place up in the mountains if you want to get out of here," he said. "We could watch the leaves change."

I didn't know what the prophecy was or why people were suddenly celebrating, especially when the courtyard was still pretty full of dead soldiers. But I knew a good offer when I heard one.

I turned to Lyle and nodded. "Let's go."

THE GODDESS PROVIDES

By L.L. McKinney

Led by the bite of icy steel pulling at her brown wrists, Akanni flexed her fingers, trying to regain some of the sensation stolen by the shackles. *Clink. Clink. Clink.* The chain that bound her to the soldier bounced against the scabbard at his hip. The steady rhythm matched the thud of his feet on the cold, packed dirt.

"Make way," he boomed, his voice sharp with self-importance. Bodies shuffled aside, clearing a path.

The soldier gave the chain a yank, jerking Akanni forward. "Keep up."

Pain tore at her ankles and feet. Hunger twisted in her gut. A pounding had set in behind her eyes last night and refused to fade, but she breathed deep and slow.

I am stone. I am the mountain.

Dozens of dark eyes followed their progression.

"That's her," voices murmured, the sound flowing in and out like waves.

"Kazili Heshenae."

"Cursed."

Brown faces crowded in and around each other to get a look at the princess turned prisoner. The forsaken one. Akanni lifted her chin and met as many of those gazes as possible.

You are all going to die for what you've done.

The ground curved upward, and Akanni struggled briefly to keep her footing. The soldier did not slow. He moved with purpose, his armored shoulders back and his head high. Muted moonlight danced on the embroidered swatches of red stitched into emerald cloth at his back, made to look like bloody slashes in the fabric. It was the banner of Tosin the Lion. To Akanni, it was the mark of a betrayer.

Higher they climbed. The chill crawled up her limbs, stiffening them, but she would not falter. For three days she had marched, exhausted, humiliated, but she would not break. Not yet.

The wind carried the scent of soot, iron, blood-soaked earth, and winter cold. The smell of war. Fire flickered in the torch stands now lining the path. The crackle was like whispers on the air, warning of the danger ahead. At the top of the hill, a massive structure of leather and thatching rested at the center of the city of war tents. The trappings were extravagant, giving it the appearance of a fortress. Banners snapped in the breeze, all of them bearing the same green scarred with crimson claw marks.

The soldier stopped in front of two guards posted on either

side of the entrance. "Watch her." He handed the end of the chain to the one on the left, a wisp of a man, a boy really. He was not much taller than Akanni, and appeared younger than her seventeen seasons. His eyes, wide and uncertain, darted back and forth between her and the one who had brought her here.

"Watch her," the soldier repeated with a lifted finger. "Closely."

"Yes, sir." The boy's dark hand shook as it clutched the chain.

"And show some balls."

"Y-yes, sir."

The second guard drew back the flap so the soldier could enter, then followed him inside. Voices filled the air in their wake, quiet, muffled.

Akanni drew her shoulders back and mustered as much of her royal bearing as she could. "Tosin is conscripting children into his armies now?" She kept her voice quiet.

"I am not a child." The boy lifted his chin, even though his voice did falter slightly. "It is an honor to serve the Lion."

"Tosin the Lion." Akanni spat the words in mockery. They tasted foul, putrid, bearable only by the weight of the anger coiling inside her. "Tosin the coward."

"Watch your tongue."

"Tosin the murderer. His hands are stained with innocent blood. His soul is rot. He would be a king, but all he will rule is death."

"Tosin . . . Tosin will lead us into a new age. A new prosperity. We will be blessed. The Goddess provides. But you would know nothing of that, would you, heshen! Blasphemer!"

A rush of wind swept over the hilltop. It snatched at the cloak around Akanni's shoulders and batted at the flames in the large basins on either side of the door, nearly snuffing them out.

With a curse, the boy bent to grab a log from the small pile of wood just to the side of the basin nearest him. He only had one hand to work with since he was holding the chain to her shackles, but he managed to toss wood onto one flame and then the other. The fires slowly revived, as if wary to come out into the freezing night air.

"That's what they call me, isn't it?" Akanni kept her eyes on the peeking flames, her voice distant in her ears, hollow. "Kazili Heshenae. Princess of Blasphemy."

The boy fell silent. She could imagine the look he was giving her. Many had given it in the years following her renouncement of the Goddess. It was the kind of look often reserved for those with the white sickness, a look of disgust mingled with a pitiful contempt, but still a healthy dose of fear; for if you get too close you could contract it. Stand too near someone who had angered the Goddess, and Her disdain could afflict you as well, and nothing angered the Goddess more than blasphemers.

Well, almost nothing.

No one could have predicted the heir to the throne, of all people, would turn away from the Goddess. Not when her mother was among the most devout in all of Oramec. So devout, in fact, that as well as her duties as queen she bore the mantle of High One, chief priest of the palace.

Every day of her life, Akanni remembered her mother waking early for prayer and staying up late for the same. If she could not make it to the grand temple for worship, she would go to a little room where candles and incense burned, and offer up praise and reverence. She taught Akanni with patient hands how to make the Goddess's mark in the earth to bless it before offering thanks and prayer. She showed Akanni with gentle touches how to bring a swift and painless end to sacrifices, then till the blood with the earth and use the clay to mark her body during times of fasting.

"The Goddess visits us in our temples and prayer closets," her mother had said one time while making the mark. "But those of true devotion can earn Her rhakah, the greatest of Her gifts. That is when Her will inhabits the body as if it were a temple. I seek this blessing for myself, and for you. If it is to be yours, you must be strong, like stone, and steadfast, like the mountain."

Her mother was strong.

Her mother was steadfast.

Even when the white sickness came on her, Akanni's mother danced and sacrificed and abstained, ever fervent.

A frail heart and iron guts had finally forced her mother from the temple and into her bed, where she held Akanni's hands in her now too-thin ones.

"It is not for me to decide which path I take." Her mother's fingers like talons, the bones bulging, she was barely able to mix the clay, but she painted Akanni's face; three lines under each eye, two dots above each brow, and a stroke of her thumb from Akanni's hairline to the tip of her nose. "The Goddess provides, Akanni. Always."

Her mother was *prayerful*.

Her mother was *faithful*.

Her mother was *devout*.

The sickness claimed her still.

That was when Akanni stopped believing.

"Kazili Heshenae," Akanni repeated as the memory of her mother's final night faded, and the flames in the basin near the boy bearing Tosin's colors flared. She lifted her eyes to him. "You should run."

The color fled his face, leaving his brown skin mottled. His throat worked in a thick swallow and his eyes widened all the more, white and frightened.

He parted his lips as if to speak, but the flap to the tent swung open, the other guard holding it to the side. "Bring her."

The boy nodded and stepped quickly into the tent, drawing the chain with him. Akanni followed.

I am stone.

Inside, an oppressive heat swallowed her. Sweat prickled against her skin almost instantly, and her lungs struggled to take in air for the briefest of moments. The aches in her body intensified, threatening to drag her whimpering to her knees, but she held fast. She bit into her lower lip hard enough to taste blood. The sting struck sharp against her swimming senses.

Laughter sounded from the far side of the tent. Propped against a bed of furs, rugs, and pillows large and small, lay Tosin. His pale skin was red from the heat and pockmarked with scars, most of them his own doing. Before taking on this venture of warlord, Tosin had professed himself a holy man. He was a practitioner at the temple, no one of any true import, but despite that, he'd managed to win over many of the Goddess's worshipers. He was cunning and manipulative, and when her mother passed and Akanni renounced the Goddess, he saw that as his opportunity for more. He pleaded his case and took up the now-empty role of High One. The mantle would have fallen to Akanni's shoulders, but she had cast that aside. In that way, her blasphemy had indeed brought this trouble down on her.

"Kazili." The word poured from his lips like runover from his goblet. "You look well."

Chained for three days and nights, hauled alongside a horse like little more than cattle, she knew she stank of exhaustion and exertion and, to her furious shame, the bitter odor of how she'd had to relieve herself while walking, given no space or privacy to do so. The cold had helped to mask the smell, but in here, in the heat, it crawled up her nose, along with the cloying, familiar smell of blood and drink. Fresh slices along Tosin's bare flesh where it was visible past the layers of his robes meant he likely had recently finished letting, to honor the Goddess.

"It has been so long since last I saw you. Three seasons, if memory serves." His eyes trailed over her faintly trembling frame, and it was all she could do not to lose what little bit was in her stomach.

I am the mountain.

"It was during the High Solstice," he continued, smiling wide beneath a line of shaggy black hair on his lip. "The day of the festival."

"The day you murdered my family," Akanni spat between clenched teeth.

To either side of her, the boy-guard and the soldier both swiveled to look at Tosin.

The bastard continued to smile, though it hardened.

"That is a serious accusation, my dear. Especially coming from a heshen."

At that word, the boy-guard and the soldier looked back to Akanni, the soldier with disdain on his brown face and the boy with fear.

"Leave us." Tosin waved a hand.

"Sir?" The soldier frowned.

"She is a shackled and unarmed girl; she poses no threat. Not to the future Kazi of Oramec." Tosin lifted himself from his nest of damp-looking pillows. His body was thin, though it lacked muscle. He was not a young man, and the drink had clearly taken its toll. "Leave us."

The soldier bowed and, reluctant, turned to depart. The boy-guard fidgeted a moment before dropping the chain to the ground with a *thunk* and hurrying after his superior.

Tosin watched them go before turning back to Akanni with another of those blasted smiles. "My dear, even a heshen should be wary of speaking such lies." He stepped toward her.

Akanni stiffened, but thankfully he moved away and over to the opposite end of the tent. There, a basin of water was waiting. He undid the sash at his waist and let the fabric fall from his body. Akanni averted her eyes until she heard the splashing of him settling in.

"What has led you to believe that I, one of the Goddess's chosen, would kill the ruler of Her people?" Tosin flicked a bit of water over the side.

Akanni knew she should hold her tongue, but the pain of the last few days was hot and fresh, and it fanned the flames of anguish from her time in exile. The combination made her temper short and her tongue loose. "I saw you," she bit out. "With the man in the cloak."

She remembered that night clearer than any other, save the night her amma went to be with the Goddess. It was late, and she had just returned home after a trip with her father and twin brother, Seth. They'd gone to a neighboring kingdom for a period of weeks to witness the marriage of one of their cousins.

Amidst the cushions spread around her, Akanni had rocked with the jostle of the palanquin as it bore them on. The smell of old pine and citrus polish swirled heavy in the air. Beads rattled and clacked against one another, hung with silk to shield the windows and door from the sun, which had thankfully gone down some time ago. The rhythmic clatter punctuated the relative silence, along with the beating of feet and braying of beasts outside.

"Nnn, rouse yourselves, my children." Her father's voice was heavy in the shadows that filled the space between them. "We are home."

The palanquin was large enough to hold the entire royal family, though Akanni always took to curling against Seth like he was a large, warm pillow. She stretched her tired limbs and sat up. Her brother did not move, though his eyes went from her to their baba.

"Have you given any thought to our earlier conversation?" Seth said. His voice did not hold the deepness of Baba's, still a boy's tones. He hated when Akanni teased him about it.

Even in the darkness, the look her father shot him was cutting. "There is nothing to think on. It is blasphemy, and we shall speak of it no more." Stroking his silvery beard where it lay over his belly, their father glared at the ceiling. "Goddess keep me, I cannot have two heshen as children." Even though her father had been supportive in her decision, as supportive as one could be, his words still stung.

Seth tensed beside her. Apart from their mother, he was the most devout in the family, and if their father's words stung her, they were like a blow for him. When their mother passed, Seth dove even deeper into the teachings and worship, drawing ever nearer to the Goddess as Akanni pulled away. He did not approve of her renouncement and spent no less than an hour every day praying that she would come back to the Light before being judged.

The palanquin jerked then rocked as it was lowered. Father did not wait for his attendants before rolling to clamber out, grumbling about going to bed. It was a shame to let him leave in such a dark mood, and Akanni made to go after him, but a hand on her shoulder held her fast.

"Amma was supposed to perform the bahet for the wedding. Her absence was keenly felt by all, but mostly by Baba. Give him until morning." Seth's voice was soft, forgiving. Their father was a kind man, usually full of smiles and laughter for his children, but without Amma . . . that man had faded.

Akanni nodded and patted Seth's hand. "Do not stay up too late." Even though he sounded as if he'd already forgiven their father for the insult, it would likely send him to Amma's prayer closet for some time.

He squeezed her shoulder and dropped his hand.

In the palace, amidst the alabaster stone and trappings of jade and silver, where the visages of ancestors watched over them silently, Akanni called for a bath. She settled into the warm waters, drawn from the nearby shore, and let her attendants see to scrubbing her rich, brown skin then smoothing it with scented oil. Nimble fingers worked at her hair, undoing the plaits against her scalp and washing away days' worth of dust and travel. More oil made her scalp tingle and left her coils smelling of citrus.

Dressed in her gown and with a light robe wrapped around her frame, she dismissed her retinue and made for her bedroom. The quiet of the palace was haunting, but not

unpleasantly so. As she came around a corner, she drew up
short then pulled back. Peeking around confirmed what she
thought she saw.

Tosin, the priest. He exchanged quiet words with a man
in a cloak, the hood drawn up, handed him something, and
then waved him on. The individual drifted into the shadows
and was gone, leaving Tosin to adjust his robes and start in
her direction.

Akanni drew back and took a steeling breath. Tosin
always set a chill in her spine. She did not like him here,
walking these halls, praying in her mother's place. But the
palace clergy needed a head, her father had said, and since
Akanni herself refused, it had to be someone the people
trusted.

When he came around the corner and saw her there, he
paused, a look of surprise crossing his gaunt face.

"Kazili." He bowed. "Keeping late hours?"

"Just coming back from a bath. It's soothing after travels."

Tosin smiled and drew in a slow breath. "Plum citrus." He
tasted the air. "Sweet as you are."

The shiver from before returned. "I had best get to bed."
She stepped past him without waiting for him to bow as was
custom.

"Good night, Kazili," he purred in her wake. "The Goddess
provides."

Akanni's steps quickened. She reached her room and
bolted her door behind her. There was something foul about
that man, and she almost wanted to call for another bath

after having spent those few moments in his presence.

Instead, she drew the gossamer curtains in around her bed. Travel worn and weary, she drifted easily into sleep.

The sun had not yet risen when she woke to the sound of alarm bells and shouts from the guard. She jolted from her bed, taking up the dagger she kept hidden beneath her pillow. Still in her nightgown, she threw open her bedroom door.

Something slammed into her and took her off her feet. Pain rolled through her body as she tumbled across the floor. She blinked against the blackness and the beating of her heart, her gaze drawn to movement across the room. Crouched on the ledge of the large window left open to let in the sound of the sea, the cloaked figure from the night before sat, bathed in moonlight. She blinked and he was gone.

Akanni stared, not entirely sure she'd seen anything at all. She pushed herself up, her elbow twinging where it had struck the stone of the floor. The alarm bells continued to ring, and the voices continued to cry out. It was only now, with her door open, that she could make out their words.

"The Kazi, he is dead!"

"Fire! Fire in the prayer closet!"

Shock, cold and unyielding, dropped through Akanni. She sat frozen on the hard floor. Words from the hallway crashed into her thoughts as they washed over each other.

Her father was dead. Poisoned. And the sun would rise to the discovery of her brother's charred remains at the base of her mother's now-ruined altar.

"The wrath of an angry Goddess fulfilled" was the lie Tosin spun. It would not have worked, except as she wept at her father's bedside the next day, Tosin had her room searched and recovered a vial of the toxin that had killed her baba.

"The Kazili wanted the throne, and plotted against her father!" Tosin had railed. "The prince must have uncovered her plot, and she killed him as well. The body was stabbed through the heart. There was blood on her dagger! Blasphemy! Murder!"

Akanni could hear him riling up the guard as she raced through the palace with those most loyal to her and her family, intending to flee.

"Hunt down the Kazili Heshenae! She must pay for her sins!"

Tosin's voice chased Akanni from her home that day, and across the savannah for three seasons hence. During that time, she told her story to the few who would listen. Some joined her. Others . . . well. Her small encampment remained on the move, trying to gather numbers and strength, going from allied country to allied country to seek the aid of any who would see her returned to her home and her throne.

But even as she worked, so did Tosin. He spun his web of lies to reach farther and farther. Many people believed him. Those who did not feared going against the High One. And the evidence against her, false as it was, was condemning. So Tosin named himself the Lion, then took command of her family's armies to begin the hunt. He would track down the heshen and bring her to the Goddess's justice. Then, Her will fulfilled, he would see to it the throne was secure.

So Akanni lived in exile, training, planning, managing to stay three steps ahead of Tosin, until three nights ago, when a contingent of his men discovered her with a small band of attendants, trying to get word to the lord of a local city, hoping to gain another ally. The attendants were slain, and Akanni captured.

And here she stood, defiant still. "I saw you with the man in the cloak. The same man who left the poison in my room after he used it to kill the Kazi." She had told the guards of the intruder, but when they searched the grounds, they found no trace of him. Then they dismissed her story altogether when they found the vial. "You had him drug my father—did he slay my brother, too?"

Tosin gazed at her, still wearing that look of slight amusement. "You always were smarter than any girl has the right to be."

"Mark me, Tosin. I will end you, and then I will find the one who helped you murder my family." Anger coiled through her like a living, wild thing, ready to pounce. She was still shackled, but chains could be used to kill.

Tosin's laughter brought on the familiar chill along her back. It wasn't the amused laughter from before, but more a bitter, cruel thing that curled his lips. "Should we let her in on our little secret?" he said, but not to her. His eyes moved to somewhere over her shoulder.

Akanni spun and came face-to-face with the last person she ever expected to see. Her lips worked uselessly at first, but she took a breath that was half gasp, half sob, and forced a single word free.

"S-Seth?"

Her brother stood over her, far taller than he had been when she last saw him. His face was set in the hard lines of their father's. He watched her with rich, brown eyes. Their mother's eyes, but his were not gentle like hers. They were cold, glassed with a deep sadness.

"Sister."

Shock maintained its iron grasp on her mind. "W-what . . . what is this?" Her voice was small in her ears, pathetic.

"This is the will of the Goddess," Tosin said from behind her. Water sloshed as he climbed from his bath. "Once I have slain the Kazili Heshenae, I will bring her body to the great temple and lay it as a sacrifice on the altar. From the ashes, and by the blood of the devout, our prince will be reborn. It will be rhakah, the Goddess made flesh, like the days of old. You see, I said I would secure the throne, but I never said for myself."

Akanni trembled hard enough that her shackles rattled. Tears streaked her face. "It was you," she whispered, her eyes on her brother's unchanging face. "The m-man in the cloak. It was *you*."

"Yes. It was me." Seth's voice had deepened with the approach of manhood. Both of them had one season before they were of age.

She dropped to her knees, doubled over. "W-why?" she asked the dirt between sobs.

"Because it was up to me to set things right." Seth shifted, and his hands pressed to her shoulders as he knelt in front of her. "You had strayed so far from the path, and Baba refused to bring you back. I . . . begged him. He said it was not our place, that we should give you time."

Seth's hold tightened. "But time is not something we had. Baba was fading. I saw it, I know you did. He would not see the next turn of the seasons, and you were moving further and further from the Light. He would be dead, and with you being the eldest, Amma's throne would pass to a heshen. The Goddess would surely destroy us all. I swear to you, sister, I do this out of love. Love for our people. Love for the Goddess. Love for Amma. If she could see you now, see how far you have fallen, she would weep."

Akanni wept. And as she did, Seth's fingers stroked her hair like he used to when they were little.

"I went to Tosin with my concerns. He prayed and fasted, and the Goddess granted him a vision, a way for us to avoid the destruction of Oramec, of so many innocent lives. This . . . this plan. It broke my heart. I did not want to see the truth of what needed to be done. I thought I could avert this future another way. At our cousin's wedding, I asked Baba to consider passing the throne to me. He refused, even when I told him of my fears. Do you know what he said? 'To the Deep with the Goddess.'" Seth's voice trembled. "Can you believe that?"

Akanni stopped crying. Her fingers curled in the earth.

I am stone.

Her heart pounded in her ears, but she heard her brother's words ring clear.

"I asked. One last time, when we returned home. He said it was blasphemy. Him! Accuse me of being heshen, after what he said!" The anger in Seth's voice would have frightened her before, but an icy hardness had poured through Akanni and encased her wailing heart. "I knew what I had to do. I knew it would be hard, but . . . all trials are."

"And so you have completed this one," Tosin said from somewhere above her. "The Goddess will be pleased."

"And when your body is burned on the altar, sister, your sins will be purified. You will be able to go to Her." There it was, the joy and lightheartedness she was used to hearing in her brother's voice. So much of him seemed the same, and yet was different.

She hoped, she prayed, that at least his habit of keeping a dagger hidden in his usual spot had not changed.

"Get her up," Tosin snapped.

Hands gripped her shoulders. That's when Akanni snatched at the rim of her brother's right boot. Crouched as he was, he couldn't pull away fast enough as her fingers curled around the hilt. Twirling the weapon easily in her hand with the ability three years of daily training had taught her, she drove it up and into the soft, giving flesh of her brother's belly.

He screamed.

Something warm and slick poured over her hands as she

worked the knife back and forth. Getting her legs underneath her, she surged upward, throwing his body off her. He fell over, clutching at his guts as they spilled into the dirt.

"Guard!" Tosin bellowed, even as the flap of the tent was already drawing open.

In that instant, the pain, the anger, the fury Akanni had worked to contain exploded outward. Fire swept through her entire body. She let it consume her, then let it flow. White flame erupted from her skin. The guards and the soldier from before, having rushed for her with weapons drawn, recoiled. Fear took their faces and lit their eyes. Their swords crashed to the ground as they turned and fled, leaving Tosin to his fate.

The white flame ate away everything it touched. The pillows, the rugs, the posts that held the tent in place. Soon, it would all come crashing in, but not before she finished what she was here to do.

She faced Tosin, who cowered where he had leapt back into his bath, as if the water would save him. She stalked toward him, through the flame. It licked at her skin, harmless.

Tosin shrank in on himself as she drew near, the whole of him shaking enough to send ripples racing through the dirtied water.

"W-what . . . what is this?" His voice cracked in terror. He glanced about, for possible escape, his straggly black hair whipping about, but there was nowhere to go. All was flame and ember and ash. "What are you?"

"This . . . is rhakah," Akanni said.

The disbelief on his face pleased her.

"She came to me, in the dead of the night. Me, of all to be chosen, a nonbeliever. I was tired, starving, and weeping where your soldiers had tied me in the cold to sleep, certain I was going to die." Akanni had never been more certain of anything in her life. The cold was crushing. Near starving, her body was failing. She had failed. There was nothing left. "I wanted to die." She had welcomed death. Prayed for it. And as she lay there, the life slowly seeping from her, she heard it.

"My child," a voice whispered in the darkness. "My daughter. My love. Hear me."

"A-Amma?" Akanni whispered, certain she was near the gates to the Garden, and her mother had come to take her the rest of the way.

"I am all and nothing. I began before, and I will end after." The words echoed around Akanni, sweet and low. The voice's edge danced against her mind like a blade. "I have heard your prayers, and I come for you, wayward child."

The darkness parted and light filled the void, then coalesced into a single orb, bright and shining. The moon, Akanni realized, just as the lights of stars sparked to life around it. The sky stretched over her, clear and bright.

"This will not be your last night, if you but promise me . . ."

"P-promise . . . ?" Akanni continued to shiver.

"Promise me you will end them. The heshen. Blasphemers, who do foul deeds in my name. Who plot against my people. Promise me, lost one, and I will give you what you want most."

A spear erupted from the ground before her. It jutted into

the air, and on its spike, Tosin's head, bloated and discolored in death, gazed at her.

"Promise me," the voice repeated. "Harden your heart, for it will be tested. Whatever it takes, do this thing. Be strong, like stone, and I will make you the mountain."

Akanni saw the face of her mother in those stars above Tosin's rotted head, and the faces of her father and brother. Then all began to fade into the Deep's black.

"Promise me . . ." the voice whispered, flaking away.

"I—I . . . I promise," Akanni gasped.

A feeling like fire filled her arms and gathered in her palms. Light sprang forth from her fingers. It engulfed everything around her, white hot. She wanted to scream, but she could not. Nor could she move. So, she lay there, as the light brightened, until it consumed her.

"When I awoke," Akanni said as she stared into Tosin's terrified face, "I realized what had happened. That I should be dead. But She spared me, for this moment."

The flame began to creep toward Tosin where Akanni's will had held it back. He whirled and splashed, scrambling to try to get away, but the fire took him. His screams ended in cracked yowls as his tongue burned. Flesh peeled from muscle. What water remained in the tub bubbled and thickened red.

Akanni turned, indifferent, as the remains of the tent continued to falter around her, burned to nothing. She approached another spot where the fire had held back at her bidding.

Clutching his stomach with red-licked fingers, sweat prickling his ashen brown face, Seth gazed up at her in a mix of wonder and confusion. Coughs wracked his body, and blood dappled his lips. "H-how . . ."

"*I* am the mountain."

The last of the tent's trappings fell away. Tosin's camp flickered into view, the fires all around the hill still lit, almost mirroring the stars above. Soldiers who had come, looking to try to help, surrounded her. Those same brown faces that had watched with scorn as she was marched up here now twisted in shock and fear. The boy-guard was not among them. She wondered if he'd run. Several of them did now, racing down into the camp. They would not get far.

Kneeling, Akanni pressed her hands into her brother's blood where it spilled across the ashy sands. He'd fallen still, finally, their mother's eyes staring at nothing. Carefully she tilled the blood and the earth, making the mark of the Goddess. Then, with fingers crusted with clay, she pressed them to her face.

Three lines beneath each eye. Two dots above each brow. Then she stroked her thumb from the line of her hair, down the center of her face, and to the tip of her nose.

Standing, her legs trembled but held. She turned to face the camp, now in a full panic, as she allowed the fires to consume the corpse behind her.

"Well done, my child." The familiar voice rose in her ears, sizzling with power. "Take what is yours."

Akanni's chest heaved and her eyes burned, but no tears came.

I am stone.

Her palms grew hot as the flames around her intensified.

I am the mountain.

She lifted her hands toward the camp.

"The Goddess provides."

HEARTS TURNED TO ASH

By Dhonielle Clayton

Jackson broke up with Etta on a Thursday night, and her heart started to disintegrate on Friday right before dawn.

Hearts can do that. According to Ms. Mildred, Etta's grandmother who doesn't want to be called a grandmother, and who Etta always thought was wrong about everything. Soul mates aren't supposed to break up. Not when worried mamas had the conjure woman cast the stars, tie a fortune string made of the universe from one heart to another. Not when fates had been written.

But Etta didn't know that was the reason for her pain.

Not yet.

Etta sat straight up in bed. The moon winked in her window, tiny pearls of light scattering across her new diorama of the Eiffel Tower on her nightstand.

Heat seared in her chest like a lit firecracker. She rushed to the bathroom. Her breath tangled in her throat, a pink flush fighting to push through the brown of her cheeks. She pulled down the collar of her nightgown. Beneath her skin, she could see her heart: a smoldering coal. Her veins illuminated like snakes desperate to escape the destruction.

The blood vessels in her eyes left red spiderwebs across the white. Her pupils dilated, the black swallowing the hazel. Jackson used to tell Etta that her eyes were his favorite thing about her face. He'd goad her into closing them, then he'd trace his deep-brown fingers across the lid and down over the eyelashes until his soft fingertips rested at the corners. He'd count the few freckles she had on them, little dark stars.

"Open your eyes," he'd say. "Let me see you."

And she always did.

Then he'd let his hands, strong from lifting lumber and building fences on his grandfather's land, knead the shape of her shoulders, and rest his palm on her chest. He'd thump his thick fingers to the thudding rhythm of her heart, excited from his scent, anticipating the taste of his mouth.

Etta's hand found that spot.

His spot.

But now, her heartbeat was almost gone.

"Don't ever give your heart away, Etta." Ms. Mildred's words puttered out between puffs of a clove cigarette.

Etta was only around seven years old when her grandmother issued this warning.

They'd been headed into town for something that Etta couldn't remember anymore. She'd been stuffed into Ms.

Mildred's blue Cadillac, her little-girl limbs looking for space among the antiques in the back seat. A stuffed robin in a wire birdcage stared down with glassy eyes, piles of striped hatboxes slid back and forth, and the sounds of clattering teacups became a melody underscoring her grandmother's words.

"Your heart is the core. Where you house how you *really* feel about things. It's precious. It's to be protected like a pearl."

The car swayed like they were in a boat and trapped in some storm of Ms. Mildred's own creation as she barreled down the long stretch of road that connected their house to the outside world. Or at least it always felt like that to Etta. They were the only family aside from Jackson's who lived so far away from town. Far enough so white folks couldn't meddle and the Black ones felt it was too much trouble to turn down their gravel driveway and travel the two miles to the Big House to be nosy.

Dust and gravel pummeled the windows. Ms. Mildred cursed before looking up at Etta in the rearview mirror. Etta felt like her grandmother was the most beautiful woman in the whole world, even more beautiful than her mama. Not a single wrinkle marred the brown of her grandmother's skin, and Etta had always thought that it would smell of maple syrup and roasted pecans if she ever let Etta get close enough to sniff it. She wasn't the kissy type of grandmother. She had the same freckles Etta had, but they'd been expertly placed so that when she smiled—which was rare—they took the shape of a scattered heart. She always wore a deep shade of red lipstick and told Etta that it let everyone know she would bite until she got blood.

"Did you hear what I said?" she'd asked Etta.

"Yes, ma'am," Etta replied.

"What did I say?"

"Never give your heart away."

Ms. Mildred nodded, then blew smoke rings, the white clouds smelling like Christmas. "Don't let nobody take the center of you." She beat her chest so hard Etta thought her fist might pierce her own skin. "But do you *really* understand what I mean?"

"What about love?" Etta asked.

"What about it?" she replied.

"Aren't I supposed to get married?"

Ms. Mildred burst with laughter, the cackle escaping from deep down in her belly. "Love ain't got nothing to do with marriage, honey."

"Do you love Granddaddy?"

Ms. Mildred almost bit down on her cigarette. "I like him fine. But I didn't have to give my heart away to have your mama with him. And I had children with other men, too."

"Uncle James, and Aunt Peggy."

"And I liked their daddies just fine," she said. "I just see these little girls running around here with no sense. Nose wide open. Brain full of rocks. Distracted 'cause some boy told them they were pretty. There are so many other things to do is all I'm saying. Don't be no fool, Etta." Ms. Mildred's eyes found Etta in the back seat, and she watched as her grandmother's forehead creased, fold upon fold, an accordion of thought and feeling and memory trapped in brown skin. Ms. Mildred launched into more fussing: "Don't let love take you too high, 'cause you'll be a kite without a tail, and before you know it, caught in a storm cloud. And lightning ain't kind. Love ain't worth being electrocuted for. Or your heart turned to ash."

One of the things Etta remembered the most about this conversation was the lightning, how she wanted to be that kite or one of the rods her daddy had installed on the roof of their house right before he left them and never came back. She wanted to feel that electricity. She needed to know how it felt.

"What if I gave my heart to a girl instead?" Etta asked.

"That would be better. Women are much better about taking care of hearts. But the point still stands."

"I love you, Ms. Mildred," she'd squeaked out.

"And I love you, too, Cookie."

Now Etta's mama found her on the bathroom floor and scooped her up like she was nothing more than a baby again, not a girl of seventeen. Her mama hadn't seen her in several days because Etta had been in and out of the house and off with Jackson. She grunted as her mother carried her back into the bedroom.

"Something's wrong with my heart," Etta whispered. The words jagged rocks scratching at her throat as she struggled to get them out. "It's burning."

Mama inspected her, pulling down her nightgown and gawking at the sight of her chest. "What happened with Jackson?"

"Why?" Etta croaked. "Shouldn't you call the ambulance? Shouldn't we go to the hospital?"

"No medicine from that place can fix this." She ran her cold fingertips across Etta's achy skin. It was a momentary comfort. "Now, tell me what happened."

"We broke up."

A gasp escaped Mama's mouth. "Why?"

"I don't really know. I don't under—"

"What you mean, you don't really know? This isn't possible."

"What does it have to do with . . ." Etta sucked in a deep breath as pain erupted through her.

"You need to go see the conjure woman, Madame Peaks. Only she can stop this." Mama pushed the frizzy curls off Etta's forehead.

The picture of the conjure woman drifted into her mind like a reflection broken into shards. A pair of filmy eyes. A pursed red mouth. Luminous brown skin. A scarf wrapped around her head like a dollop of cream. Etta had little-girl memories of the woman—her mama dragging her there when her daddy left, to ask for a root to bring him back; the way her house seemed tilted, almost; and how at thirteen, she and Jackson had found a weird map from the woman in his mama's basement.

"He was your soul mate."

Mama had told her the stories of how she and Jackson's mama had their stars cast, and Etta had felt like her connection to him fit, slid into place like when the right puzzle piece finds its match. The pull always tugged at her whenever she thought of him, whenever she saw him, whenever he showed up in her dreams; she had to see him, touch his skin, wrap herself in his scent.

"Your skin's yellowing. Your heart is dying fast."

"I don't understand why this is happening." Tears flooded Etta's cheeks. "I don't even understand why we . . ." She couldn't finish the sentence. The thought of the word sent another bolt of pain through her.

"When soul mates break up, the shock in the universe has consequences." Mama rubbed as many tears as she could from Etta's cheeks, then left the room for a moment.

If Etta's pulse could race, it would've as her mind filled with worries. She'd always known her family's and town's superstitions were more than just that, and that roots and conjure were as everyday as the herbs in most folks' kitchen gardens. But the magic, if you could call it that, always felt like something far away, a horizon she could never touch, a thing that didn't affect her life. Or so she'd thought.

Mama returned with steaming mugs.

"Drink this," she ordered.

Etta took long, slow sips. "What was I supposed to do?" She balled her fists but didn't have the energy to bang the bedside. Her heart steadily slowed a little after each labored beat.

"You're supposed to stay together. You were matched. You were destined." Mama touched Etta's cheek, her brown fingers warm from the mugs. "You're supposed to make sure it worked."

"Why is it all on me?" Etta's lungs squeezed, and she coughed. "What will happen to him?"

"He'll get what's coming. Worse than a heart dying." Mama rushed forward with a bowl. Tiny trickles of dust the color of pulverized rubies made their way out of Etta's nose and mouth. Mama caught each little bead for safekeeping. "You must hold these close, otherwise she won't be able to put your heart back together again."

"When's the last time you saw Madame Peaks? What if she's not even alive anymore?"

"She's not a person who dies, and stays dead." Mama closed her eyes for a moment before answering. "I've seen her three times. The first when I was pregnant with you. Jackson's mama, Mrs. Mary, came with me. Y'all were due a week and three days apart. And we'd been dreaming of y'all together. Best friends. Partners. I knew it was the right thing to do to have your stars cast."

"You've told me this story a hundred times."

"Listen again." Mama nibbled her bottom lip, puffy from the hot tea. "The second time I saw her was when you were around four years old. Just to make sure it had took. She said everything was as it should be, as it had been written. And the last, right after your daddy left us."

"How do I find her?" Etta replied, out of breath.

"With conjure. With roots."

It felt impossible.

"Why'd you even do this, Mama?" Etta winced, the burning sensation in her chest back.

"I never wanted you to have to be alone like me."

Etta kissed Jackson first. They'd just turned eleven years old that summer and they were out on his grandfather's farm, which touched the back of her grandmother's farm. She'd conscripted him into helping her collect materials for her next diorama. She loved creating little scenes in shoeboxes and hatboxes and fruit crates. Really, any box she could find, she'd make a little world within it. She liked to create tiny visions of the future she wanted—her far away from this too-hot place, her pressing her feet onto the cobblestones of old cities, trying to absorb magic through her shoes, her being able to sketch new skylines to make replicas of later.

They'd climbed as high as they could in her favorite magnolia tree because she'd wanted one of the white flowers from the very top—the perfect ones that hadn't been messed with by squirrels.

Jackson sat beside Etta, brown legs dangling and blending with the rich color of the tree boughs. He looked around for one of the flowers. "I think they're all gone. Blown away."

"I'm too late," Etta had said.

Jackson stood, then climbed onto a higher branch and disappeared into the leaves.

"Come back. There's nothing up there." Etta counted to

ten, but Jackson didn't return. "Jackson Eugene Williamson, I'm coming after you." She squeezed a nearby branch, preparing to hoist herself up and follow him, but he jumped back down beside her, holding an abandoned bird's nest.

"Maybe you can use this?" he asked with a shrug. "I've been watching it, and the family left a week ago."

Etta thought she could do a thousand things with that nest, and she felt like he knew that, which made her heart almost flip. "Should we kiss?"

"Why?" he asked.

"Why not?"

He shrugged again. "Okay. I guess that's a good reason."

She leaned forward, puckered her lips, and clamped her eyes shut.

It took a while but Jackson finally brushed his lips across hers.

Their eyes both snapped back open, and they said "Yuck" in unison.

The first time Jackson told Etta he loved her, they were fifteen years old. He'd left her a message in one of her dioramas, and used the Valentine's candy hearts with the words on them to arrange it.

She pretended to be mad that he'd desecrate one of her masterpieces. Littered her image of what twilight in Cairo might look like with his note. But she let the candy stay in there until the ants crept through her window and ate it all.

And she loved that he said the word *love* first.

Being loved by him grew so big it became even better than the dioramas.

Mama dragged Etta out back. The sun had barely started to rise, a hint of its yellowy forehead peeking over the line of magnolias that marked the edge of their land. They raced through the gardens, ducking under a trellis of vine tomatoes and butter beans and bright, plump squash.

The chicken coop sat to the left, and even their rooster wasn't up yet. Rows of fields stretched out as far as Etta could see, always reminding her of the beautiful cornrows Mama would braid into her hair, but these would bloom with melons and cabbage and potatoes instead of zigzagging curls. The slaughterhouse and smokehouse lurked to the right like twin shadows. And the Big House where Ms. Mildred and Granddaddy lived sat out in the distance, the white porch wrapping around its front like a perfect ribbon and the little oil lamps in the windows illuminated like eyes gazing out into the dark.

Dew coated their ankles, and the warmth of the day started to heat up their skin.

Etta walked as fast as she could with Mama toting her like a basket ready to spill its contents.

"We're almost there," Mama whispered.

"How far does Madame Peaks live?" Etta asked.

"She doesn't live close by or far away."

"What does that mean?"

"You'll see."

At the edge of their land, Mama gave Etta a tiny bottle containing her heart fragments, set her against one of the magnolias to rest, then took out a little shovel and dug up one of its roots. She used a knife to sliver off three pieces. Etta heard her thank the tree.

"What are you doing?" Etta craned to see.

"Building a conjure door. Madame Peaks left this town—this world—when I was a young girl. But I always knew how to find her." Mama pulled a letter from her pocket. "Now, once you go through, hurry on up to her house. You'll see it. There's no getting lost." Mama got to work unpacking ingredients from her satchel and setting them on the ground.

Etta nodded.

Mama read the letter aloud. "Three magnolia roots to create the frame. A pinch of saltpeter to awaken them. A spoonful of cayenne to charge the conjure. A bowl of salt to purify the door. A cup of brick dust to protect the traveler. And a drop of the traveler's blood."

Before Etta could react, Mama had pierced the knife into the flesh of her fingertip and taken blood.

Mama scrambled back as a tiny fire popped and crackled in the heap. The air filled with a creaky, stretching sound. The roots grew into long braids, twisting and twirling until they were the length of long ropes. They coiled together into a wreath, gathering all of the ingredients from the pile like careful hands, then bloomed into a large trellis bursting with crimson flowers.

Etta's eyes grew wide with wonder as a doorknob appeared within it.

Etta hobbled through the entry. She turned back to face her mama.

"You coming?" she asked, reaching back.

Mama shook her head no. "You've got to do it alone. But I'll be waiting for you right here. Go straight to the house. Don't wander. Don't be curious."

Etta gulped, but quickly the pain in her heart reminded her to move. Across a long thicket of grass sat a house, and it hung over a cliff like a tiny lip. She thought that one day the house might catch too much wind and tip over, tumbling down onto the rocks. The old lady's treasure scattered like bones to be picked clean by vultures looking for nest objects.

A bottletree twinkled in the morning light. The blue glasses caught sunrays and any evil thing that might wander this far into her yard.

Her mama had a tree like this, tucked inside the garden so Ms. Mildred wouldn't see it, and Etta remembered the night they'd put it up, the summer she'd turned nine. An ivory moon had overwhelmed the sky, its glow washing the plants with light. Mama had lined up a series of glass bottles of every color, shape, and size on the grass. They'd danced around the tree, tying the bottles to boughs and branches.

Etta approached the house with caution. Staring at the porch and how it wrapped around the house like a crooked smile. Bulbous red globes dangled in the big front window.

Through the glass one could see shelves upon shelves of glass containers full of unrecognizable things. A tattered sign dropped like a spider above the doorway and in faded cursive lettering announced: MADAME EMMA PEAKS'S CURIOSITIES AND ROOTS.

Mama's money felt like a ball of fire in Etta's pocket. She'd given her several bills. She didn't know how much it cost to repair a heart.

Would it be fifty dollars?

A hundred?

More?

Etta was afraid, but her heart couldn't beat any faster. She took a deep breath and walked up the staircase. It wheezed and whined and announced her presence. Before Etta could raise her hand to knock, the door crept open.

"Come in, child," a voice called. "I've been expecting you all day."

Etta stepped inside the parlor. Clear jars revealed diseased bits of human viscera: pus-coated eyeballs, carbuncled flesh, gangrenous toes and fingers, spotted livers, lesion-covered kidneys, ribbons of blood vessels. The skulls of small animals paraded along an oak desk. Tonics and remedies, tinctures and salves, syrups and balms were featured for sale. A mortar and pestle and a bundle of brass surgical tools caught the red glint of the globes in the window, morphing them into demonic instruments.

The bones of a skeleton were stitched together with brass pins; a marionette flung across a chair, strings tangled, arms and legs sprawled out every which way.

A chandelier of half-burned candles sparked with flames as Etta walked beneath it.

"Where are you, Madame Peaks?" Etta called out.

"In the back. Come."

Etta followed the voice. A hallway stretched before her, winding narrowly like a dark river. Pockets of gloom and dead air lurked about, while candlelight quivered in splotches along the floor, sprouting into sturdy, infrequent stripes.

Etta pushed open the kitchen door. The woman slumped over a sink, her spindly back curved into a question mark as she rinsed herbs. "Have a seat, child. Be gentle with yourself. I can feel your fragile heart."

Etta slid into the nearest chair at her table. "How?"

"That's for me to know." She turned around and stared at Etta with foggy eyes. She wore a heaping pile of black fabric. Her brown skin held deep folds. When she walked toward Etta, her cane scratched across the floor like sharp-nailed claws.

"Can you fix my heart?" Etta handed her the tiny perfume bottle, then reached into her pocket and revealed the crumpled bills.

She took the money from Etta's palm. "I can do you one better. I can either fix it or give you a new heart."

"A new heart?"

"Yes. You got to decide whether you want me to grow yours back or if you want to select another."

"You have that kind of thing here?"

"I have everything I need, and *yes*, that means hearts, child. Let me show you."

✦ ✦ ✦

When they were thirteen years old, Etta and Jackson found a conjure map in his parents' basement. It was tucked away in a hatbox and up on a shelf, and Etta never knew how he'd found it all the way up there.

They spread it across the floor, brown foreheads slick with sweat as they gazed over a map of the constellations littered with red lines that Etta felt sure were blood. Their baby pictures sat tucked into opposite corners, and pen marks revealed their full names, birth time, weight, and other numbers neither of them could decode.

"What does this all mean?" Jackson asked, his nose crinkled with curiosity. She loved the way he bit his lip when he focused and how his head cocked to the left.

"Didn't your mama tell you?" Etta asked. "We supposed to be together forever."

"Forever is a long time. What if you leave our town? You said you wanted to travel once we graduated high school."

"You can come with me." She couldn't imagine doing anything without him. They were inseparable.

Jackson loved Etta, and Etta loved Jackson. That's how it went.

"And leave them to work the farm? I couldn't do that."

"It wouldn't be forever. We'd come back. Don't you want to see what's out there? Aren't you tired of Blue Hill?"

"No." He dropped his gaze back to the map, and they didn't say another word to each other that day.

+ + +

"Before you decide, I'll show you the hearts. Follow me, child." Madame Peaks led Etta down a set of staircases into a cellar. "It's been so long since someone has come needing a heart. I've got quite the collection as of late." She shuffled forward, and reached for something in the dark. A candelabra illuminated in her hands. "Come, let me present you with a few to consider."

The walls were covered in glass sarcophaguses, each boasting a heart.

Etta's eyes widened. "Where did you get all of these?"

"They were traded or collected."

Etta didn't know what that meant, but she was sure afraid to ask questions.

"I'll present a few of my suggestions." Madame Peaks stopped before the third one on the left. "The iron heart. Shiny, bright, still malleable in case you change your mind about love later in life—or the universe presents you with someone worthy. Doesn't rust." She shuffled forward to the fifth one. "The amethyst. A semiprecious stone and variety of quartz. Will protect you against your heart feeling intoxicated by love."

Etta marveled at how this heart twinkled in the light, shades of purple glittering almost like a trapped star.

Her mind became a tangle of indecision. She didn't know how she could ever choose another one.

But before she could even think through the first two, Madame Peaks held the light up in front of two others.

"This one is my personal favorite. The gold heart. Took me many years to acquire," she mused. "It's definitely too soft for a person so young, and I'd need to work on it to increase its strength. But it sure is a beauty." She tapped too-long nails on the sarcophagus, then stepped forward to one final glass coffin. "Lastly, a thorned metal heart. I bargained for this one. The ridges should provide ample protection. They open and close when attacked."

Etta grabbed her chest.

Madame Peaks took her hand. "It's time to choose, child."

"How could I possibly?"

"You ain't got no choice. You can have any of the hearts here. I'd probably pick the amethyst one. Saw your eyes get big as coins. Or I can regrow the one dying in your chest."

"Will it hurt if you fix the one I have?"

"It's never easy. I suppose like love itself. But if I do, you'll have to relive the relationship—the high and the low, the sweet and the sour, the light and the dark. It's what conjure requires."

"You spending too much time running around here with that boy," Ms. Mildred told Etta right after she turned sixteen. "You haven't made a single diorama this month. This year even. You promised me one."

Etta was undoing the plaits in her hair and preparing to go meet Jackson. He'd said he had a surprise for her, but he was never good at hiding things. Not from her. She'd seen him whittling wood and collecting light bulbs, and she couldn't resist. She'd sneaked over to the woodworking shed he shared with his daddy to see what he was up to. And it was the greatest thing: he'd made her a life-size diorama of a traditional Japanese teahouse. "We're in love," she replied to Ms. Mildred, bracing herself for one of her grandmother's bites. "And we've been busy. Too busy for me to make those silly dioramas anymore."

"We?"

"Me and Jackson."

"So much *we* and not enough *I*, Cookie. You hardheaded." She sucked her teeth. "And he's a wanderer who doesn't want to see nothing. The dangerous type. You'll be in trouble soon. Mark my words."

"No, I won't. I'll just be in love," Etta replied.

"You better hurry up." Madame Peaks sniffed Etta once they got back upstairs. "Sage and amber."

"What?"

"You smell."

"What do you mean?"

"When a soul is being taken, this scent, your scent, is released. Calling death. The body is a discarded, charred building left behind once the soul is gone." She bent forward over Etta with an ancient-looking stethoscope, pressing it to Etta's chest. She closed her wrinkled eyes as she listened to the slow chug of Etta's heart. The tiny flutters sent a buzzy lightness through Etta; any moment now she'd drift away like a feather.

"It's winding down, turning to dust, girl."

"I don't know what to do."

"You know the options. First, regrow the heart you got. Second, choose one of mine from the cellar. Third, find your beloved again."

"But I can't. It's over. He doesn't want me anymore. I lost him."

"Women don't lose men. There's nothing you could've done. Men leave women for all sorts of reasons. Sometimes it's too hot outside. Other times, their bellies ache. It could be too windy that day. It's when women tether their hearts only to the whims of men that they turn to ash."

"My mama said you cast our stars."

"I did. But the universe has other plans."

"What will happen to him? Will his heart die, too?"

"No."

"Why not?"

"He got something else coming his way. Don't you worry. You won't suffer all the consequences. But for now, focus on yourself and stop worrying about him. You've got to grow your own tree."

"How much will regrowing a heart cost?" Etta asked.

"Everything you have, child." Madame Peaks led Etta to the chaise in her living room. Etta laid across it. Madame Peaks lit incense. Clouds of smoke drifted up and around her head. Flies paused on the windowsill, brown moths froze flat against the windowpane, cinder and smoke rose through the old floorboards like wisps of steam, candle flames stretched into long bars of light.

Mirrors fogged. Liquid boiled in the jars. The walls erupted in flames. Madame Peaks took deep breaths over Etta. "Ashes cannot be remade into flesh."

"But won't I die?"

"Your old heart will, but your soul will wait for the new one to bloom."

"How?"

"The roots always provide."

Etta was too weak to protest or be afraid.

"But you must promise me something, child."

"Yes," Etta replied.

"Never give your heart to another."

Etta thought of Ms. Mildred. "So I can never fall in love again?"

"No. You can, but hearts are your own to keep. They're to keep you alive. Give your affection. Give your love. Give your time, but nothing so vital to your own survival. Be careful with giving away parts of yourself before you understand them fully. You're free of the stars now, so choose wisely in the future. After you know yourself. Love is not supposed to poison your own well."

Etta nodded.

Madame Peaks hunched over Etta, her breathing turned into a hissing wind. Papers scattered everywhere, glass jars crashed onto the ground, the red globes in the window wobbled, threatening to drop.

Red dust poured out of Etta's nose and mouth and swirled. Madame Peaks opened the tiny perfume bottle and its contents joined the rest.

The ash hovered above her like a thunderous cloud ready to expel lightning.

Her chest felt empty and hollow.

"Open your mouth, child, quick."

Etta let her neck drop back and opened her lips like a baby bird ready to receive whatever the woman had. She placed a blue-petaled chicory flower on Etta's tongue.

"Swallow it whole," Madame Peaks directed.

A warmth burst through Etta's chest, and the tiny pulse of a heart drummed.

"You rest now. The new heart will take a day to grow. I'll watch over you."

Etta's eyelids closed at Madame Peaks's command, and she muttered a promise to her—and to herself: "I'll never give my heart away again."

"Rest, child. The cycle of light and dark will begin. You will remember your favorite moment with your beloved and your worst moment. The only way to the light is through the dark."

"I will never be able to not remember the way you look," Jackson told her the first time they'd taken all their clothes off in front of each other.

"Is that a good thing?" Etta had asked; a deep blush rushed through her like she'd been electrocuted.

"You are someone I will never be able to forget. A melody I can never erase," he whispered in her ear.

She ran her fingers over his brown chest, tracing the lines of his muscles, then letting them tangle in the soft curls that covered his skin. His hands found the curves of her body, leaving their warmth.

"It's just not working," Jackson had whispered. His bare legs hung over the side of Etta's bed. The moon had just started to rise outside the window behind him. He wasn't even supposed to be in her room. Mama didn't like company upstairs. But Etta always broke the rules for him.

"What do you mean?" Etta arched her back. "We've had the best days together. That big diorama you made me was the most beautiful thing in the whole world. Did I not tell you that enough?"

"I don't know . . . it's just been hard."

"What's been hard?" Etta tried to touch his cheek, but he jerked away, flinching like she was a stranger touching him for the first time.

"I feel like I should be doing something else. That this has had its run. I need to be on my own for a little bit."

"What do you *really* mean?" Etta replied. The scent of him wrapped around her, pulling her to him despite his painful words. "Am I not pretty enough?"

"You've always been the most beautiful girl I've ever known."

"Did you meet someone else?"

"No."

"Then, what is it? What could it possibly be?"

"I don't know," he said with a sigh. "It just doesn't feel right anymore."

"We can make it feel right again. Just tell me what I need to do." Etta hated the pleading tone in her voice.

"I need to figure it out," he said. "Alone."

"Please. We're supposed to be together. Our mothers matched us."

"I know."

"We're destined."

"Destinies change."

"Not ours." Etta pressed her mouth against his. He let her. The soft pad of his bottom lip grazed hers and she tasted the chocolate he'd eaten before climbing through her window.

Etta woke to the sound of a bird tapping against the window. She thought she was back home in her bedroom and she'd roll over and see her diorama of Paris staring back at her, but the conjure woman's living room sharpened into view.

"How are you feeling?" Madame Peaks asked.

Etta pressed a hand to her chest. The pain was gone. "Is it done?"

"Almost." Madame Peaks motioned to the table. "You can watch for yourself. There's a mirror jar. It'll show you what's happening inside your chest."

Etta picked it up and thumbed the glass. Inside, a nest of branches interlaced with the flesh of a heart, and tiny green stems coiled around it, holding the promise of flowers. A sense of peace washed over her; the sadness of losing Jackson a bruise lightening, the soreness of it easing out.

"Be more careful with that one. Get to know it better."

The image of him drifted into her mind, but it didn't hurt this time. She'd seen the good and the bad, she'd remember how she'd drowned in him, forgetting her grandmother and Mama and her friends and her dioramas, forgetting herself. "I will," she told the woman.

LETTING THE RIGHT ONE IN

By Patrice Caldwell

A vampire stands outside my window with a question on her lips.

I peer down at her. Her skin glows blackish-blue in the moonlight. She waits for my answer, hands in her jean pockets. Her backpack is thrown over her left shoulder.

The Prozac bottle I knocked down earlier rolls across the slanted floor of my room. My tattered copy of *Dracula* is strewn across my bed. More books decorate the floor, all illuminated in the same moonlight that colors the vampire.

My parents' yells come from downstairs through the too-thin walls of this house that still doesn't feel like home. I don't think it ever will.

I glance back to my window to the vampire just outside. The heat from our kiss still lingers on my lips.

What am I going to do?

I met the vampire yesterday at the central library. Technically, it's Mainville's *only* library. I'd been a regular since we moved here nine months ago. In that time, I had read over two hundred books.

The genre didn't matter, as long as it featured my favorite tortured souls: vampires.

I started with classics like Polidori's *The Vampyre* and Stoker's *Dracula* and Octavia Butler's *Fledgling*. Then I moved to series like The Vampire Diaries and standalone novels like *Sunshine, The Silver Kiss, The Coldest Girl in Coldtown,* and *Peeps.*

I'd been drawn to vampires ever since I saw *Blade* with my dad years ago. Though some had found families, like Rose's friendship with Lissa in the Vampire Academy books, they never fully fit in. They were all eternal outcasts. Black sheep.

Loneliness clung to vampires like a too-snug coat—just as it does to me.

Yesterday, the head librarian looked up from her desk at the front just long enough for me to wave. Then I immediately headed downstairs and took a right to where the *R*'s are. I'd just finished a reread of the Vampire Academy series and was moving on to rereading The Vampire Chronicles. I just needed to grab *Interview with the Vampire* and then I could be—

But when I turned the corner, I saw her.

A girl. In *my* section. A section in which I hadn't seen anyone in the nine months I'd spent there.

Her hair was dyed the coolest shade of pink that perfectly contrasted with her dark-brown skin. She had my book— *Interview with the Vampire*—in her hands. She was browsing through it. Laughing.

"Are you checking that out?" I asked. My voice came out sharp. Who was I to be so possessive? This was a library, after all.

The girl quickly looked up, snapping the book shut. "You can have it. I've read it a few times already."

Another Black girl who loved vampires!? Who *was* she? "What were you laughing about?"

"How surprised Louis is when he realizes that his family's slaves know that he and Lestat are vampires. Oh, Louis." She laughed again.

"No one listened to Black people. Not then and certainly not now," I said.

"Exactly." She cocked her head slightly and stepped toward me. Thick, coarse curls framed her face and stopped just past her shoulders. Even her slightest movements seemed incredibly graceful, like those of a dancer, aware and in control of every muscle in her body. She was maybe a foot taller than me, and her eyes were a dark brown. I lost myself in them.

She cleared her throat.

I blinked, snapping myself away from her gaze, the moment gone.

"I said you can have it."

She held it out to me. I took a step toward her, but as if my legs lost their footing, I tripped, falling headfirst toward the ground. In a blur, she grabbed my arm. A jolt shot through me. Her skin felt ice cold. Lifeless.

I laughed, shakily. "I'm not usually such a klutz." I pulled myself upright.

She tucked her hair behind her left ear, then smiled, averting her gaze to the ground. "It's fine." She laughed again, filling the empty space with warmth that sent shivers down my spine. "I am."

"Yeah, right," I said before I could stop myself. "I mean, you just don't seem like the clumsy kind."

She shrugged. "Some things never leave you."

I furrowed my brow. What an odd thing to say.

She shook her head. "Here you go." She placed the book in my hand. I took it and we rounded the corner. Out of habit, I glanced up at the security mirrors placed in corners and under the stairs so you wouldn't run into someone coming around the corner.

My eyes widened. Impossible. I dropped the book.

Though I was there, clear as a sunny Mainville day, she was not.

She glanced at me, taking in the confusion warping my face, then quickly moved out of the mirror's view. "I should get going." She stumbled backward.

"Wait," I said. I grabbed the book from the floor.

When I turned around, she was gone. Vanished. As if she'd never existed.

When I got back home, it was dinnertime. Mama was in the living room, sitting at her desk behind the couch, and Daddy was in the kitchen humming to himself.

"Could you quiet down in there?" Mama demanded. "These bills aren't gonna pay themselves."

I cleared my throat to announce my presence. Daddy gave me a small smile, but the light didn't reach his eyes. It hadn't in a long time. Not since we left Chicago, and his friends and job there. Not since we moved here—for me.

Mama said he'd find a job. Hadn't taken her long—she was a doctor. He had started at his old company right after college and quickly worked his way up to the senior staff position he held when we left. He never said so, but I knew he missed it.

I adjusted my jacket, fumbling with the zipper. The guilt gnawed at me. I took a deep breath to calm myself. *It's not your fault.* But it was. It was my fault my friends stopped talking to me. My fault Mama became so worried about me and moved us here. It was—

"What grand adventure did we have today?" Dad interrupted my thoughts, grounding me back in the now.

I half rolled my eyes. "I'm seventeen, not five, Dad."

"Doesn't mean you can't still have grand adventures."

"Never mind grand adventures," Mama said. "She needs to be thinking about college. Did you consider that internship Shayla mentioned?"

Her best friend in Chicago had offered to let me shadow her for the summer at the law firm where she'd recently made partner. Shayla was the first Black woman there to do so. I guess they both thought I could be another.

"No, ma'am," I said finally.

"Well, you can't just sit around here all summer. Dr. Freeman said you need structure, and I think that—"

"Samantha," Daddy interrupted, "she just got in the door. Can she remove her shoes? Take off her jacket? She's your daughter, not one of your patients."

Mama flinched.

That was my cue. "What's cooking here?" I asked too cheerily. "The food smells great." I placed my bag, stuffed with all the books I'd checked out, on the floor.

"Welcome to Chez Dad." He made a grand gesture toward the pot of chili. Mama laughed. Another argument averted.

Mama made the table, setting out plates, and Daddy served the chili in big scoops. "So what are you reading now, Ayanna?" Mama nudged the books on the floor with her foot.

"Oh, nothing," I said quickly.

She's trying, said a voice in my head. So I took a deep breath. "Uhh, just *Interview with the Vampire* and the next books in the Sookie Stackhouse series. The hold came in for them."

"Sookie Stackhouse? Is that the one about the werewolves?"

I shook my head. "Well, there are werewolves—there are a lot of creatures actually—but it focuses on this waitress who's telepathic and falls in love with a vampire, and the hot mess that ensues." I explained the series to her between bites of chili. "The series wrapped up a while ago, but I'm just now getting into it. I'm also rereading some favorites, so I have those books, too. I'm thinking about reading *Salem's Lot*—" I stopped as I caught Mama's frown. "What?" I said, already dreading her answer.

"Have you considered calling any of the other girls in your

class?" Mama wrung her hands. "I met a girl named Veronica who was visiting her grandmother at the nursing home today. She seems nice; maybe you can invite her over sometime and—"

I cut her off. "I'm fine, Mom." It always came back to this. Me needing to make friends, as if I hadn't tried.

Crease lines settled on her brow. The room grew silent save for the scraping of our spoons against the bowls.

Mama likes to say that we moved here to be closer to her mother. Mama grew up in this town, and my grandmother had been living alone since my grandfather died two years ago.

Truth is, Grandma didn't need us around. Mama didn't start to worry about her "being alone out here" until my friends stopped talking to me, until I quit sports and spent more time in my room with books than I did with "people my age."

Grandma had her own life here. A social calendar so full we barely saw her. As for me, my classmates had their groups, their cliques formed since pre-K. Books became my lifeblood.

"Thanks," I said, gobbling down the rest of my meal. When I finished, I took my bowl to the sink and washed it off, then grabbed the book bag. "I'm going to go read."

Daddy placed his hand on Mama's. She quickly removed it. The facade was starting to crack again.

"Don't stay up too late," she said.

But I was already up the stairs to my sanctuary.

My therapist, Dr. Freeman, once told me that some people are just sadder than others. That some of us are naturally sensitive. More in tune with our feelings, our emotions. That it's okay. *Normal.*

But try telling that to middle-class Black parents who were one generation away from segregation. One heartbeat, one connected thread to sharecropping and slavery. Who gave up so much so their kids could have more.

Try harder.

Stay busy.

Be strong.

To them, whose parents broke their backs to put food on the table, who remembered moments of having no food in the fridge, nothing "in your head" was hard to overcome.

That was always their advice.

And it worked for a while. I joined sports team after sports team. I studied hard to be at the top of my class. I even made friends, but I never quite fit in. I was always the black sheep of my friend group, just as I was in my family.

They think you're stuck up. That you like being alone, when really you're barely hanging on. You're muffling tears at night with your pillow. If you could get rid of your softness as easily as they put their expectations on you, you would.

And those very friends abandoned me, after. So now I don't

try. I have books and therapy and Prozac. I'd rather be a loner than hate myself again.

Vampires get it. There's no place for them in our world, either. So they make a place, they create their own families. In a world that would hunt them down, they survive—they thrive.

I placed the books on my bedside table and closed my door. I took in the Twilight Saga movie posters to my right. Bella looks so uninterested in Edward. Let's be honest, she would've been better off alone—or with Alice. A collection of *Blade* DVDs I "borrowed" from my dad years ago are on the bookshelves to the left of the door.

Romantic leads. Detectives. Best friends taking on evil. The safe haven I built myself.

The facade faded as the argument began like clockwork.

"Her problem is all of those books," said Mama, snapping at Daddy in that hushed tone parents use when they think you can't hear or they don't want you to hear. But the walls of this old house are thin, and the sounds wafted up until they reached my ears.

"Well, she got it from your side of the family," Daddy retorted. I cringed.

"What's *that* supposed to mean?" Mama asked, even though we all knew. Mama's brother died by suicide. She never said so, but I knew she blamed herself. Just as she thought my depression was her fault, too. She wore guilt I didn't ask her to put on.

Dr. Freeman said that healing is a process. I only wished

my parents could work on themselves, too, so I didn't feel like I was carrying my problems *and* theirs.

Their argument continued, each blaming the other for how I "ended up this way." Each word was a slap until I couldn't take it anymore. I slipped in my earbuds, turned up the music until Brendon Urie's vocals were all I heard. I drowned myself in dreams of the girl I'd just met. The girl who was graceful yet clumsy. Gorgeous, irresistibly cute. Who loved vampires, whose touch was ice cold, and who didn't have a reflection. It could've just been a trick of the light, I told myself. But I shook reason aside.

As impossible as it sounded, I'd just met a vampire.

The next morning, I found a note on the living room table. Dad had gone into town. Mama, to church.

I breathed a sigh of relief. She'd stopped dragging me to church a year ago, after our old pastor did a sermon about how it's Adam and Eve not Adam and Steve and I walked out the door.

I made eggs and turkey bacon. Slapped some jam on bread, then headed back upstairs. Time to enact my plan I'd spent all night considering.

Using paper and pen, I browsed through all my books, my collection of films and TV shows on DVD and on my laptop. I threw out outliers like sparkling during the daytime, because it was a sunny day when we met, and turning into a bat, because as much as I love *Dracula*, the obsession with bats is a bit much and not consistent when it comes to world vampire mythologies.

Fangs (duh).

Sleeping in coffins (ugh, just ew).

Wooden stakes. (A bit difficult to test . . .
I'm not trying to kill her. I want to, uhh, well, I'm
not sure yet.)

Aversion to sunlight. (Which, given the sunny day,
is probably a no . . . are Black vampires more
resistant to sunlight??? Hm. Fledgling makes a
great case for this.)

By the time I was done, the sun was just starting to set.
I grabbed my things, then I wrote Mama a note of my own:
Going to a study group. Be back for dinner.

A lie, yes. But a necessary one. I needed an excuse she
would want to believe, and the library was closed on Sundays.

Mainville is a small Louisiana town, where the railroad
tracks that used to separate Black and white are now just
remnants of an era long gone, but never forgotten. In every
park there are monuments of some famed soldier or general who fought on the wrong side of the Civil War. It's near
enough to Baton Rouge to not be completely remote but far
enough to not attract regular visitors, aside from, according
to Dad, the occasional camera crew hoping to use the small
town as a backdrop for some scene or another in a story set in
"the American South."

Well, and one cemetery where every slave owner turned Confederate war hero is buried right next to several local distinguished members of the town's civil rights movement. The irony clearly escaped the town as it crawled and then leapt into the twenty-first century.

Nighttime fell like a shroud and settled over the misty cemetery as I pushed open the creaking gate.

I stepped right into a puddle as soon as I entered. The muddy water soaked my toes through the mesh of my sneakers. I should've worn better shoes. Not that I was used to this sort of thing. I mean, what did you wear to creep into a cemetery? What if there were grave robbers? *Were those still a thing?*

Stone angels were scattered throughout. Hovering over graves, watching over them, I supposed. Some had eroded over the years and now had moss growing where eyes had been and vines encircling their wings and necks.

If the girl from the library was a vampire, this was where she would be, right? Mainville has no abandoned houses, no warehouses to squat in. The cemetery seemed like the next best option.

I wandered through the tombstones, looking for some sort of hint—an opened aboveground tomb, an unearthed coffin—until something grabbed me.

I screamed. It yanked me back. I pulled away only to trip on a tombstone. Without a glance back at my attacker, I scrambled up and didn't stop running until I passed through the cemetery gates.

"Uh, hey. Are you okay?" called a voice. A girl emerged from the shadows of the dimly lit sidewalk.

I jumped back. It was her—the girl from the library. The maybe-vampire, her dark skin flawless in the moonlight. "What are you doing here?" I asked.

She eyed me suspiciously, then glanced around the moon-lit road outside the cemetery. "Walking down the street?"

"Right," I said. "That makes sense."

"You have a tree branch stuck in your hair."

I touched the back of my head. Sure enough, a tree branch. Then it dawned on me—I was attacked by a tree. I started to laugh, doubling over on the sidewalk.

She lifted a brow. "Are you sure you're okay?"

I straightened up and imagined how I must look to her. "Yeah. Yeah, I'm fine."

"Oh my god, you're bleeding." She pointed to my left leg. My jeans were ripped, and blood soaked the fabric just below my knee.

"Here." She handed me a first-aid kit from her backpack.

I opened the kit and doctored myself up, and all the while she stood there. Her eyes didn't widen, her breath didn't grow ragged. She barely flinched as I cleaned up the blood.

"You should be careful. That cemetery isn't safe."

I laughed shakily. "Why? Because some*thing* might find me in there?"

"Uh, no, because of this." She pointed to a sign next to the gate. CEMETERY CLOSED FOR CONSTRUCTION. UNSTABLE GROUND. "This whole town is built on a swamp."

How did she know that? She must've just moved here. After all, Mainville is small—I knew everyone my age.

As if she read my mind, she replied, "It's Louisiana." The girl laughed. "Besides, my aunt's really into small-town history. She's an antiques collector."

Antiques collector? What a perfect vampire job. "So you've been with her your whole life?" I imagined them traveling from town to town, never staying long enough to be detected. *Classic.*

"Um, not really. Just recently. Since my parents died."

"Oh," I said. "I'm sorry."

She smiled. "It's okay. Are you doing anything right now? I mean, aside from robbing graves."

"I wasn't rob—"

She laughed.

"You were joking."

"Uh-huh." She kicked a pebble around with her foot. Then she cleared her throat before continuing. "I, uh, heard there's this diner, Shirley's, that everyone visits. I figure even grave robbers have to eat."

"I'm never going to live this down, am I?"

She shook her head. "Nope. So you in?"

"Sure! I like food."

She laughed again, and I wanted to kick myself. *I like food. Really?? Just bury me in this cemetery right now.* "Maybe I should get your name," I rushed to say.

At which she laughed even more. "It's Corrie."

"Ayanna," I said.

"Nice to meet you, Ayanna." She smiled at me and I blushed.

Only when we were halfway there did I wonder: *Did I just get asked out by a vampire?*

Several minutes later we were at Shirley's. The diner in town. The only one.

One diner. One church. One cemetery.

We were seated at one of those booths. You know the ones, striped colors. Me across from Corrie. Meh diner light that complemented no one. Except her. She was even prettier than at the library. And her lips were the brightest pink.

My eyes trailed down to her crisp, white button-down that plunged into a V—

"Hon."

The waitress stood before us. Corrie looked expectantly at me.

"Sorry," I said. Heat rose to my cheeks. "Um, I'll have the chicken tenders and fries, and you—" I turned to Corrie.

She grinned. "I ordered a milkshake."

Way to go, Ayanna. Was it obvious I'd been checking her out?

The waitress gave me a knowing smile. Yup. Definitely obvious. Invisibility would be great right now.

No, I reminded myself. *She clearly likes you. Why else would she randomly ask you out?*

I took a deep breath and relaxed. Moments later we were deep in conversation. First we raved about our favorite *Buffy* episodes and our favorite book adaptations.

"You can't tell me you seriously liked that movie," Corrie said, referring to *Queen of the Damned*, which I'd started gushing about. "I mean, come on. It totally messed up the book."

I stared at her in disbelief. "First of all, Aaliyah was a genius, and her starring as Akasha was a gift."

"*Fair.* Rest in power," she said.

"Second, the soundtrack is everything."

"True."

"And third—"

The waitress came by and placed down our food. One massive order of chicken tenders and an even larger basket of fries. Corrie's milkshake was bigger than her face.

"Thanks," I said. "Do you have any garlic powder? You know, like *garlic* fries?"

Corrie didn't bat an eye. The waitress came back a moment later with a shaker full of garlic, and I shook it all over the fries.

I offered the basket to Corrie, bursting with curiosity. If she was a vampire, how would she react? "Want some?"

"Never had garlic fries before, but first time for everything." She took a handful, dunked them in ketchup, and stuffed them in her mouth.

I wilted. *Maybe I got a bit ahead of myself on this whole vampire thing.*

"So you were saying about *Queen of the Damned*?" she prompted.

We got in a heated debate over whether Tom Cruise or

Stuart Townsend was the better Lestat that ended in laughter and a truce.

She reached for the final fry. "We'll split it."

And as she broke it in half, I smiled. Maybe it didn't matter if she wasn't a vampire. For the first time, I didn't feel so alone.

We took our time wandering back to my house. I didn't want the night to end.

She was the first to break the silence. "So why did you move here, if you don't mind me asking? Doesn't seem like this is your kind of place, either."

I started to brush it off. Then I looked up at her, calm running through me. A sense of ease. Of belonging I hadn't felt in a while. Three hours talking at Shirley's, and it felt like not even twenty minutes.

"Last year I got asked to homecoming by this guy . . ." I paused, taking a sharp breath as the memory flooded back to me.

"Did you like him?"

"No," I admitted. "We were just friends. Not even that. My friends convinced his friends to have him ask me. He walked up to me at my locker and was just like, 'You want to go to homecoming?' It made sense, you know. My friends were all dating his friends, and we were the two oddballs."

Corrie looked skeptical. "Your entire friend group was dating his friends?"

I laughed, embarrassed. "Yeah. They're Slytherins. I can't act like it was incidental."

"And you?"

My cheeks warmed. "Total Ravenclaw. You?"

"Gryffindor . . . Slytherin?" She nervously shuffled from side to side. "I don't know."

I glanced doubtfully at her. "You've never read them, have you?"

She shrugged. "Well, what can I say? As we know from Anne Rice, vampires and witches don't mix."

I cracked up.

"So you were saying?" she reminded me.

My giggles broke off as the memory returned. "Right. He asked me to homecoming. My mom lost it, as in I've never seen her so happy. She took me dress shopping. Makeup done. Hair. She tried to give me her pearls. It was the first time I felt like I could be the daughter she wanted me to be, instead of . . . well, me. But then he left me on the dance floor for someone else." The shame felt as fresh as if it had happened yesterday. "So I came home early. My mom found me on the bathroom floor, dress soaked in tears. The next day, my friends barely spoke to me. They said I ruined their homecoming plans, whatever those were. That it was my fault he left me, that maybe if I would loosen up more he would've been into me. They felt we had grown apart. We stopped talking after that. I've struggled with depression my whole life, but after that I just felt so isolated—so alone. My parents agreed I needed a new environment. For healing." I paused. "Sorry. Total downer, right?"

Corrie shook her head, and sympathy filled her eyes. "More like you deserve friends who treasure how amazing you are."

"You're just saying that."

"No, I mean it." Corrie took my hand. "You're smart. Clearly. Your friends . . . that dude, they have their own stuff they need to deal with, but you're certainly not to blame."

I nodded. "I know that now. But thank you. I wish I had met you then."

She smiled at me, and I found myself again staring at her lips. "But then you never would've met me now." She gazed up at the night sky. "Besides, I get it."

When she looked back, her full gaze was on me.

I cleared my throat. "May I kiss you?"

"Yes," she said.

I kissed her. Right in front of my home. Her arms wrapped around my body, electricity and heat rising through me. I kissed her like there was nothing else in the world, like . . .

Something sharp pierced my lip. "Ouch!" I touched my mouth. I tasted copper. "Did you just—?"

"I'm sorry," she cried, pulling back. Her hand immediately went to her mouth, hiding her . . . *fangs?* "I didn't mean to, I—" She stepped into the shadows cast by the trees surrounding my home.

"Corrie, wait," I pleaded, but she was already gone. Vanished again. Leaving me, alone, at my front door.

My phone buzzed. A text from Mama. Dinner's been ready. Where are you?

I glanced around once more, hoping she'd reappear. I thought of all the things I could say to her. To tell her I wasn't afraid. But she was gone. And, like always, it didn't matter what I wanted.

+ + +

Mama had laid the table, and Daddy had cooked. Salmon with pilaf and green beans. My favorite, and they both knew it.

The highs and confusion from my evening with Corrie evaporated. Dread settled in their place.

Mama pulled out a chair. I sat.

Daddy reached over and placed his hand on mine like he had Mama's last night. That scared me even more than whatever he was about to say. "We want to tell you something."

"This isn't working," Mama announced, blunt as always. "And it's not you, baby. It's us."

Daddy nodded.

"We need time. We need some space from each other." Mama smiled, and that only made it worse. "Now, we would never ask you to choose."

"Best you stay with your mother," Daddy cut in. "You need the stability."

"What about you?" I whispered. Every syllable felt like he was punching me in the heart.

"I'm going back to Chicago. They offered me my position back." The way he said it was so easy, like he wasn't about to rip our family in half.

Divorce. Divorce.

Suddenly I was slipping past them. Up the stairs to my room.

"Ayanna!" Mama called as I slammed the door.

"Give her space," Daddy said, but she rushed after me.

Mama tried to push open the door. "Ayanna, I—"

"I'm fine." I glared at all the vampire memorabilia around me. Even my supposed sanctuary couldn't protect me now. "I just need space. Okay? I need some time."

I waited until she left, glass shards in my chest, and then I knocked down the books, the shows, the films. I ripped down the posters from the wall. Even my Prozac bottle tumbled to the floor. Down it all went, until I was crumpled on the ground, crying.

All I wanted was to go back to laughing at Shirley's.

I could stay with Mama here, where every sentence she spoke was riddled with guilt. Or with Daddy, who saw depression as some sort of family curse.

"I can't do this anymore. I just can't," I murmured. I looked to my things, scattered all over the floor. I was seventeen. I could run away, but what would I do? Where would I go? Sooner or later I was going to have to make a choice.

A knock at the window breaks through my teary haze. I stand up and move toward the glass.

When I look down, she's there. Corrie. The vampire. On the side of the house. Climbing it in a way no human could. I swear I see the glint of fangs in the moonlight.

My phone buzzes. A text from Dad: Please come back down. Your mother and I love you very much. We'll figure this out. I promise.

But I don't *want* to come back down. Don't want to listen to their arguments, their tears. Never asking me what I want. Never once really bothering to try, any more than my "friends" back in Chicago. Well-meaning isn't enough.

I open the window, and the curtains sway in the breeze. The hot Louisiana summer air rises. I look at my list on the floor with all my notes.

How can I care so much for someone I just met? Feel so connected to a girl I barely know? A calmness settles within me. For once, I want to live my way. By my own rules. By my own choices.

"May I come in?" she asks, brown eyes shining up at me.

My heart flutters. My lips curl into a smile. And I nod, because it's the only thing that feels right.

"Yes."

TENDER-HEADED

By Danny Lore

Akilah buzzes apartment 3C, because the witch has sto-len *another* hair-braiding client.

Everyone on their block knows Auntie's a witch. Akilah's mama knows: "Don't go crossing Jayleen's auntie," she says. "Be polite, keep out of her way, leave her alone."

Akilah's homegirls know, too: "I don't know why anybody gets that ol' woman doing their hair," Tiana says, "when you're cheaper, faster, and less creepy."

Jayleen's daddy is Auntie's favorite nephew, so even though they've been dating for a year, Jayleen never gives Akilah their opinion on the matter.

Except today.

"Lala," Jayleen pleads. "Don't start with Auntie."

For once, Akilah isn't trying to hear it. When Sonia came around Akilah and Jayleen with a head full of fresh, beautiful extensions, Auntie had to be responsible. No one else on the block braids like Auntie does.

Akilah holds up a hand to keep them quiet. "I'm tired of this." She buzzes again; she knows the woman is upstairs, so she'll do it for however long it'll take. "That's the third this month. Last week it was Derek, and I've been doing his hair for half a year. How long am I supposed to put up with her poaching my clients?"

"You kind of poached them first."

Anyone else would get the full brunt of Akilah's irritation, but even now Akilah can't keep that momentum up with Jayleen. Her mama says it's because Jayleen's too sweet, too honest, but Akilah suspects it's because of the way sweatpants settle on the curve of Jayleen's hips. But *still*. "There ain't no *way* that Auntie's so gentle or amazing that it's worth twice the money." She buzzes a third and fourth time, barely seconds in between. "Bet their hair smells like musty old ladies and strawberry candies anyway."

"Maybe you need to treat your clients better, Lala." Even annoyed, Jayleen uses Akilah's nickname.

Before Akilah started braiding hair, everyone went to Auntie unless their parents did it. Akilah heard how much people paid and was aghast; she learned to braid on cousins who wriggled and whined, and she realized that, if her clients could put up with a little roughness, she could get a full head done in half the time it took Auntie. So, she charged less, and soon enough, most of the girls and guys in her school who rocked braids were coming to her.

And then the first one went back to Auntie. And then the next. And the next. It's become a cash flow problem.

"Oh, whatever." Akilah sucks her teeth.

"So what are you going to do, huh?" Jayleen moves to block Akilah from pestering the poor intercom. Akilah exhales in a huff. "You're gonna fight an old woman over a few bucks?"

"Your aunt isn't just an old woman, and you know it," Akilah hisses. "I'm not some bully—and I'm not stupid. I just wanna see what's so special." Jayleen frowns, confusion in their dark-brown eyes. "She's gonna do my hair."

"What?"

"You heard me, Jayleen," Akilah says. "Or maybe you didn't, because you're all ready to step in with some Old Lady Protect Squad crap. I'm gonna see what the hype is about and then show all of *you*"—Akilah jabs Jayleen in the chest firmly—"that I'm better for the money."

Jayleen presses their lips together for a moment, and Akilah almost dares them to say whatever else is on their mind. Jayleen turns to the intercom and presses three of the apartment buttons at once; the door clicks. "Fine. Just . . ."

Akilah pushes the door open and turns to look over her shoulder. Jayleen is hovering, but they're not moving to follow Akilah upstairs. "Just what?"

"Don't go rushing her, okay? Have some patience."

Akilah has been in Auntie's apartment once or twice before, but always with Jayleen. Nothing has changed since last time. It's an old woman's apartment, with overly embroidered flower patterns on the couch and armchairs, slightly yellowed and crackling wallpaper, a dated dark-wood coffee table. Akilah remembers using the bathroom there once and finding one of those crocheted doll-dress toilet roll covers on the back of the toilet. There are herbs drying on the windows that might be the same ones Akilah saw here last time. The orange near-setting sun comes through the window, hitting the shimmering line of a pair of spiderwebs in the corner.

Aside from the webs, the apartment is clean when Akilah steps into it. It smells strongly of incense, frankincense or myrrh—Akilah doesn't know the difference between the two. All she knows is they both remind her of annoyingly long church sermons. The TV is on, and a daytime court show is playing. It bothers Akilah that the door is open, because it means either that Auntie ignored the buzzer but opened, or that Jayleen called her.

"Just give me a minute, honey, I'm just finishing these dishes." Auntie comes out of the kitchen, wiping her hands with a dishrag. She looks Akilah up and down, not dropping her smile. "You've gotten bigger since last I saw you." Akilah hasn't gotten bigger since she hit five foot three at fifteen, and that was two years ago. Old people seem to think that's the highest compliment they can offer. *You've grown.*

"How much to fix up my head?"

Auntie strolls up to her and holds up a hand to touch her hair. Akilah's hair is pulled back into one thick puff. The amount Auntie quotes is twice what Akilah charges, but before Akilah can say anything, Auntie cuts her off. "We both know you don't need me to do your hair, but it's still time and labor . . ."

Then Auntie tugs, just enough to make Akilah wince.

It's a month ago, in Akilah's living room. The room smells like the rice and beans Jayleen has on the stove. Jayleen stays near the room entrance. Akilah doubts it's more comfortable there; Jayleen probably doesn't want to get involved in Akilah and Sonia's argument.

For a beat, Akilah is lost: Had she been here a second ago? Had it smelled like rice and beans or incense? Had it been dark outside or had the sun still been shining bright? She remembered *this moment—until suddenly it isn't a memory, and her brain snaps back into this present.*

She remembers what the argument was about and gets back to it. "I don't have to finish your head, you know that, right?" Akilah walks around the chair so that she's in front of Sonia, cell phone in her hand, frowning.

Sonia's mouth is dropped, and Akilah must screw her face into a frown so she doesn't laugh. The expression probably isn't any better. "I already paid half up front, and I'm not paying the rest just because Tiana called you—"

From the corner of Akilah's eye, she sees Jayleen's eyes narrow suspiciously. No, no, that's a distraction from what she wants, and she isn't trying to get into that. "This isn't about Tiana, and it doesn't matter why—"

"What does Tiana want?" Jayleen interjects.

Akilah doesn't wave Jayleen off, but only because she doesn't want to fight with them. She wants to ignore the question. She clenches her cell phone tightly. She knows Jayleen's not going to grab it, or look at it, but Akilah knows the last text message she sent, the last one she read from Tiana, and the last phone call, and it makes her fingers curl even tighter.

The sun is back, glinting off the webs in the window. Akilah blinks, squints, readjusting to the living room. Not her living room, but *Auntie's*, with its old-lady furniture and church smell. Readjusting to Auntie looking at her, waiting for Akilah's response.

"What in the hell . . . ?"

If Auntie notices what happened, she doesn't respond. "You can pay half today, half later. I know where you and Jayleen hang out. I'm not worried about you shorting me."

Akilah is off-kilter, and for a moment thinks of backing out. She doesn't *need* to give Auntie money for anything. She could take her friends out for dinner with that money, instead of trying to prove to herself that Auntie isn't shit. She thinks about the flash she just experienced and wonders if that's not the right move.

But it irks Akilah to watch her clients go back to Auntie. There is no way that Akilah's braids are lesser, or her attitude so annoying . . . No way that the witch's thin fingers and slow movements are worth it.

She sucks her teeth and pulls out her wallet.

Auntie takes the money delicately, folding it up and putting it in her jeans. She gestures with her head toward a folding chair propped against the couch. "Why don't you take that seat, Akilah, honey, while I go get my product." She turns and starts walking toward the back of the apartment. "You're not tender-headed, now, are you?

Auntie stands up while doing hair, with Akilah in the seat. So she can keep watching her shows, she explains. She takes her time starting, running her hands through Akilah's hair as she decides how to tackle it. Akilah reluctantly admits that this process feels nice, when Auntie parts her hair into sections with a rattail comb, the air from the fan hitting Akilah's scalp. When Auntie starts applying grease to the parts, it's a strange sensation for Akilah to not lift her arms to try to do it herself.

"What kind of grease is that?" Akilah wants to twist around and look at the jar. Before she gets a chance, Auntie pauses and passes it over. It's in a small Tupperware. "Oh. It's some homemade stuff."

"I mix all my products myself," Auntie answers casually. "Sometimes from scratch, sometimes with store products as a base. It's better, I think. Lets people know I care."

Akilah sniffs at the Tupperware to hide the fact that she makes a face. She tries to parse the smells. At first, it's just hair grease, but then other scents follow. Not quite floral, but a bouquet nonetheless—seven, eight smells at once that Akilah wants to differentiate between, like potpourri and dried orange slices and suddenly cinnamon, and then there's another tug from Auntie and—

She's eight years old and Akilah's nostrils are filled with the smell of a hot comb, all too close to her head. She eyes the tool with all the distrust that it's owed as it heats on the stove, the metal surrounded by blue and orange flame. Her head, she knows, is "prepped" for it, sprayed with heat protection after a wash. Still . . . prep does not make this pleasant. Prep still means that hot, hot metal is going to touch her hair.

"Come on, Lala, up." Her mama pats the kitchen stool, and

Akilah obliges. She sits as still as possible, but still, at eight, it's hard. *Eight-year-old energy and a hot comb don't make for best friends.*

Out of the corner of her eye, she sees Mama test the hot comb's temperature and hiss. "There we are. Okay now—" Akilah's older brother comes dashing into the kitchen. He's eighteen, and too old, Akilah thinks, to run around the way he does. "Jamal," Mama hisses again, although this time not from the heat.

Akilah does, though, yelping as her hand rushes up to feel the new burn along her edges. Her eyes start to blur with tears as the tender skin stings. She sniffles, and Mama curses as she puts down the comb.

"Imma need you to put the brakes on in my kitchen. Making me burn your sister's head—"

Akilah frowns deeply in Jamal's direction. He's blurry, but she can see he barely reacts, having already stopped running. He certainly doesn't look at Akilah. "I need some money."

"You need some sense."

"Just forty bucks," Jamal counters.

"I don't have it." Mama says it in a way that means "I'm not giving it to you," and even at eight, Akilah understands that.

Jamal's eyes light up something fierce and angry, with an expression that Akilah always thought looked too much like an adult on him. "What do you mean, Ma? I need it."

"You don't need—"

"Yeah, I do!" he yells, and he slams his hand against the washer so hard that Akilah jumps in place.

She didn't understand why Mama did this. Didn't just give

Jamal what he wanted when he acted like this. Now he's gonna yell and slam things, and Mama will join in, and maybe she'll give him the forty dollars eventually, or maybe she doesn't, and he leaves the house in a huff again. Either way, if Mama just did it, they didn't have to do this, he wouldn't run in all ready to fight about it, and maybe Akilah's forehead wouldn't—

"Ow!" Akilah winces.

Auntie stops braiding; when had she started? "Something wrong, honey?"

Akilah reaches a hand to her forehead, confused by the lack of heat, but she realizes there's no burn there either. It's been a long time since she last used a hot comb, and even longer since she used one with Jamal in the house. For a second, she'd been burned fresh, her mama and Jamal's voices loud and sharp in her ears, as her feet dangled on that stool . . .

But her feet touch the floor now, and all Auntie is doing is braiding. Akilah doesn't even recall handing back the grease, but that, too, is gone. She glances back to look at Auntie. "What did you do?" This time, her voice sounds strange to her ears—too old, compared to how she'd sounded before, too low. This time, it takes a moment for her sense of the past to catch up and click into place with the present, to comprehend that this is how she's supposed to sound.

Auntie blinks, keeping her expression placid-pleasant. Akilah hisses as Auntie uses a large clip to keep some of her hair to the side. It's too tight, but Auntie adjusts it as soon as Akilah squirms. Akilah spies a spider on the web in the window, slowly making its way across the glimmer of spider silk. "What you paid me to do. Fixing your head. Now stay still."

This time, when Auntie tugs, Akilah has a sneaking suspicion about what comes next, but doesn't have enough time to react—and if she did, how would she stop? There's no stopping the sudden snapping back in time, not when—

"What?" Akilah's a few years back now, and her brother is in front of her and her mother again. They're outside the building, and it's strange—Akilah's a teenager, bigger than when she was eight in front of the hot comb, but Jamal's the same size he was back then. Still larger than her, still larger than her mom, and still ready to pop off at a moment's notice.

Akilah knows what this fight is about immediately, even if the details haven't caught up yet. It's always about his wallet. Always about filling it. So what matters aside from the amount?

"I said chill, Lala," Jamal snaps. "And stay out of this. This is between me and Mom."

No, it's not, because Akilah was supposed to have a calm day with her mama, getting those slender cornrows that her mother had perfected post–hair straightening. Just them and Akilah's homegirls on the steps, watching people move past. Instead, Jamal's shown his ass again, and Tiana and Mama are cringing, and Akilah's tired of watching it happen. She wants to go back to a few minutes ago, when her mother was redoing a part, and Akilah could feel her hands along her scalp.

But Jamal is still Jamal, and she isn't about to fight him. She does the only thing she can. "How much you need?"

Jamal blinks, his tirade halted in its tracks. "Lala, what are you talking about?"

"I've got money," Akilah explains stubbornly, even before her mother opens her mouth to argue. "What do you need today? Twenty? Forty?" She whips around to her backpack, digging in to find her wallet. She'd been saving to go out this weekend, all her allowance for the past couple of weeks and a little extra from fixing a classmate's braids when the ends came loose.

She shoves cash in his hands, nearly everything she'd put aside. "Take it," she tells him. She hopes he'll pretend to be gallant, to have a chip on his shoulder about taking money from her, but she knows him better than to expect it. He glances between her and Mama and Tiana—Tiana who watches, memorizes every action and twitch and word—before shoving the cash into his pockets.

It's like sun breaking through clouds, because he suddenly smiles. It's like the morning that you wake up and you realize your braids have finally loosened up, that the headache is gone, except that just comes from the way Mama's shoulders unclench as Jamal suddenly wants to remember they're family.

But Akilah solved it.

Now Akilah's getting whiplash, struggling to remember the year. How her legs aren't as spindly anymore, and they don't shake under her while she wonders if she handed over enough for Jamal to relax. Her hair is halfway finished now, and when she reaches up a hand to check on it, she could have sworn Mama was further along . . .

No, not Mama. *Auntie.* The witch.

Akilah jumps up from the chair now. "Don't touch me!"

she snaps. Auntie flinches at Akilah's volume, but recovers quickly, crossing her hands in front of her as if waiting for a child to stop having a conniption. And maybe she is, because all at once Akilah is seventeen, eight, sixteen, and fourteen, and it's all dizzying, it's all too much. "I don't know what you're trying to do to me, but I know—"

"Now, maybe I'm just old," Auntie starts, and Akilah cringes despite her rage, because she knows how this speech sounds. Witch or no, it always sounds the same. "Maybe I'm out of touch, but I don't get you, Akilah."

"There's nothing to get between you and me," Akilah assures her, gesturing. Her gaze shoots to the side at the slightest movement; a small spider crawls on the end table. Two spiders. Akilah takes a step toward the door. She doesn't know magic, but she knows *normal*, and this ain't it.

Akilah shouldn't suddenly feel like Auntie is as tall as Jamal, as short as Mama. Her scalp shouldn't ache as if divided into three different styles all at once, her forehead shouldn't sting like a burn.

"Oh?" Auntie questions. "When you first started braiding around here, I was glad." Akilah snorts. "I'm getting up there in age, and I don't need to be fixing everybody's head all up. And Jayleen doesn't braid unless they see my arthritis acting up." Akilah didn't know Jayleen could braid.

Akilah's head shouldn't, couldn't be jerked back then, as if Auntie's hands and combs were still separating knots and curly chaos, but—

—No, that's wrong. Jayleen has offered to braid her hair, a few

months ago. Akilah's in tears. Jayleen's hand is on her back, rub-bing small comforting circles as Akilah hiccups and sniffs. She isn't cute right now, but Jayleen touches her like she is. Jayleen offers to braid her hair as if it might help.

Akilah doesn't even really say no—her throat hurts too much from crying to speak. The mortification from Tiana's attitude still rings too loud in her ears for Akilah to even manage a nod or a shake.

She doesn't get it. Tiana is her best friend, but still caught her off guard. Tiana's snap back—Well, we'd be able to go if you didn't give Jamal all your damn money—made Akilah still. Jayleen had almost jumped in, would have snapped back if Akilah hadn't deaded the situation. Because Tiana's right, isn't she? That Akilah is the one with the job, and it's only fair that she treats her friends if she has the money . . .

It isn't the first time that Tiana's been annoyed when Akilah couldn't front the money for them to go out, but it's the first time she's used Jamal's name, buried the knife as deeply. Akilah doesn't want to fight with Tiana or Jamal, doesn't know how to make them both happy . . .

No, that's wrong, too. She sniffles, pulling away from Jayleen even as they gently scratch between her braids. Tiana wouldn't be pissed if only . . .

Akilah's breath goes jagged with tears that were cried months ago.

Another spider, three of them now, crawl up from the back of the couch. Akilah feels sick.

"I suppose Jayleen stopped braiding when you started your

business. Didn't want to step on their girlfriend's toes. But I always assumed if you were going to braid hair, you were going to do it right. No rush jobs, no rotating chairs of clients to squeeze in another dollar." Akilah doesn't speak. "It was a shame to see my old clients again. Saying that you're rude, that you're rough on their heads—"

"That's not *it* and doesn't give you any right to be doing magic on me!"

Auntie tilts her head. "You paid me to fix your head, didn't you?"

Her words ring with a different kind of importance, and Akilah freezes. She freezes before she sees the spiders—the ones under the couch and from the kitchen and down the hall and over the television. She can't move even before she sees the spiders moving to form a circle around Auntie, or the couch and folding chair and drapes sharing the same spider-web glimmer.

Akilah does not turn to look at the walls behind her.

"In the old days," Auntie says, "I would have been petty. So many young upstarts who think that talent and attitude and rudeness all go hand in hand. Who don't think about why they want to rush things. I would have said to hell with it—if weaving and braiding is so important to you, you can do it for the rest of your days." The webbing stops reflecting light and begins to glow. It's a blessing that Akilah is frozen in place, because otherwise she might collapse to her knees. "But I've grown a little wiser in my old age. And there's better ways for me to deal with youth. You always have a reason for your behavior." She unfolds her hands. "So instead, I just teach you about yourself."

Something brushes against Akilah's side and she screams.

"Auntie!" The body that touches her is Jayleen's. Akilah's never seen them as pissed off as they are now. For a second, Akilah can *only* see Jayleen, their strident, protective anger, the way they position themselves between the two women.

Jayleen's voice breaks the spell still over Akilah, and she can feel her legs again. She looks past them, back at Auntie. The spiders are gone. The glowing web is relegated again to normalcy in the window. Akilah shudders, and Jayleen puts an arm around her side, pulling her in. Jayleen's hands banish the crawling feeling that lingers.

"Jayleen." Auntie doesn't match Jayleen's volume, but echoes the angry beats, reminding them they're talking to their elder.

Jayleen lowers their voice, but the emotion is still there. Does Jayleen know what Akilah saw? "That wasn't fair."

"Fair?" Auntie repeats. "She came into my house with that attitude and wanted to see what I do."

"That's not what you do anymore."

"Isn't it?"

Jayleen lets out an exasperated noise, shaking their head as they turn back to Akilah. "I'm sorry, Lala."

Akilah's voice shakes. "You didn't . . ." She pauses and clears her throat. "You didn't do this to me. You don't owe me an apology." She glances over at Auntie. "What *you* did"—Akilah gestures—"was messed up, I don't care what kind of witch or whatever you are—" She catches herself and takes a breath. "You're not the only one who should apologize to me." She deserves better than Jamal and Tiana, who cared more about her wallet than her peace of mind.

She thinks about Sonia's braids and the rush jobs. Of pushing Derek out of her chair so someone else could take his place. How many times she'd done that just to keep her brother and friends smiling back at her.

Jayleen reaches up and touches Akilah's unfinished cornrows. Akilah braces for a tug, a jerk backward into memory, but instead there's just the warmth of Jayleen's fingers. It's the gentle relief of Jayleen scratching between her parts without messing up what's already been done. And with that comes a slow blossoming of past senses: the warmth spreads first, and then touch, sound, and then Akilah gently settles into her past.

Akilah is on the couch and a bad rom-com plays on the screen. On the floor, Jayleen leans their head back into Akilah's lap as they look up at her. It's a week ago, Akilah knows, a rare moment between hustles. She's not shocked by this moment, not confused by being suddenly thrust into it. Instead, the room slowly warms, pleasantly snug, as Jayleen reaches up and plays with Akilah's hands. Massages her hands because Akilah did four heads of hair today, and she's so ready for a nap.

But... "I could just sit here and massage your head, you know?"

"Oh yeah?" Jayleen teases. "And how much for that?" Akilah swats the side of Jayleen's head. "Ow! Come on, I'm playing with you—but you don't gotta do that. You need to rest."

Akilah shakes her head. "I'm not gonna charge you. And you sure you're good? Because I can get us some food." Jayleen shakes their head, and that's the first moment of confusion Akilah feels. It's an alien reaction, and she runs through the list of other options. "Or you said you wanted to go to the movies. We could—"

"We can just chill," Jayleen says, and no one says the word chill *like Jayleen. No one who talks to Akilah, anyway. "You don't gotta pay for food, or the movies, or nothing. You can get to snoring, for all I care." Akilah swats them again, and Jayleen laughs. "I mean it. I'm good. You're good."*

"You good now?" Jayleen asks. Akilah doesn't know how to answer that, but nods nonetheless. Jayleen's hands feel cool, the way Akilah knows it'll feel when the sun finishes going down.

"I look like a fool," Akilah says, reaching up and feeling her unfinished hair. Jayleen's hand touches hers, and she thinks about how many times Jayleen has checked in with her. Told her she didn't *have* to do anything. Spend anything. Is surprised when the thought doesn't trigger another flash, that instead it just feels good. Feels like something Akilah should have noticed a long time ago. Should get to feel with more people than just her partner.

She glances over at Auntie. "No offense, but—"

Auntie waves her off. "Like I said, girl, it isn't about money for me. I didn't finish your head, so you don't owe me money." She pulls the money from earlier out of her pocket and puts it on the end table, patting it. "Here's your refund. I made my point." She glances between the two teenagers.

"And I can think of somebody that'll finish that ol' head of yours for free."

Jayleen looks away from Akilah. That soft, kind memory hadn't been one of Auntie's tricks, had it? Akilah almost speaks, but her phone buzzes. Two texts from Tiana. She swallows the lump in her throat that threatens to smother how nice Jayleen's hands felt.

"Could you, please . . . ?"

Jayleen kisses her on the forehead while pulling the phone gently out of her hands—the thing that Akilah hadn't quite gotten the strength up to asking. "Of course."

KISS THE SUN

By Ibi Zoboi

The sun is our unrequited love. Every day he lets us know that we are not meant to be together, staring down at us like that from afar. Untouchable. But still, lust burns bright in his eyes. We are the same, you know. He doesn't see that. He sees our costume of deep brown and black skin, of fiery girl, of reluctant human. He thinks that is all we are—soucouyant, fireball witches—so he doesn't want us. At dusk, when we are shielded by the waxing moon and we can finally undress out of our human skin to reveal our true selves, he has already retreated to his palace beneath the sea.

Then we are left to contend with our fireball bodies, the night sky, the jealous moon, and our victims. Still we fly, we feast, we play, and we wait for his return at dawn. Then, and only then, can we steal a sweet kiss—this brief merging of firesouls, if only for one small moment in the dawn sky.

Tonight, other flames compete for the island people's attention. Burning tires are lighting the dark sky so bright, the island people won't be able to see us. They are protesting again, so they won't care about us soul-sucking flying fireball witches; we, the soucouyant of Kiskeya Island who fly through the warm, damp air inhaling unsuspecting souls with our fire breaths. This time, the uprising is against the opening of a new resort along the shores of Bassin-Bleu, where the white-sand beaches are, where La Siren brings her maids to rest and dry their fins and meet their lovers, the seal-skinned fisherboys.

Foreign businessmen and developers have torn down the tin-roofed cottages, the cinder-block bungalows, and the pastel-colored gingerbread houses along the eastern coastline to build a sea of twenty-story luxury hotels.

Four of us are climbing the hill overlooking Toussaint Valley. The hill is not the tallest peak on our island by far, but it's just high enough for us to stay out of sight, and low enough for us to launch toward the night sky.

"They'll have to find a new beachfront brothel, those whores," Martine says as she holds one of the handles on the large cooler she and Veronique are hauling up the hill. It's filled with cubes of ice—our healing balm after flying as balls of flame all night.

"Why do the mermaids have to be whores? Why not the fisherboys, eh?" I ask them. I'm carrying another cooler on top of my head. It sits on a piece of bundled cloth, balancing perfectly. None of these soucouyant girls can do this while climbing up a steep hill. Many of them are thinner than I am, but they still have the girth and curves of a soucouyant. Although they are not as graceful. I am bigger, taller, and more commanding. That is why I lead them. Well, one of the reasons why.

"True-true, Solange! The fisherboys are the most whorish of them all," Veronique says. "Once their mermaid girlfriends leave for the ocean, they rub their Black bodies with coconut oil for the white tourists at the resort to gawk at and pay good money for. Whores."

"They are both whorish creatures," Martine adds. "Blame them both. That's why the developers want that piece of our island: so they can have their fantasies. 'Take your pick, ladies and gentlemen. Girl fishes of the sea, or muscle boys carved out of onyx?'"

"Not all boys," someone says, quiet-quiet.

I turn to see Giselle lagging behind. She's the fourth to join us. Five more should be coming soon. "No, not all, Giselle," I say, knowing how sensitive she is. "Gerard is one of the good ones."

"He loves only me," she adds, raising her voice and rushing past Martine and Veronique to catch up to me. Her arms are swinging, hands empty.

Martine and Veronique chuckle. "Only you? Stupid child," Martine says.

"You did not think to bring ice, Giselle?" I ask before Martine berates her even more by bringing up her boyfriend's cheating.

"You must not know of the blackout," Giselle says. Her short afro glistens with oil; so does her deep blue-black face.

I stop and look down the hill. Dusk is settling over the island, and it's only now that we notice the lights haven't come on in the island people's homes. Still, a protest of burning tires and a blackout have not stopped our game in the past. Streaks of orange and dark blue paint the sky, and as soon as it's dotted with stars and a pale yellow full moon, we will take flight.

"Maybe you should run back home to your love, Giselle," Martine starts. "You wouldn't want him to be lonely with only the darkness keeping him company."

"How long has the electricity been out?" I quickly ask, interrupting Martine's impending bullying.

"Not long. Just as I was going into the kitchen at the resort, the workers were there taking out the meat. But the generator kicked in just in time. Too many people around, so I couldn't steal the ice," she says, glancing back at Martine.

"Were you able to steal a kiss from your one and only?" Veronique mocks.

Martine laughs.

Giselle quickly turns around, and they almost bump into her. She places her hands on her hips, furrows her brows, and says, "You are jealous. You would rather inhale the souls of innocent boys than fall in love! You are the real whores!"

"Ey!" I shout, setting the cooler down on the ground. "I will have none of this! Martine and Veronique, let her be."

"Let her be? She couldn't even bring her own ice, and we're supposed to let her be goo-goo gaga over this boy?" Martine says. "Giselle, your boyfriend is fucking everybody! There. I said it. Get over it."

"Martine!" I yell, wanting to slap her face.

"I know about the mermaid," Giselle says quietly. "I let him have her. She only comes every so often, so it's okay. He needs the balance, you know. I'm fire, she's water. Sometimes, my heat . . . It's too much."

"Oh my goddess! This child can't get any dumber!" Martine says, pressing her palm against her head.

"I am not dumb!" Giselle shouts, stepping closer to Martine. A dull red-orange light begins to pulse beneath her dark skin. Her anger will make her shed prematurely tonight. That's the last thing we need.

So I gently grab Giselle's elbow, pulling her back. Her skin is warming up, too. "She's not dumb. She's in love," I say.

"In love? Gerard is not the sun, by far," says Veronique.

"We're not all trying to kiss the sun," Giselle says, deepening her voice. "Some of us need bodies to fall in love with. Human bodies. Not for their souls, but for their . . ."

"For their what, Giselle?" Martine asks. "You know, if he hurts you, he will become disposable. The moment that you start to cry over this fisherboy, he is gone!"

I don't say anything to that, because Martine is right. Vengeance is now the sole purpose of our fiery lives because of what's been done to soucouyant girls on this island over the years—the taking of our bodies without permission, the stealing of our skin to sell on black markets to foreigners. Vengeance is the game we're playing tonight. Our lives have become all about this game. It wasn't always that way. Soucouyant would fly on the night of a full moon and aim for any victim—any soul that would quench our thirst for life, more life. Shed skin, fly, and feast. That was it. Then we would go back to our regular half-human lives. Now this is unacceptable. We have to choose our victims wisely, and we make it a game so we don't live bored and redundant lives like the humans on this island. Make it fun. Make it useful. So I tell Giselle the truth, but I mix it in with some sweetness to cool her down a little.

"Yes, there are others," I say softly, looking directly into her large, round eyes. Giselle's smooth skin looks almost navy blue in the late evening sky. She's one of the darkest of us all, the prettiest. But some of those boys would have her think otherwise. "Gerard needs more than just a water girl to keep him balanced. He needs earth and wind, too—all four of the elements. That doesn't make him a bad person, Giselle. You two just need to talk it out."

"What are you saying, Solange?" she asks, her shoulders dropping, her lips turned downward.

"Gerard goes to see La Diablesse at the top of the mountain." Martine cuts me off.

"Shut up, Martine!" I shout. Then I add, "He asks for one of those goat-footed girls, yes."

Giselle raises her chin as if trying to hold on to the ounce of dignity left in her. But, thank Goddess, her red-orange glow has cooled to a dull yellow. "Oh, is that all? A goat-footed diablesse? You think I will be jealous of a girl who has a hoof for a foot?"

"I hear they are ruthless in bed," Veronique says. "Make those fisherboys writhe their greasy bodies out of shape from pure ecstasy."

I narrow my eyes and purse my lips at Veronique, but she doesn't see me. "I'm sorry, Giselle. Just talk to him."

Giselle holds her head even higher and clears her throat. "And the wind? You said he goes to the wind for a girl."

"He fucks the loup-garou, Giselle! Those nasty shape-shifting girls," Martine says. "Well, girls one minute, beasts the next. Fickle like the wind. I tell you . . . That's why I don't keep no man or boy. The sun is my tried and true!"

We're all quiet for a bit as Giselle drops her head and starts to fidget with her hands. The dull yellow glow is gone now. Her anger has settled in her human body. I'll give her a moment before I ask her why on Goddess's green island did she not find another way to bring ice.

"You did not say anything about the tourists. At least he stays away from them," she says, still holding to a tiny piece of hope.

"Giselle, those pale-skinned tourists are his favorite!" Martine says. "The ones with skin like the moon, with hair flowing over their shoulders in waves. *Steups!* Typical. I guess he considers them magical creatures, too. That slimy eel of a boy!"

I reach over to pinch Martine's arm and pop my eyes out at her. But she only rolls hers at me and crosses her arms over her large bosom.

Giselle is broken now. Her whole body melts even as she

stays standing. But it's not anger, so her skin doesn't glow. It's disappointment, maybe. Sadness. So we let her have this moment without uttering another word.

But the sound of approaching footsteps and voices slices through our short-lived silence. The other soucouyant girls are coming.

"We need to settle this now," I say. "Giselle, how do you feel?"

"Yes! How do you feel?" Martine repeats, stepping closer to Giselle. It's clear she doesn't have a victim's name for tonight. None of us do. That's why we're prying one out of Giselle.

"I feel fine," she whispers.

"Liar!" Martine shouts.

"Who is a liar?" someone from down the hill shouts even louder.

I step closer to Giselle until all three of us surround her. "Come on, Giselle. Let it out," I say. "How do you feel?"

She inhales deep, scrunches her face, and through clenched teeth says, "I feel angry. Angry, Solange! How could he do this to me?" Her voice shakes. Tears well up in her eyes, and the fiery red-orange resurfaces on her skin in just seconds. But she can't shed just yet. She has to hold on to it, for her sake. For our sake. We have to shed together. This is our strength.

Martine and Veronique sigh.

"Good," I say. "But I don't want you to be angry, Giselle. Push it back for a little bit. Hold on to it. You might win tonight. You might be the only one of us who gets to kiss the sun. If and only if you feel like hurting him. Do you?"

She closes her eyes and nods slowly.

"You want to stop him from hurting other girls?" I ask.

"No," Giselle says. "I want to stop him from *loving* other girls."

"Yes!" Martine exclaims. "We have our first soul for the night!"

"Yes we do!" someone shouts.

The other girls are closer now, and I can see their heads bobbing up the hill. Lourdes comes into view. She's all smiles even as she still wears her uniform from the resort—a red pinstriped shirtdress dotted with yellow hibiscus flowers. We've all changed out of our uniforms for fear that any of the island people might see us coming up the hill and report us. That wouldn't matter, though. My mother, a soucouyant herself, owns the Golden Sun Resort. She would simply feign ignorance and accuse the tattle-teller of making up backwoods stories. My mother would claim that she is a woman of Christ and she doesn't believe in the island's stories of magical creatures. That little fib has worked for years.

Still, my mother doesn't know about this game we play. I don't know what she'd do to us, to me, if she found out.

"Mr. Donald Hightower," Lourdes says when she reaches us. "The Don for short. American. New York, I think. Rich, for sure. And he has his preferences."

"But I'm sick of consuming old rich white men," Veronique whines. "I think they give me a rash."

"Ah, but the vengeance is so sweet!" Lourdes says, who's

all legs and teeth. The knee-length uniform fits her mid-thigh, and she's always grinning wide-wide.

"What has he done?" I ask. Lourdes is good for just throwing out names for our game. She thinks it gives her an edge, but it doesn't. "We don't go after innocent men, no matter how rich, no matter how white."

"Ha! Old rich white men and the word *innocent* don't belong in the same sentence, Solange. Especially if they're here in Kiskeya. We all know they come for holiday to titillate their shriveled-up, incompetent loins with the likes of us—Black island girls, tender and sweet. Again, his name is Donald Hightower, and he's staying in the Tropical Suite at the Golden Sun Resort. How long until sundown?"

"We have another one. So we'll have to take a vote on who we aim for first. What is Gerard's full name, Giselle?" Martine says.

"But wait, I want to know what Donald Hightower did. A cheating island fisherboy can't be as bad as an old rich white American man," I say.

"The better question is *who* did he do?" Lourdes responds. "Stefanie. Let them see your face."

We all turn toward down the hill because none of us is named Stefanie. Soon, a light-skinned girl wearing a bright pink sundress appears. Her hair hangs over her bare shoulders in narrow ringlets, and her lips are a deep rose, naturally probably. When she steps closer, I notice the brown freckles dotting her cheeks.

"Why did you bring her here, Lourdes?" I shout. My own

voice startles me. The words burst from my lips like rolling thunder. "We don't need to see the victims. Your word is enough."

"Ah, Solange. She is not just a victim. Stefanie, why don't you—"

"Why don't you let her speak for herself?" Martine asks.

The light-skinned girl clears her throat and raises her chin to say, "Lourdes says that I am one of you!" Her voice is like caramel, too soft and too sweet to be anywhere around us on a night like this.

We all laugh. Every last one of us. The joke resonates so deeply that we become a chorus of laughter—a harmonious melody forcing our bodies to bend forward as we hold our tight, aching bellies from the sheer ridiculousness of what this sun-yellow girl has just said.

"Bullshit," I say. I'm the first to wipe the smile off my face and stare the girl down. "How dare you? We will devour you right here if you've come to insult us, little girl."

She steps back, but it's Lourdes who shields her. "Do you want her to show you?" Lourdes asks.

"Impossible!" Martine says. "She's too pale. Soucouyant are black like night. It's the only way to hold the fire that lives in us. This sponge cake of a girl will burn her own skin if she starts to shed."

"*If* I start to shed?" the yellow girl says, and in an instant, that familiar soucouyant red-orange glow begins to pulse beneath her pale skin. "Lourdes tells me that you have a race and there's a prize. I want to play."

We all gasp—one collective inhalation of the warm island air.

"She's faking it!" Veronique shouts.

"It's a trick!" another girl hisses.

"You can't play," I say. "We don't know where you've come from, and you are not of soucouyant stock. We don't have any pale skins among us. The prize for this game is to have kissed the sun and become even darker than we already are. Our mothers know to check the tips of our ears when we are born to make sure that we will be dark-dark, as if we've been hugged by the island sun. If you are indeed a soucouyant, your own soul would've burned you alive when you first started to shed at the age of nine. You are too light. Your skin defies tradition. You can't take the heat."

"But I am here," Stefanie says. "I did not die. I did not burn. Let me race you. All of you. I will prove to you what I am."

"Please, Solange," Lourdes says, coming closer to me. "We have nothing to lose by letting her race. If she's not a soucouyant and she sees us shed tonight, I will personally handle her."

I make sure to look deep into Lourdes's narrow eyes. The splotches on her face have cleared up. I almost slapped some sense into her when we found out she'd been bleaching her skin. Doing such a thing as a soucouyant is like suicide. She's always been the hungriest of us all—the first to shed and the last to get back into her skin, never even trying to get close to the sun. She just wants to feast. This hunger for souls is her weakness, as well as her hatred for her dark skin. She loses focus while flying. Too eager. And maybe, too trusting of this light-skinned girl.

"Vote!" I shout to the girls. It's always been the nine of us, with the rest of the soucouyant girls on the island doing their own thing. No one has ever asked to join our race until now. So if this yellow girl wants to join us, I know that it is vengeance she seeks. And maybe, just maybe, she wants to be kissed by the sun, too, and make her skin darker, like it ought to be.

"Our ice is melting," Veronique says. "Did our visitor bring her own? That will determine how we vote."

"I don't need ice," Stefanie says.

"So what do you do with your skin while you fly?"

"That is my business," she says.

With that, we let her be. Our great-grandmothers used to store their skin in wooden mortars. That was when the air was pure and not polluted with all kinds of chemicals and toxins. That was also when the island people didn't know where to find us to steal our skin. Now we have to keep our skin cold in ice, away from the harsh elements, so it doesn't shrivel up into a floppy mess. And we have to stay hidden deep in the hills. The protest tonight is also a welcome distraction. The other five girls have rolled an even larger cooler up the hill, and they've already agreed that they would share it. I have my own ice-filled cooler. Giselle is the only one left without somewhere to keep her skin cold. So I offer.

"No. I'll be fine," she says. Her eyes are fixated on Stefanie. "It will be a short race."

I glance back at the light-skinned girl before picking up my cooler. I notice how Lourdes is all over her, pointing to the sky, toward the moon, and showing her the best path to the sun when he begins to creep out from his palace beneath the sea. "Just over that huge flamboyant tree at the edge of the third hill," she says.

I look back at Giselle. Still, she stares at this girl out of the corner of her eye. It's not suspicion painted on her face. It's something else. Something much worse.

"Vote!" I yell again. The girls pause and look at me. "We have Gerard . . . What is his last name, Giselle?"

"Pierre-Louis. He lives in one of the jalousies along the Petitville hill," she says with her voice as distant as the moon.

"Gerard Pierre-Louis of Petitville, and Donald Hightower, an American tourist and businessman."

"What are their crimes?" someone from Lourdes's group asks.

"Infidelity and—"

"Attempted rape," Stefanie says with her brows furrowed and her fists clenched.

"Rape," I repeat quietly while looking at Stefanie. I swallow hard and nod at her—a silent apology on behalf of my mother. As owner of the resort, she's supposed to keep all girls safe from those preying tourists and businessmen. But the fisherboys not only cheat, they help those men and women get whatever it is that they want for the right price, including girls.

"Surely, rape is much worse than a philanderer, Solange," Lourdes says. "We aim for the Don first."

"The Don or anybody else like him would not even think to touch us girls if it weren't for the fishermen and their sons," Martine says. "Traitors!"

"Does it even matter?" Stefanie shouts.

"Oh, a temper," Martine says. "I guess maybe you are a soucouyant after all, but I'll have to see this."

"Okay, enough!" I say. "Stefanie, you can't vote. We need an odd number in case we have a tie. Plus, we don't trust you yet. All in favor of aiming for the Don . . ."

Six hands raise, including Giselle's.

"All in favor of Gerard the fisherboy . . ."

Martine and Veronique raise their hand.

"There. I don't need to vote. You've made your decision," I say. "Thank you, Lourdes."

She smirks, only looking at Stefanie and not me.

"No. Thank *you*," Stefanie says.

Then I clear my throat and raise my chin. "Let me repeat the rules: Shedding is a solitary act. Please give each other enough privacy. Keep your moans and groans to a minimum. The best way to deal with the pain is to bite down on a piece of cloth and grunt if you need to, or take deep-deep cooling breaths. The start of the race begins at the moment of shedding. Take flight as soon as you are fully formed. Remember, our smoke consumes the souls, not our flames. Please don't burn down my mother's resort, or else we all lose much more than this race. If you have the name of the first victim, then you know the face and the location. Your fire instinct will guide you. Asking for more information will be cheating. And no, it would not give you an edge. Your anger does. The hungrier for vengeance, the quicker the shedding, the faster the flame. So, inhale the soul for energy, fly fast and fly far, touch the moon, kiss the sun. Stay up there for as long as you can until the earliest signs of daybreak. Fly as close as you can. If you kiss our beloved, bring back some of that sunfire with you. We will only know the winner once we've all settled into our skins. The darker the skin, the closest to the sun. In the unfortunate event that you do not reach the victim in time, you know what to do, and keep it to yourself. Our first victim is Donald Hightower, nominated by Lourdes. The Golden Sun Resort. Tropical Suite."

"Is that all?" Stefanie asks.

"Oh, this game is too easy for you?" Martine says. "You are free to leave, you know."

"What she means is"—Lourdes interrupts—"I made it sound much more complicated than that."

"You told her the rules before you even brought her here?" I ask, but I put up my hand so Lourdes doesn't respond. I don't need to hear her excuse. I will know what her true intentions are soon enough.

A loud bang makes us all jump, and we turn our heads down the hill. More flames are raging on the streets as night falls over the island. The National Guard trucks are rolling into town from the capital. I'm sure my mother is looking for me right now. All our mothers are. But they also know that this is the night we feast. We are safe. Others are not.

Someone hisses. It's Veronique. The skin around her arms

glows and begins to bubble up like molten lava. She quickly runs behind a bush, leaving Martine to drag the cooler to where they'll be shedding.

Beads of sweat form on Giselle's forehead. She knows better than to fan herself. She's one of the lucky ones who gets to sweat while she sheds. It eases the pain. She looks around for a spot. Soon, she's out of my sight.

Almost all the girls are, except for Lourdes and her friend. She's helping her with her clothes. "Careful now, you don't want to burn them," Lourdes says.

I squint to get a better look at the two of them now that darkness is beginning to wrap around us. "What are you doing, Lourdes? This is a race, and we're not on teams."

Lourdes raises both her hands off Stefanie. "You're right. Stefanie, this is your race to win. Good luck, child."

But Lourdes doesn't stray too far from her. Stefanie sits on the ground with her legs crossed and simply stares out into the late-evening air as if she's meditating. Soon, she is all red. Her skin doesn't bubble like ours does. It's like blood. Smooth. Liquid. She's quiet and still as if her skin will simply melt off without her even crying out in pain.

My shedding starts at the bottom of my feet—a tingling sensation, then it's as if I'm standing on hot coals. I have to slip off my sandals. I can't even stand. I find a spot behind a lime tree where I can still keep my eye on the new girl and Lourdes, and from where I am, I spot Giselle, who is also watching Stefanie.

Shedding is several simultaneous sharp, grazing pains as

if many knives are peeling away my skin from bottom to top. I used to sob like a baby, the pain was so unbearable. It moves up my legs, and that burning sensation reaches my bones, where I can feel everything start to melt into thick liquid. We are volcanoes when we shed. Heat rises up from the pit of our bellies until our souls combust into flames.

I waver between clenching my jaw and fists and taking in deep breaths. I don't follow my own rules by biting down on the balled-up hem of my skirt. At this point, I can either submit to the pain or fight it. The worst part of it all is when I hear my soucouyant sisters cry out in agony. Our collective hearts are melting into bloodfire. To the island people, we are the sounds of the warrior ancestors who succumbed to the great big revolution that drove out the colonizers centuries ago. That is not true. We never succumbed. We are still here.

Do you know how hard it is to not be able to release pain with our voices, to not be able to scream into the air with hopes that the deep aching will finally release us from its deathly grip? Our very breath has become like tiny grains of cayenne or Scotch bonnet seeds. Everything burns. Until it doesn't.

Shedding human flesh is liberating.

In the frenzy of it all, I had opened the cooler and sat my round behind on hundreds of cubes of ice, and that is where my skin rests as I combust into a blazing flame, crackling and whipping the warm night air.

Four girls have shed before me, and one of them zooms up into the now starlit sky, aiming for the Golden Sun Resort.

I stay high enough above the treetops, searching for the light-skinned girl. She's still there, slowly turning into a dim firelight barely strong enough to take flight. Ah! That's the only way she's still alive, poor girl. Her flames don't burn as bright, as hot. She's not a fireball, she's a lit matchstick of a soucouyant, if I can call her that, and here she is wanting to be part of this race.

I press my fireball body against the night air and begin to aim for the resort, but the presence of two soucouyant flames keeps me where I am, circling the hill and careful that my flames don't lick the treetops. Stefanie has completely shed now, and she leaves her skin at the edge of a bush. Her flame is still a dull, yellow-orange ball of potential. She flies past me, slowly, as if the air itself is molasses. Poor child.

But it's not Stefanie's weak flight that makes me pause. Lourdes and Giselle have already shed, but they're circling the hill just as I am. They're not joining the race. I fly higher so that I am above them, watching. I've never won a race, because I'm always keeping an eye out for any cheating. Of course, we don't have eyes out of which to see, or lips out of which to speak, but as flames, we still have feelings and intuition. We are still living energy, another state of matter. We are humans become gas, so we still have to eat.

I've never seen a soucouyant stay behind while a feast of human souls awaits. Sometimes, our hunger for any human soul is sharper than our thirst for vengeance. None of us would give up consumption for anything. Even if we didn't reach our voted victim, we would feast on our own and not mention a word of it to anyone. The human we'd consume would be our own secret.

But there are no humans left on that hill. What are Lourdes and Giselle waiting for?

Then I spot it—Stefanie's skin left unprotected on the cool ground. No ice, no cover, no guard.

I watch as Giselle and Lourdes circle each other. Giselle's flame is mostly blue, her hunger and vengeance much deeper than Lourdes's, who is an even mix of orange, yellow, and turquoise. Her crackling flames extend much farther than Lourdes's, too. It looks as if she's out for blood and soul, except it's not the Don's or even Gerard's. The second that Giselle shoots for the ground, I know for sure that she's out for skin. New skin. Stefanie's skin.

Lourdes lunges right behind Giselle, and immediately, I aim for the both of them. My flame latches on to theirs when I reach them, but they are too strong, too angry, and they roll out of my grip.

But Lourdes catches up to Giselle, and the two flames become entangled until they look like one giant, rolling fireball. I throw myself into their chaos, but their battle is so fierce, so hot that I bounce right off them as if they've become a solid bubble of flames. They've encapsulated themselves so that nothing can penetrate their little war.

I can no longer tell them apart. Soucouyant energy is like a human face. The way the flames dance and how the colors reveal themselves tell us who is who. But it's as if one flame has consumed the other. Soucouyant are souls, too. But this is a taboo, one of only two. We do not consume the flaming soul of a sister soucouyant. We do not enter the skin of a sister soucouyant. These are not simply the rules for our game. It is tradition. It is a mandate from our foremothers.

Hunger pounds against my soul, and I'm sure by now that one of the soucouyant has reached the Don. He is probably a shell of white man now, body and no breath. It's time for me to feast, but my sisters are locked in a tiny war for a light-skinned girl's skin.

In an instant, I recognize Giselle pulling away from Lourdes, and she quickly descends to the ground, as flame, then as firelight, then as soul. The skin suctions around the soul, and it fits like a sock to a foot. Skin doesn't discriminate. It needs a soul, any soul, just like a soul needs skin so it can become fully human.

Lourdes flies away, and I am left alone to watch Stefanie's skin become Giselle's body. She curls herself into a fetal position on the ground, hunger gnawing at her core because she hasn't feasted, and she begins to weep.

There is nothing left for me to do but to fly into the night, feast, and gain some energy to deal with this at dawn.

The very old are not as sustaining as the very evil. Vengeance is not in my soul when I find a grandfather wandering the hills at night. I don't eat the full meal of life force and memories. I take tiny sips or a small bite only, leaving my victim with a fever and shortness of breath. They don't see us coming, you know. Maybe they notice the light, then the unbearable heat. The older women think it's menopause.

But it is us. We shift from flame, to firelight, to smoke, to heat in seconds. We wrap ourselves around their skin and inhale deep-deep. My inhalations are shallow. I don't seek death. Then we rise as smoke and shift back to firelight, then to flame, gaining more and more energy as we fly. I pray that my victims survive. Thank Goddess, they have strong, wiry spirits that can bend away from death.

I am not like the others. I have mercy. I show restraint. And I am not afraid of being charred by the sun, if it comes to that. I am not ashamed of my black fireskin. I know that this is the source of my power, our power. This is why I lead them.

Still, after my small meal, I aim for our beloved sun. He's at the tip of the horizon now, and the other soucouyant are waiting for his arrival, too. One of us circles the air with such energy, such velocity that I'm sure it's with the Don's soul stirring in her fire belly. It's Martine. Of course.

As soon as the sun hits the horizon and the edge of the sky lights up, Martine zooms toward him until she is so close, we can't tell which is flame and which is sun.

I begin to lose strength. I can feel my flames becoming smaller, weaker. I let my fireball self fall and fall, until I am firelight, smoke, soul, skin, and finally body. My feet are now firmly planted on the ground. I am upright and half-human again. Half-girl.

And so is Giselle-in-Stefanie's-skin.

We are all back in our own skins now, and some of us have to catch our breaths and gather our thoughts. Only one flame is left in the sky, circling the hill with an anger so hot, she can easily aim for any one of our souls right now.

So I grab Giselle-in-Stefanie's-skin to shield her.

"What is going on?" Veronique asks. "Why are you protecting that yellow girl? She didn't even race like she said she would. She was down here all this time."

Before I can answer, Lourdes appears. Her face tells the story—eyes narrow, lips pursed. "I should kill you!" she hisses, looking directly at Giselle-in-Stefanie's-skin.

"I won fair and square," Giselle says.

"That wasn't the game you were supposed to be playing," Lourdes says.

"It doesn't matter. I won!"

"Wait. What is Lourdes talking about?" Martine asks, appearing before us with her skin darker than it's ever been. Clearly she won the real game. She kissed the sun. But no one cares, because they're slowly figuring out what Giselle has done, what Lourdes intended to do, and what Stefanie truly is.

"Life is the game I'm playing. Life here on this island," Giselle says, tossing her new long, curly hair back over her shoulders. She looks at her hands and arms as if they are brand-new clothes. "I never wanted to hurt Gerard, really. Or that old white man. He's done nothing to me. I don't care. But now . . ." She twirls, whipping her hair around to make her whole self spin like a tiny hurricane. "Look at me! I am pretty-pretty. Now Gerard will love me and only me!"

The girls gasp and mumble among themselves.

"Wait, now!" Martine shouts. "She did not . . ."

"She did," I say, quiet-quiet.

But a loud screeching makes us all turn to see Giselle's actual body speeding toward us. "Give me back my skin!" Stefanie-in-Giselle's-skin shouts.

Before I can protect Giselle, Martine pulls me away so that Stefanie lunges straight for Giselle. Lourdes jumps in. I try to stop them, but all my soucouyant sisters are holding me back now.

"Stefanie, you'll be hurting your own body, you know!" I yell. "Giselle can always fly out of that skin, and you won't have one to get back into!"

"Let them fight," Martine says. "Giselle has committed a taboo, and she deserves to be punished."

"Lourdes planned it all along."

"Well, Stefanie should destroy them both!"

With that, I pull away with such force, I knock three girls down. I aim for the fighting girls who are throwing punches, pulling hair, and are out for blood, skin blood. It isn't supposed to be this way. We are sisters. Skin sisters.

I pull Giselle-in-Stefanie's-skin away and dare the other two to hit me and have to deal with my mother. That works.

"Why are you protecting her?" Lourdes shouts. "You always protect her!"

"Because she carries the most pain in her flames and in her skin!" I shout back.

"And I don't?" Stefanie-in-Giselle's-skin asks. "Do you know what a curse that light skin will be? The men . . . the boys . . . And even the women with their jealousies so thick, I can't even breathe around them. I eat them, you know. Before tonight, I consumed those jealous girls. If I'd known this was what you planned, Lourdes, I would've destroyed you, too!"

"You can't harm a firefly, stupid girl!" Martine yells back. "I saw your flame. You are a weak soucouyant. Maybe now with Giselle's black skin you can reach your full potential."

"Ey!" I yell louder than all of them. "Stop it! Stop it now! This is a travesty! This can't be good. Things are going to be bad-bad for us."

"As if it hasn't always been bad! Look at us! We are flames, yes, but this island throws us away like old coconut shells. Useless and ugly, they call us," Giselle-in-Stefanie's-skin says. "The world throws us away as if we are a muddied and soiled disgrace. If jealousy and the desire of men and boys are the hardest things to deal with in this skin, then I gladly accept. I will take pretty over ugly any day. Any day!"

"You were not ugly, Giselle," I say, reaching for her hand that is not her hand. "Ugly is what the imbeciles on this island say. They all want to be drunk from the rum of the world— white beauty, wealth, shiny things that will choke them if they put them on too tight. You know that is not true-true. What is real is what we are. We are fire, Giselle, and this skin is what protects us, is what gives us our light, our life."

It's quiet for a long moment. This bit of truth settles over my sisters, and I know that I've reached her. But then she asks, "Do you like your new skin, Stefanie?"

Stefanie looks down at Giselle's shapely body wrapped

around her own firesoul. Even without ever getting close to the sun, Giselle's skin is so beautifully dark, I'm sure it carries the memory of all the powerful soucouyant before her who have gotten close to the sun. "Take it back," Stefanie says with disgust painted all over her face.

"I didn't think so," Giselle says, looking her old skin up and down as if she's gotten rid of smelly trash. "And I dare you to try to take this skin, my new skin, away from me. All of you. Watch!"

With that, she descends from the hill.

Stefanie-in-Giselle's-skin doesn't move an inch, but I know she is plotting. And so is Lourdes.

I look around at all the deep-brown and black faces of my soucouyant sisters as they watch Giselle-in-Stefanie's-skin walk away victoriously. From how some of their eyes stare with envy, with longing, with wishes, I know for sure that Giselle has won the game. The big-big game. She did not feast, nor did she kiss the sun. But with Stefanie's freckled light skin and long, flowing hair, maybe, just maybe, she *is* the sun to them.

Next time we shed on the night of the full moon, more of my soucouyant sisters will aim for her, to kiss her, and inhale her firesoul right out of that sunny skin. And still, she will be their unrequited love.

THE ACTRESS

By Danielle Paige

"More tongue," executive producer **Michael Winthrop's** voice screeched through the mic of the PA standing over Reid Hamilton and me on the *Hearts Eternal* set.

By the time Rhiannon Heart was fifteen, she'd fallen down a well, fought and won against leukemia, shot a man in self-defense, spent time in juvie, fallen off the wagon, spent time in rehab, and oh yeah, discovered she was a witch and fallen in love with a vampire. But she had never been kissed until two seconds ago.

I wasn't Rhiannon. I just played her on TV. I was Gamine Belle, and I had never been kissed until two seconds ago either.

"It's supposed to be a kiss that makes every girl at home want to be her. That makes them want to drop their . . ."

The mic squawked again, and this time, Morgan the PA put her hand over it, preventing me from hearing the end of Michael's comment. But my brain could fill in the blanks. I was getting notes about panty dropping from a sixty-year-old man in a glass booth a hundred feet away from me.

Reid shrugged his shoulders and squared his jaw, but thankfully his cheeks burned as red as mine felt. At least he understood the embarrassment, too.

I was a professional. I had been acting since before I knew what acting was. I had been in commercials for diapers when I was in diapers. I went on to soaps and then finally a prime-time gig on the vampire teen drama *Hearts Eternal*, which had become the number one show for the prized demographic of eighteen to forty-nine.

The production assistant rocked back on her heels, clearly listening to her headset.

"I won't tell her that. You come down here yourself."

I glanced up at her gratefully, but as I looked from her to the boy I had kissed and back again, I realized everyone in the glass booth had heard what Michael had said, and the boy I'd just kissed had heard it, too.

Which was embarrassing for both Rhiannon Heart and me. Both my character and I had major crushes on Reid and his character, Wolfe. I'd had a crush on Reid from the moment I met him, even though I had always been skeptical of those girls who experienced instalove in books. But he smiled at me and I literally felt my pulse quicken, my eyelids flutter. I was smiling without the prompting of my mother or a director.

"Gam . . ." Right now, Reid said my name, reached for my hand, and squeezed it. I willed the tears not to come.

"Well, what are we waiting for? Reset. Go again." I heard Michael's voice over the loudspeaker. He'd given up on talking through the PA.

Before Reid and I could respond, Harris Radner blew onto the set, looking like he was one of the cast members' older brothers. He was only a few years older than Reid and I, and he had piercing green eyes and chiseled features. He had chosen to be behind the camera as a writer-producer, and he was my favorite grown-up on set. He wrote the best scripts, including this one.

He put a gentle hand on my shoulder. "Hey, Michael's a jerk and a dinosaur. Just focus on Rhiannon and Wolfe. You're young. You're beautiful. You're in love. You're about to have everything you want . . ."

I tried to listen to Harris. I tried to dismiss Michael as a dinosaur jerk. But then the mic squawked again.

The PA mouthed *I'm sorry* and walked away. I tried to smile back at the PA, but all I could think about was the fact that I'd somehow kissed wrong. And everyone knew it.

My stomach clenched. What should have been a seminal moment had become my most embarrassing one. The set, which usually felt cavernous, was now claustrophobic. The lights above, which usually barely made a dent in the sub-zero temps of the set, suddenly felt warmer than sunlight. I thought I was imagining it, but I could see perspiration forming on Reid's brow. The lights flickered when I looked back at him.

"Hey, we've got this," he said with a reassuring smile that

only increased my anxiety. I looked away. I did not want him to pity me.

The lights went out again as our director, Marnie, called "action," but when my lips were supposed to meet Reid's again, I felt my stomach sink, and the world was suddenly on fire.

Well, not the whole world, the set.

When I opened my eyes, Reid was already on his feet and grabbing my hand. I let him pull us away from the flames.

The fire alarm went off, and Marnie began yelling for everyone to get out of the building.

While we were standing outside in front of the studio, fire trucks blaring, I could already hear the sound of cameras shuttering.

It was *TMZ* or *ET* or *E!* or some other show known only by letters. Behind them was the usual collection of fans carrying signs declaring their love for Reid. There were also a few signs rooting for our coupledom, both on-screen and off. Some part of my heart lifted at the sight of my name linked with his— *ReGam forever!!! RhiWolfe Afire.*

Today notwithstanding, my character and I and the fans had come a long way since I was cast two years ago. Then there had been an onslaught of tweets that felt a million times more painful than this morning's embarrassing moment. When it was announced that a brown girl was playing the blonde, blue-eyed protagonist of the *New York Times* bestselling YA series Eternal Damned, my notifications blew up with threats, insults, and calls for a boycott of the TV series.

I read the tweets over and over again. To add insult to injury, there was a flash flood on the way home from school just as I stumbled on the tweets. My driver and I barely escaped the car, and I wound up with a sprained wrist. Even as the doctor put a cast on my arm, I couldn't stop looking at my feed. I knew the script. I'd seen it happen before with everything from Star Wars to Harry Potter. Fandoms could be cruel fandoms. But there had been no way to predict what it felt like to have the hate scroll on your screen, pinging at regular intervals. The words stung even though I knew better. Even though I knew they were ignorant. Even though I knew they weren't true.

I stayed quiet at the instruction of my publicist. At the advice of my mother. At the insistence of Michael. Michael was the one who engaged first, defending the choice to cast me, defending my talent. Even though I knew he didn't really believe in me.

But it was Reid's single tweet that stopped the hate storm.

> Gamine is the best thing ever to happen to Rhiannon, to me, and to the show.

And just like that, the tide turned, and I got more tweets congratulating me than wanting me dead.

When he came to my apartment to make sure I was okay, I didn't feel grateful to him, but angry. A single tweet from him had calmed the internet waters. I hated that his endorsement mattered and my words, my being didn't. And I hated that I had to explain that to him.

I liked that he noticed I was upset, and that he acknowledged that he saw the difference in the way we were treated, but knew that he couldn't understand what it felt like to be me. At least he wanted to.

"Ignore them," Reid insisted now, not even looking toward the photographers. He took a blanket from one of the paramedics and began to unfold it, but his eyes were still on me.

"Are you okay?" he asked. "Michael's a jerk . . ."

"At least he can't say it wasn't hot anymore," I offered awkwardly.

"Gam . . ." he said, his voice laced with so much pity it nearly broke me. "If I had known it was your first time, I never would have. . . . we could have . . . practiced."

I could feel my cheeks warm. I dragged my fingers through my curls before tucking them behind one of my ears like I did when I was nervous.

"Hey, it's okay . . ." he said, pulling me closer to him, using the blanket we shared.

"I just thought you'd only want to have to do it on set." *Said no girl ever.*

He was freaking Reid Hamilton, and even though I was a star in my own right I was not immune to his obvious charms. Neither was the rest of America under thirty-five.

"Was I that bad at it?" I asked.

"You were great. It was great. But I wish you'd told me you'd never . . ."

"It's embarrassing. I'm sixteen."

"I think it's sweet . . ."

"Right," I said.

"Hey, you know that there's a difference between an on-screen kiss and one off-screen—" he began.

"Yeah, Michael totally explained that to me," I countered.

"You've seen them yourself—the kiss for the cameras is for the cameras. It's about making sure that it looks passionate, but at the exact same time, it's about making sure that the camera gets our best angles. It's not real. It's not true."

I heard what he said, but it was still my lips on his. My heart beating in my ears. It felt real—even if it wasn't to him.

"That wasn't your first kiss, that was Rhiannon's," he said. I was struck by how long his lashes were and how insanely beautiful and brown and deep his eyes were. When I looked into them, everything and everyone else fell away. He didn't have the square jaw that the other boys on the show had. His face was thin and long and punctuated with a dimple on his left cheek that shot through me every time he smiled. His wavy hair, usually pinned down with gel, was mussed in the hasty exit from the studio. "Whenever you have your first, whoever has it with you will be lucky."

Shows like *Hearts Eternal* were way stations on the way to the big screen, but Reid was all humility. He didn't seem to take his fame for granted, even though the whole world seemed ready for him to make his big-screen break. For some reason he kept turning down every movie script his agent brought him. He always had an excuse. Too close to *Hearts Eternal*. Too far from his range. I teased him about being Goldilocks looking for something perfect. But I secretly wondered if maybe it had all been too easy for him. Maybe he was scared life wouldn't be the same once he got out of the *Hearts Eternal* nest.

But I never said that to him. I wasn't ready for him to leave *Hearts* yet. I wasn't ready for him to leave me yet.

As the "root for" couple, every other scene of ours was together. Sometimes I had scenes with his evil brother and other times with my best friends—one who was a witch, the other a vampire. But it was Reid that I ran lines with. It was Reid that I did homework with. It was Reid that I ate lunch with, and it was Reid that I went to movies and got meals with even when we weren't working.

"I got another script," he said as we stood in front of the studio, backs facing the photographers.

"What's this one about?" I asked.

"Psychic alien assassin . . . wait for it . . ."

"Who falls in love with his victim and has to decide whether to love or to kill," I finished.

He laughed.

"Close—psychic alien killer who's charged with killing the president but falls in love with his daughter and has to decide whether to love or to kill."

I raised my hand dramatically.

"I would see it."

He shrugged. "I don't think it's me, though."

"You get more scripts than I get food from Grubhub."

"I'm being a brat, aren't I?" he said.

I was his costar, and I had only been offered a handful of roles, two out of three of which were teen prostitutes. I would kill to be offered the chance to lead an epic space battle. But every role I really wanted involved my agent pitching me to studios, not the other way around.

Reid saw how unfair the business was. He was trying to learn from that first onslaught of tweets and everything that came after. Enough to know that sometimes I wanted him to be quiet when it came to the difference in our careers. And that sometimes I just wanted him to listen when I wanted to vent about it.

I swatted him with the end of the blanket. He retaliated by ballooning the blanket over our heads and engulfing us in it. I laughed.

"Hey, maybe we should have practiced," he whispered.

"Practiced what?" I demurred. I wasn't sure, but it almost sounded like Reid Hamilton was flirting with me.

I was close enough to see his chest move as he breathed. Which meant he was close enough to hear my heart beating double-time in my chest.

He whispered my name and left it hanging there.

I met his gaze and I could have sworn that the whites of his eyes were almost luminescent. It was a trick of the light, I reasoned. And as his smile spread, the light was forgotten.

Was it really possible? Was Reid going to kiss me?

But just as suddenly, he stepped back and unblanketed us. And the daylight crashed in.

"Want to go get froyo?" he suggested as I tucked my hair behind my ears and tucked away my expectations.

"I should really get home," I said, thinking of Mom.

"We saved like three hours with the fire. Come on. You can help me read *President Alien*?"

"That is not the name." I laughed again.

"Would I lie to you?" he said, and I nodded.

When the car dropped me off at home, I was full of frozen yogurt, and the morning's fire was in my rearview.

When my mother answered the door she was clearly upset. The studio had called and told her about the fire.

"I should have been there."

"Mom, I'm fine."

"You're not fine."

"I'm fine. It was just a freak thing. The electrical or something. The crew will get it fixed, and we'll be back on set in two days."

"Honey, it wasn't a freak thing, and it wasn't an accident. It was you."

"What are you talking about?"

Mom wasn't good on her own. Since Dad had divorced her when I was five, she'd been practically my shadow for most of my life. My decision to have a closed set clearly upset her. She paced the room.

"I don't know how to say this except to just say this . . . You are not like other girls. "

"Mom!" Sometimes she criticized me, but I'd never have expected her to agree with Michael and call me a freak.

"I know you're upset about today," I told her, "but I am allowed to have a little privacy."

"No, honey, not just you, the whole family. You don't know your power."

"Are you seriously going to do this today? Michael insulted my kissing, and then there was a fire. Isn't that enough? I should have taken you with me so you could have had a front-row seat to my humiliation. Is that honestly what you're saying?"

"Listen to me. Look at me," Mom said suddenly. "I am not talking about today. I'm taking about your whole life."

"I am not listening to another word," I said, tears forming.

My mom opened her palm, and a tiny flame erupted from it.

"What the hell?" I screamed.

"We all have different gifts. Some of us control air, some fire, some water. Some of us control all of the elements. Others control minds. Still others control space. Some of us control all of those things—"

"And you control fire?" I asked, still absorbing the new reality.

"And so do you," she said.

I heard a voice in my head that wasn't mine—it was my mom's. *I control more than that.*

I jumped.

Honey, I know that this is a lot. I wish I'd told you sooner.

"How is this happening?"

"You might have all of my gifts or just some of them—

sometimes they skip a generation. Your grandmother could barely cast a spell."

I didn't want to hear any more.

I got up suddenly and walked toward my room.

"I need a minute."

"Honey, there's so much more to tell you—"

I slammed the door.

I looked at myself in the mirror and began removing my makeup. When I was done, I took a long look at myself. Who was I? I tried to wrap my mind around what my mother had told me. I studied myself for a beat. I put up my palm and concentrated. Nothing happened.

I wasn't playing a witch. I was one.

I flashed back to the day I'd auditioned for *Hearts*. I'd been sitting in a room filled with blonde Barbies who were thinner and taller and a couple of years older than me. I was the only one who had dressed up in the school uniform that Rhiannon wore to her supernatural school in Noelle Harking's Eternal Damned series. I had been a fan of the series since I discovered it when I was seven. With the books coming out each year, I felt like I grew up with the little witch who starts at a new school, gets bullied, and has to decide whether to use her powers for good or for evil.

"That was great, Gemma, thank you for coming in," the casting director said when I finished the audition monologue in which Rhiannon finally tells the boy she likes that she is a witch.

Something in the way the casting director said it told me I

wasn't getting it. That she thought I was great, but she wasn't going to pick me. And it wasn't just that she got my name wrong.

I got to the door and turned back and walked back to her.

"I know I'm not what you are looking for," I said.

"Gemma—" she said delicately.

"Gamine," I corrected. "But I know this character—I can be this character . . ."

She blinked up at me. I had her attention.

"I know there are tons of people who think they know this character—and some other girls out there look just like you think she should look—but when I read this book, I felt it on the inside. I felt I could be her."

Before she could respond, I clicked my heels back across the floor and out the door.

Three days later, I had the job.

Now I looked at the mirror again and then stormed back out to see my mother. She was still sitting in the same spot. The television was on but she wasn't looking at it. She looked up at me.

"Honey, I . . ."

"Can you tell me one thing?" I said over her. "You said you could control things. Did I or did you—did we make this happen, too? The acting, the roles, everything that I thought I earned—did you . . . magic it?"

Mom's face fell as she realized what I was thinking. "Oh, honey . . . no. Everything you did was yours. Not even a hint of magic."

"How can I believe you?" I asked.

"I actually thought this life would be easier for you than your old life was."

"I'm on television. Thousands of kids are watching me. Thousands follow me. How was that supposed to work? How is that the way to keep a secret this big—one that you didn't even bother to tell me?"

"Your life is your own. You don't have to see other kids on a daily basis. You see me and a small crew. If anything witchy happens, you're on a show about witches . . ."

I studied my mother for a beat. This woman who was always so calculating and so smart had somehow missed the point of everything.

"Mom, you've made this big show of how close we are my whole life, and yet you've been hiding the most important thing about yourself. About me."

"I never thought of it as a gift. I thought of it as something I had to control. I hoped that you would never have to deal with it." She paused and wrung her hands. "For most of my life, being a witch wasn't a good thing." Her face looked pained, as if she was remembering something.

I went back to my room and shut the door again. I felt a twinge of concern for Mom's younger self for whatever she'd gone through, but she didn't get to make me feel bad for her when she'd hidden who we really were my whole life.

I threw myself on the bed, knowing that sleep would not come tonight. A bitter laugh escaped my lips. This morning I'd thought the kiss was going to cause a shift in my life. Now I was someone who had been kissed but there was something else, something much more seismic. I was a witch.

In the morning, I woke up to a ton of texts from Reid making sure I was okay and asking if I wanted to have breakfast. I ignored them, not wanting his pity pancakes. When I slipped out of my room I found a note on the kitchen table from my mother. She was off getting chocolate croissants for us from my favorite bakery. She would be back in a few minutes. The only thing I knew was that I wasn't going to be there when she got back.

When I got downstairs, I walked through the building, past my doorman, and out into the street. Before I could decide where to go, my phone pinged.

An hour later I was at Freds with Harris, the writer-producer who'd been on set yesterday with a front-row seat to my kissing debacle.

"What do you want to drink? I'm ordering a bloody Mary. Do you want one?" he asked in a rush. Harris was only a few years older than most of the cast. He'd been directing since he got his big break with an indie slasher movie about kids trapped in a superstore.

I declined the drink and ordered an omelet with egg whites.

"Skip the egg whites. Live a little."

I'd been on a diet since I was born, it seemed. I shook my head.

"I can't afford it," I said.

"I say you're perfect. Girls want to see themselves, not stick figures on the screen."

The waitress cocked her head at me.

"Okay, regular eggs."

I didn't even know what real yolks tasted like. When I took a bite a few minutes later, I was surprised at how good they were. They melted in my mouth. Another reason to hate my mother—a lifetime of deprivation.

"Thanks for this," I said, filled with gratitude.

"Don't thank me yet," he said gently.

The eggs I'd been enjoying threatened to come back up.

"Michael's firing me. Is that why you invited me? That's why you wanted me to order the real eggs."

Anger welled in me.

"He can't do that because of the kiss. He can't fire me."

"It's more than that. He says it's your look."

"My look? What's wrong with my look?"

"You know he wanted someone different when the role was cast—he made no secret of it."

"I know that. But I thought he had come around. Everyone has. I can't change who I am—"

"Hey, I would never suggest that. I think you're perfect just the way you are—but your character is growing up. I think it could be time to show Michael that you're more grown up, too. What I mean is your wardrobe, the hair— time to lose the pigtails and trade them in for a blowout. And the overalls . . ."

"You think a makeover can save my job?" I said hesitantly.

"It's Hollywood. We think that a makeover can save the world. I know it sucks that this is the way it is. But I want it to work."

"I want it to work, too," I said. I forced a smile. I had been through so much more.

He planned the whole day. The best salon. A private stylist at Barneys, upstairs from Freds.

When we emerged from the store into the LA sunlight, Harris turned to me and asked, "How do you feel?"

"Different."

"Different good or different bad?"

"Good. I guess everyone has to grow up sometime."

It was a strange afternoon. I'd never spent so much time alone with Harris. He was funny and kind and laid back, and he made me feel better about everything. I felt myself relax, and I was finally feeling better despite the fact that my job was in jeopardy, I had to kiss Reid again, and oh yeah, I was a supernatural being with powers like the one I played on TV.

A thought occurred to me that dampened my improved mood. "Is Michael going to be okay with the show paying for a makeover?"

"He will be when he sees you. Let me worry about Michael, okay?" he said with a certainty I didn't quite share.

"Okay," I said, and flipped my hair, which was blown straight for the first time in ages and reached well past the middle of my back. In my hands I held a few shopping bags—the rest had been sent to the studio.

Harris laughed, and I pulled my hair behind my ear in response.

"Don't do that."

"Do what?"

"Be self-conscious. You are stunning. You always have been. Down deep you have to know that. Own it," he said.

Impulsively, I gave him a hug, and he patted me on the back.

Harris's words followed me home up to the apartment, back in front of the mirror in my room, where I was hoping to find something. Or someone. I think I was looking for myself. Instead, I saw a girl playing dress-up. But no amount of makeup was going to make me what the studio wanted.

Suddenly, somehow I knew that I could change my face with enough concentration. Focusing hard, I widened my eyes, lengthened my nose and sharpened it. I elongated my face and raised my cheekbones.

Magic could make me the girl that they wanted. But I couldn't bear looking at her. She wasn't me.

I closed my eyes and the bedroom quaked. When I opened them, the mirror cracked and the pieces flew toward me. I crouched down on the ground as glass shattered around me. The bags containing the new clothes Harris had bought began to smoke. I grabbed a pillow from the bed and smothered them before a fire could start. I caught a glimpse of myself in a shard of glass hanging from the mirror's frame. My face had returned to itself.

It was my choice what kind of person and what kind of witch I was going to be. For now, I wasn't ready to change a thing.

Reid showed up a few minutes later. He looked and smelled like he had just gotten out of the shower. I liked him like this, free of the pancake makeup and preppy clothes that the role required. He wore an orange sweatshirt and jeans, and his signature sunglasses were propped on top of his head. He almost looked like a normal sixteen-year-old, except for his devastating good looks. Instantly I knew I could trust him, I had always trusted him, and the words burst forth. "I'm a witch, Reid. I can do things just by thinking about them. I started the fire, too."

He put his hands gently on my shoulders. "Let me handle it," he said, pulling out his cell phone.

"What are you doing? Who are you calling?" I asked. The lights flickered and I took a deep breath, trying to calm myself. I did not want to hurt Reid.

I could protect myself, but if I couldn't do so while hiding my power, where would I end up? Dissected by a lab or caged by the government or used by them as weapon? I shuddered, thinking about what could happen to me

With a flash of movement, Reid crossed the room in less than a second. He deposited the mirror shards in a trash can and the offensive new clothes outside the door.

"What are you?" I asked as he finally stopped moving and stood in front of me again.

He opened his mouth and revealed teeth that did not look like ones that took an hour in Sandy's makeup chair.

I sat on one of the chairs and caught my breath.

"You're . . ." I began.

"Yes," he finished.

'Why didn't you tell me?" I asked.

"I didn't think . . . I didn't know if you would accept this. Accept me."

"Of course I accept you; you're Reid."

"And you're Gamine. What happened here?"

I told him what Harris said about Michael wanting to fire me. And about the makeover.

"He's a jerk!" he said.

"He's just the messenger."

"You're perfect. I wouldn't change a thing."

"I'm not perfect. I'm something else."

"I'm something else, too."

He reached for my hand and squeezed it gently.

We sat like that, side by side, hand in hand, until my mom got home.

"I was out looking for you," Mom said, looking more harried than I had ever seen her.

"I'm sorry I worried you," I said. I was still mad at her for keeping the secret, but some part of me understood she had wanted to wait until I was ready.

Mom hugged me and spoke to Reid over her shoulder.

"Thank you for this," she said.

He nodded, understanding.

◆ ◆ ◆

When I walked Reid out, I had so many questions about where he got his blood from, about whether he had ever killed anyone, about daylight. When blood rushed to his cheeks in a blush, was it his own? But he spoke before I could ask him more.

"Are you okay?" he asked. "I mean, of course you're not okay . . . but . . ."

"I will be," I said firmly.

"What do you do when you find out everything you are isn't what you believed?" I asked, after staring at the new space between us for a beat.

"I'm so sorry your mom didn't tell you. I'm sorry that I didn't tell you either. I'm sorry about a lot of things," he said, his words coming out in an apologetic rush.

"What are you talking about?"

"I was scared to leave *Hearts* because I was scared that someone might find out about me. I was also scared to leave without telling you—" he said. He glanced down, looking more vulnerable than I had ever seen him, as if he was afraid that when I looked at him again, I might reject him.

"Telling me what?" I asked.

"How I feel about you. How I always have."

I had missed this huge thing about Reid. But the thing that really mattered . . . who we were to each other. I hadn't missed that. And, finally, after all this time, he was confirming it.

He stopped himself. "I know there could not be a more inappropriate time for me to say this."

I laughed. I couldn't help it. And when he joined in, I knew it was going to be okay between us.

I leaned in, ready to kiss him.

He leaned back.

"Did I do something wrong?" I asked. The porch light flickered, mirroring my anxiety.

He shook his head. "When you kiss me, I want it to be about us."

"Well," I said, "we'll be kissing in front of the whole world on Monday when the studio is back up and running."

"No we won't," he countered firmly.

"Wait, did Michael tell you he's firing me?"

"He's not going to fire you—everyone loves you. The audience loves you. And I . . . I just meant that we aren't having our first kiss in front of the whole world. Rhiannon and Wolfe are."

"Oh," I said. Had Reid just come close to saying he loved me?

"One day, if I'm lucky, I hope we have *our* first kiss," he said, squeezing my hand gently.

On Monday after a long weekend, Rhiannon and Wolfe filmed their kissing scene six more times. Reid was right—it didn't feel like a real kiss should feel. It felt like work, but I was glad I got to do it with a friend anyway.

When the cameras weren't rolling, Reid and I got to

know each other as our real selves, girl and boy, witch and vampire . . . But Reid was right, it took time to adjust to my new light.

Reid and I didn't have our first kiss until three months later, after the season ended. We spontaneously met for coffee and talked and then walked down to the pier. It was something we'd done a hundred times. It wasn't planned. But it was good. It was sweet and funny and awkward.

It was my real first kiss.

And it felt like magic.

THE CURSE OF LOVE

By Ashley Woodfolk

Aunt Gigi always told me that for women in our family, red lipstick was a weapon.

"Don't wear it unless you ready for the attention that comes along with them lips, Bree," she says as she steps into the bathroom behind me. I lean closer to the mirror and smooth the crimson-tipped wand across my lips again, defiantly applying a second coat. Aunt Gigi raises her eyebrows and peels her sheer mahogany pantyhose away from her thick brown legs inch by inch.

I purse my scarlet-stained lips and turn to face her. "Yeah, I know. With great power comes great responsibility, or whatever."

Aunt Gigi finishes undressing and twists the knob to run her bath, standing in her bra. With her hairless arms crossed over her big boobs, she watches me as I finish getting ready, the way she always does. I brush my fringe of black lashes with even blacker mascara, just the way Gigi taught me. I twist my thick braids into a messy bun, the way Gigi used to do for me when I was small.

Gigi looks proud, smug, or maybe a little bit of both. I wink at her reflection in the mirror.

"You liable to drive them boys crazy," Gigi says with a smirk, and I know her words are as much a joke as they are a warning.

"They can look but they can't touch," I reply. Aunt Gigi's own rose-tinted lips slip into a wide grin. She's stunning when she smiles, even to me.

"That's my girl," she whispers just before dipping a red toenail into steaming, lavender-laced bathwater.

Giselle was usually just getting home when Aubrey was heading out for school, and that morning was no different. Aubrey didn't know where her aunt spent most nights, but the gorgeous woman and beautiful girl regularly collided like stars in the single bathroom of the one-story bungalow they shared.

Despite her aunt's warnings, Aubrey often made light of the darkness that lurked in the prettiness of her face, but the absence of the other Dunn women in their too-empty house was a haunting they both tried, and failed, to ignore.

That day, Aubrey walked quickly past the portraits of her other aunts: Claudette and Madeline, Elizabeth and Abigail. She'd studied the paintings for hours when she was younger, taking in the women's bushy, black hair and dark, flawless skin, their pouty lips and luminous eyes.

It was the last portrait she always avoided—the one of

her own mother, Josephine. But that day, for the first time in nearly a year, she looked right at it.

The whole town told stories about the Dunn women. And Giselle had told Aubrey the truth as soon as she was old enough to understand.

Aubrey used to wonder how they could give up their beauty—something that was so tangible, so . . . powerful. But she was starting to realize that it wasn't that simple. They forfeited their youth, too, and eventually their very lives.

She stared at the portrait of Josephine, remembering what her mother had said the day before everything changed.

He's worth everything, Bree.

"How did you know?" Aubrey whispered, looking for answers in her mother's flatly painted eyes.

"How did you *know*?"

"Get in, loser," Talia yells in my direction the second I push open my front door. I skip over to her car, which is idling at the curb, and Talia smirks as I climb inside.

"Hey, jerk-face," I say, unzipping the front pocket of my backpack and dropping my house keys inside. I reach for her radio and turn up the song that's playing. I bounce a little in my seat.

"About time things got back to normal," Talia says as she shifts the car into gear. It's the first time I've ridden to school with her in weeks.

I'd been avoiding her for more reasons than one. But I called her last night, and things are good now. Though it's difficult for people to be angry with anyone in my family for long, Talia seems to have a special talent for it, at least when it comes to me.

It's why I love her so much—I know her anger (and her affection) is real.

"Sorry, boo," I say. I lean over and kiss her cheek. "Love ya, mean it."

That's when it happens—the familiar rush of warmth. The prickle along the back of my neck that can only mean one thing:

He's close.

I had no idea he was in the car before I climbed inside, because Talia has darkly tinted windows. But I can *feel* him.

He's one of the many reasons I've been keeping my distance the last few weeks, and he's sitting in Talia's back seat.

"Hey," Vince says, and his voice is heat, melting all the ice in my veins. In that one word I hear *I want you* and *I need you* and *I love you.*

I wish I couldn't hear him at all.

Against my will I remember how hot his breath was when I nearly let him kiss me last month, at that party. I remember how his eyes and skin shimmered bronze, like a key, in the golden glow of the porch light, and I could imagine him unlocking the cage around my heart that Aunt Gigi had always warned me to keep shut tight.

Talia had failed to mention that her brother would be riding to school with us. I wouldn't have worn the red lipstick if I'd known.

I'm a little pissed, but she and I are so newly mended, I don't want to break us again by scrambling out away from her just to get away from him. I swallow hard and find his eyes in her rearview mirror so I don't have to look at him directly.

"Oh," I say. "Hi."

The whole ride to school, Aubrey thought ceaselessly about her aunts and her mother and all they'd given up. She did everything she could not to think about the boy in the back seat, for whom she might be willing to make the same ultimate sacrifice.

When Talia pulls into the school parking lot, I hop out of the car so quickly I nearly trip over the untied laces in my boots.

"Later," I mumble, without looking at Talia or Vince as I walk away. But I don't get very far before I feel Talia's warm hand encircle my wrist. She yanks my arm back hard to stop me, and I scream, "Ow!"

"Seriously? We're back to this already?" Talia nearly shouts. Other kids leaning against their parked cars turn to stare, and Vince lingers by the still-open back door of Talia's 4x4.

Things have been uneasy between me and Talia ever since she realized I was keeping a secret. I'd never kept a thing from her before this thing with Vince.

So as soon as I left that party without saying why, everything changed. And while I thought I'd patched things up with a phone call and the Dunn charm that had yet to let me down, things aren't as "fixed" as I thought. Talia's clearly still full of sparks, a wildfire just waiting to be stoked. I try to tread lightly.

"Back to what?" I ask, lying with a question that only seems to make Talia angrier.

My friend crosses her arms. "You think you're too good for my brother. That's it, isn't it? You think you're too good for both of us. That's why you haven't wanted to ride with me to school, right? That's why you've been avoiding Vince since that party."

"That's not it," I say. And then I try to explain. But when I tell her that I smell like lavender and honey, and that I'm wearing red lipstick, I can tell I'm not making any sense. When I explain that I'm blessed with beauty and bleeding desire, Talia actually laughs.

"Riiight," Talia says, rolling her eyes. "Conceited much?" There's a venom in her tone that poisons the comment, turning the would-be tease toxic.

I wish I could laugh it off, but I can't. Because Talia is a friend I love too much to lose. She's angry about something she doesn't even understand; something I'm only just beginning to.

Then Vince is there, and my heart is suddenly trying to beat its way out of my chest. I don't want to leave things unresolved with Talia. But I can't stand to be this close to Vince.

Don't wear it unless you ready for the attention that comes along with them lips, Bree.

You liable to drive them boys crazy.

Before he can get any closer—before he can look at me for longer than I'm able to hold his gaze, or worse still, brush a fallen braid from my shoulder—I move away from his tender eyes, his dangerous hands.

"Wait for me after school," I call to Talia, who still looks pissed. "I'll explain everything, I promise."

But that afternoon, goddammit, it's Vince who finds me first.

It happened when she wasn't watching—a slow kind of falling for Vince.

It all started with him noticing.

He noticed the way she spoke softly, so one day he stepped closer to hear her when they were talking in the dense and crowded halls of their high school.

He noticed that she was often cold, so a week after their close conversation, he offered her his scarf as they stepped out into the crisp afternoon air.

A month after that, when they and a few of their friends were gathered in a dimly lit basement, he noticed her cautious eyes. He saw the way she made herself small until she couldn't anymore and all her loveliness burst forth in a brilliant grin or a dazzling look or a charming comment. He noticed how she steered clear of the boys who threw themselves at her, and how she manipulated some of them, but only the ones who refused to listen to her very firm nos.

He waited until Talia skipped up the stairs for another

drink. He waited until the other guys scattered. He stepped closer to Aubrey and asked, "Why do you hide?"

Though she didn't—couldn't—answer, she looked him right in his eyes and said, "It's for your own good."

He believed her. And it was then that she began noticing him, too.

It stayed that way for quite a while—each of them noticing, and quietly appreciating the other. They found a delicate balance, and they loved each other, but never too much and never at quite the same times.

But it all went to hell the day Aubrey made a joke in Talia's car, and the rich sound of Vince's laughter, the unexpected light in his eyes when he looked at her, the warmth of his hands when he gently touched her shoulder—all caught her off guard. She gasped and he stopped laughing and Talia stared at the two of them until she began to grin.

"You into my brother?" Talia asked Aubrey that night on the phone, and Aubrey denied it all.

Then, at a party that weekend, Vince touched the back of her hand, the back of her arm, the delicate skin on the back of her neck. And she got lost in the softness of his fingers, the lingering sound of his laugh, the way he noticed every part of herself she tried to bury.

"Can I kiss you?" he asked. And Aubrey felt herself lean in too easily. She was too ready, too eager to say yes.

She couldn't let herself love him. Not without risking everything.

So she ran.

◆ ◆ ◆

He's waiting for me by my locker, his messy black hair some-how flickering like a flame of dark fire. And while I know loving him can hurt me, when he's standing there, looking like that, I don't know if I can keep him at arm's length for much longer.

"Bree," he says, his voice deep, deliberate, and a little bit desperate. "I just came to say I'll disappear, if you want. I'll change schools. Go live with my dad. I won't ever come close to you again."

But that isn't what I want. That was never what I wanted. I shake my head and step closer to Vince, afraid the longing alone will eat me alive if I'm not careful. I place my palm flat against his chest and let out a shaky exhale. I can feel that his heart is beating as hard and fast as mine.

"I need to talk to Talia first," I say, because Vince already knows my deepest secret, and he's somehow still here. "I have to make her understand. I have to figure out what to say to Aunt Gigi, too."

He nods and lifts my hand from his chest to his mouth. He kisses each of my knuckles and then presses my hand to his heart again, like he doesn't want to let me go.

"Are you sure I'm worth it?" he asks. And I look past him to see Talia coming toward us. I wish I had more time to come up with a plan, more time to decide exactly what to say and how, but I can feel something starting, like a fire in my veins, so I have to act now.

I look back at Vince and I think of my mother. I grasp one of his warm hands, and trace the kind curve of his lips.

"Yeah," I say. "I'm sure. You're worth everything."

That night, before Giselle got home, Aubrey told Talia the ugly truth of her family.

Of Claudette, who had affairs with dozens of men and women, until she fell in love with a man named Rudy, and the second they began their affair, her skin began to wrinkle.

About Madeline, who loved a man called Loren so deeply that she nearly went mad trying to stay away from him. On the day of their wedding, when they shared their first kiss, she lost nearly all of her teeth.

Talia frowns. She sits farther back in her seat and asks, "Are you shittin' me?"

And I shake my head. "I swear, Talia. I'm telling you the truth."

"But, I don't get it," Talia says. She takes out her phone and I get nervous she's going to leave. So I keep talking.

Aubrey told her the story of Elizabeth next. How she hated every man she met, but fell suddenly and completely in love with a woman named Esperanza after years and years of living alone. She was so enraptured that she didn't even notice when she began losing fistfuls of her curly black hair the second their lips touched.

For Abigail it had happened early—the finding of her love.

She was still in college when she met a boy named Clark, who changed everything. She was young and beautiful until she fell in love, just as they all were. She would have been young and gorgeous forever if she hadn't.

"My mother and my aunt Giselle were the last two Dunn women left," I explain. "When my mother got pregnant with me, Giselle was sure that would be the end of her. But my mother, her name was Josie, she didn't love my father. And so she stayed herself: young and lovelier than ever."

"Until last year," Talia says, really listening now, filling in the part of the story she knows.

"Yeah. Until she met Marquez."

Until then, the Dunn curse had only been a story. That my grandmother, after having a stillborn child, had traded something unimaginable to have children who stayed young and beautiful forever, and how there had been a curse wrapped inside the blessing.

"But with my mom, I saw it happen. Hell, *you* saw it happen."

"She was in love," Talia says, and I nod.

"And so, once they kissed, she began to age quickly . . . almost instantly. And I don't know for sure, because I'm a daughter of a cursed daughter, but I think that's what will happen to me the second I kiss your brother."

"The Dunn women was all beautiful and eternally young. And people was always falling in love with us. The curse only worked its dark magic if we fell in love back."

I jump at the sound of Aunt Gigi's raspy voice, as it fills the room like a thin veil of smoke. It's full of disappointment. It's full of something else, too.

"Aunt Gigi," I say, standing. "I was going to talk to you about it all tomorrow."

Gigi levels Talia with one of her serious stares like I haven't said a word—like I'm not even in the room. "Me and Bree? We the only two left."

Gigi sits down, like she's tired, and starts to peel off her pantyhose. And that's when I realize that my aunt is home hours earlier than she usually is.

"I ain't want us to end up like my sisters," Giselle says simply, sadly. "I thought if I ain't let love take me, you'd be safe."

"But wait, Gi," I say. I look at Gigi more closely and notice a streak of gray in her hair that wasn't there this morning. "What are you doing home?"

Just then, the doorbell rang. Giselle looked at Aubrey, and Aubrey looked at Talia. No one visited the strange, beautiful women—no one but Talia—ever.

The three of them walked to the door together slowly, Giselle still holding her pantyhose in the ball of her loose fist. Aubrey peered through the peephole, while the portraits of all the other Dunn women watched.

Vince was standing there, and everything about him was bronze and beautiful. But just behind him was another man, tall and dark as a shadow, who Aubrey had never seen before. She looked up at Giselle, and there was a kind of gentleness to the expression on her face—a kind of peace. Aubrey thought maybe this man was the reason why.

Aunt Gigi swipes on some red lipstick. She looks at me and winks.

"He betta be worth it," she said, but I can't tell if she's talking about Vince, the love of my life, or this shadow of a man, who is clearly the love of her own.

ALL THE TIME IN THE WORLD

By Charlotte Nicole Davis

You're on your way home from the bus stop when you realize you can stop the rain just by thinking about it.

The weatherman said there would only be a 20 percent chance of scattered showers this afternoon, and you liked those odds. You left your umbrella at home by the door. But now the ankles of your jeans are soaked black and your Steele City East High hoodie hangs heavy as a wet blanket on your shoulders. The water is cold, thinks it's still winter. It drips down your chin, seeps into your socks, wrinkles your fingers and turns them numb. The trig homework in your backpack is probably dissolving into gray paste right about now—maybe there *is* a God.

You wipe the rain out of your eyes, slick it back into your hair. Your mother cried when you came home with a buzz cut last month—you'd had such beautiful hair, she said. Good hair, your grandmother's hair. Weather like this always ruined it. Now it just freezes your bare skull.

You'd put up your hood to keep dry, but you know better. People who look like you have been killed for less.

Fuck this shit, you think, and even the voice inside your head is shivering.

And that's when it happens—the rain stops, drops suspended in the air like the jeweled strands of a beaded curtain.

You blink. Look up at the slate-gray sky. It's not just the rain. Birds are frozen mid-flight. A plane hangs suspended like a bug caught in flypaper. Back on earth, in the trees, the squirrels are still as stone.

You glance around, wondering if anyone else is seeing what you're seeing. But the street's empty. It's just worn-down houses with peeling paint and yellow grass. Some of them have been abandoned, windows boarded up. Others still have signs of life. A bicycle on the lawn, or a basketball on the porch, or a truck in the driveway with a Jesus fish on the back bumper. These houses have pitchers out front to catch the fresh water—once that would have seemed desperate, now it's routine.

Then, as suddenly as it started, the spell is broken. Time starts up once again. The birds and plane resume their flight. The squirrels scatter. The rain falls.

A chill creeps over your skin, and it's not from the weather. You run the rest of the way home.

You are Black, and you have been Black your whole life. But some of your white classmates seem to have only recently noticed.

"Did you see in the news last night about that guy who got shot to death by the National Guard in Springfield?" Emma asks your group at the lunch table the next day. "Just because, he, was, you know . . . Black . . ." She trips over the word, like it's a crack in the sidewalk. Bad luck. ". . . they decided he must be dangerous. That's the second one this week, just in Missouri. It's such bullshit." She shakes her head and sips her iced coffee from a straw. "This isn't who we are."

You and Simone exchange a look. The Look. She's the other Black girl in your grade. A recent transfer. You don't know her well. She lives in your neighborhood, but you never went to the neighborhood school—Steele City West. But now that she's here at East, you have a few mutual friends. She nods at you when you pass in the hallway, meets your black eyes with her brown ones, dips her dimpled chin, lets a brief, knowing smile spread across her honey butter face. Your stomach flutters every time.

"Who are we, then?" Simone asks.

"I don't know, the country that elected Obama and legalized gay marriage?" Emma answers. "Not . . . whatever the hell we've become now."

"Mhm. A shame no one saw it all coming," Simone says dryly. She's finished with her lunch, or this conversation, or both, because she balls up her napkin and stands to take her tray back to the kitchen. You watch her go, your eyes lingering on the curlicue of gold thread stitched across her back pocket.

The others keep talking about Springfield, but you're too

distracted to join them. You can't stop thinking about yesterday, how you made time stop. You're not entirely sure, after sleeping on it, that you didn't imagine the whole thing. That you aren't losing your mind. That was one of the more severe reactions to the Contaminant—psychosis, memory loss, violent mood swings. Other people lost their hair or their fingernails or their teeth. Other people broke out in burning red blisters all over their bodies, or they vomited their insides out. You've been careful not to use the water at home since the story broke, but still, until then, for two years and eight months: you drank poison.

Your stomach churns. You push the vegetable medley around your plate. You aren't close enough to Simone to talk to her about this, and there's no one here who would understand. Steele City East is the good school, the white school. There's no Contaminant poisoning the water in this part of town. There're no blisters splitting these kids' faces. For them, it's just a news story, and not even one of the big ones. There're four different wars to cover, the nationwide emergency instatement of martial law, the ongoing uprising in D.C., the Cat 6 hurricane bearing down on the Gulf Coast. The Contaminant is nothing. It's a footnote crawling across the bottom of the broadcast.

You're only allowed here at East because your dad is one of the custodians. It makes your friends uncomfortable when you mention that, makes them uncomfortable when you talk about the water, makes them uncomfortable when you remind them that you're Black.

So you don't. You need friends. Even in a place like this. Especially.

"Look, you guys are starting shit for no reason," Sophie is saying now. "They didn't shoot that guy because he was Black. They shot him because he was out after curfew."

"Only because his car had broken down. They should've helped him," Emma argues.

"I mean, yeah, it sucks, but laws are laws."

"The curfew didn't even exist two months ago," Trevor mutters. "They're making this shit up as they go."

"That's not the point—" Sophie says.

"What if it had been Jordan?" Emma interrupts then. "Is that all you'd have to say then? 'Laws are laws'?"

What the fuck?

Everyone's looking at you now. You are a butterfly, pinned and squirming. That sick feeling in your stomach swells.

Oh, that's RIGHT, they're realizing. It's in their eyes, like when Dorothy gets to Oz and suddenly sees everything in color. *She's BLACK.*

I don't want to be here, you think.

And then it happens again.

Time stops.

You sit up straight, grinning a little with disbelief as you look around. This can't all be in your head. It's too real. It's as if you've stepped into a photograph. The silence is complete. No chatter from your classmates, no clatter of plastic silverware. The ticking of the clock behind its cage has stopped. Your friends' expressions are frozen, too, Emma's red with embarrassment on Sophie's behalf, Sophie's face set in determination. Trevor looks like he just wants to disappear.

So do you. You stand up, careful not to bump into anyone. You're not sure what would happen if you did. And what will happen when time starts back up again? Will it look like you just vanished into thin air?

Only if you hurry. You don't know how long time will be stopped. Yesterday it had felt like only a minute. You have to document this.

You shake up Sophie's unopened can of Coke, just on principle, sling your backpack over your shoulder, and run out of the cafeteria.

The hallways are filled with students caught on their way to and from lunch, pea-green metal lockers running up and down either side, gleaming white floor tiles reflecting the harsh light overhead. The sound of your footsteps echoes emptily through the silence as you weave between people, filming it all with your phone as you go. That way you can show it to someone later, if you have to. Prove it's not all in your head.

All right, but if it's not in my head, then what the fuck is going on? you wonder. You push open the front doors and continue outside. Flags caught flapping in the wind, cars stalled on the road. The fountain in the courtyard looks like a glass sculpture.

The water, you think, walking over to it. You cut your hand through the spray, watching the drops scatter without falling.

Maybe the Contaminant *does* have something to do with this.

The Contaminant comes from a military lab uptown that dumps its chemical waste in the river. Trace metals, man-made. They haven't even added them to the periodic table yet. You still don't know what, exactly, they're cooking up in there. You don't expect you ever will.

But you know Simone's dad is one of the scientists.

That's how she ended up at Steele City East in the first place—once the story broke about the water, her father was able to pull some strings and get her transferred. You could pay her a visit, maybe. See what she knows. She must know something. More than you, at least.

The spell breaks. Time starts up once again. Your breath catches a little. You glance down at your phone, stop the video. Seven minutes and twenty-three seconds.

You're getting better at this.

You decide to skip the rest of school, spend the afternoon practicing and recording your progress. You take the bus downtown first. It'll be the perfect staging area. The city may be dying—the mall a glittering carcass, the roads cracked like parched earth—but there's still some life left.

You're cautious at first. You bring the cars speeding across an intersection to a halt, but you don't run out into the traffic right away. You don't need them starting back up just in time to flatten you. You also don't want to be seen. But you're start-ing to recognize the subtle changes that come over you when you use this power: a chill across your skin, a humming in your bones, a tingling at the base of your skull that increases the longer you're suspended. You're hoping you'll know when your strength's about to give out, in the same way that, when you're in the weight room, you know when you won't be able to lift another rep.

So you work up your courage and step off the curb, skimming along between the cars, following the broken white line like you're walking a tightrope. Catching it all on camera. Next you duck into the crowded train station and weave between the people. Then you run along the pier, the wood clomping hollowly beneath your feet, and burst through a flock of seagulls. They explode into flight around you, and when you stop time an instant later, it's as if you're caught in the middle of the firework.

You will have plenty of evidence for Simone now.

"I have to go to a friend's house to work on a group project," you tell your mom later that night. You're already shrugging into your jacket, getting ready to walk back out the door. But of course it's not that simple.

"What project? What friend?" she asks, looking up from *NCIS*. She's sitting on the swaybacked couch, in her nightgown and bonnet, sipping tea she made with bottled water. Your family brushes their teeth with bottled water, too; you cook and clean with it. You shower out of a bucket. You have to. The water that comes from the tap runs black and smells like metal.

"It's a history project, and Kristen Bennet," you lie easily.

"Do I know her?"

"Probably not." Because she doesn't exist. "Can I take your car?"

Your mom pauses the show now. "I don't know, Jordan. It's getting late. When will you be back?"

"Before curfew."

"That boy in Springfield—"

"I know."

"Hmm." Your mom eyes you up and down, watching as you hop into your knock-off Timbs. "Don't you have anything nicer to wear?"

You threw away all your "nice" clothes around the same time you cut your hair. It's all baggy jeans and boyfriend shirts now, bought with your own hard-earned money. That way your mom can't say anything about it. Though she does anyway.

"It's fine," you say, and you slip a beanie over your head.

"All right," she sighs. "Text me when you get there."

"I love you," you say, blowing a kiss, and you grab the keys and run out the door.

This seemed like a better idea when you were riding the high of your godlike powers. Now, standing in front of Simone Mitchell's front door, the rain beating down on your umbrella, the glare of the streetlight beating down on your back, you're less sure about this whole thing.

The door swings open on squeaking hinges, and a light-skinned Black man in dress jeans and a sweater stands in the doorway.

"Mr. Mitchell—Dr. Mitchell—hey," you say, fumbling over your own words. "I'm—uh—I'm here for Simone? My name's Jordan Carter. I'm here to help with a project we're working on together at school."

He furrows his brow, looking down at you through his bifocals. "She never mentioned any project to me. She just went up to her room. Simone?"

Shit.

Dr. Mitchell steps aside to let you in. If Simone doesn't play along, you'll be back out in the cold shortly.

She strolls downstairs in pajama pants and the same Steele City East High hoodie you were wearing yesterday. Her thumbs stick out of holes cut into the sleeves, nails painted cherry red. She's pulled her curly black hair into a ponytail, and she's traded her contacts for round, gold-rimmed glasses. She is as dressed down, and as cute, as you've ever seen her.

She's obviously not expecting company.

You weren't expecting to be caught this off guard.

"Jordan?" she asks uncertainly when she sees you, stopping at the bottom stair.

"Hey," you say. Your mouth is suddenly dry. "I'm here to work on the history project? Sorry, I should have reminded you . . ."

"No, it's fine." She smiles. "I should've remembered. Come on upstairs."

"Thanks," you say, relieved. You nod at Dr. Mitchell and

follow her, trying to ignore the way your heart's started jumping in your chest. This isn't exactly how you fantasized about being led to Simone Mitchell's bedroom, but the fact that it's happening at all has you wound up tight.

Focus.

Simone's house is a lot like yours: cleanly but cheaply built, creaking with age. You reach the room at the end of the hallway, and you can tell it's hers by the decorative *S* hanging on the door. Inside, the walls are black, the floor littered with skinny jeans and blouses, the desk cluttered with makeup and hair supplies. A poster of the Paris skyline hangs over her bed. You feel as if you're intruding. Probably you are.

"Sorry it's such a mess. I had no idea you were coming," she says, closing the door behind you. Her smile's gone. She crosses her arms. "You want to tell me what this was about?"

What the fuck were you thinking?

You wet your lips, pull out your phone. "It's, uh, it's kind of hard to explain. But I didn't know who else to go to. I think the Contaminant did something to me, and I figured you might be able to answer my questions because your dad . . . you know . . ."

You give up, show her the video. She sits down on her bed to watch it, gesturing for you to join her. You do, sinking into the mattress, practically sliding into her. Your legs are touching. The smell of her hair conditioner makes your head spin.

Simone doesn't speak as she watches. She furrows her

brow just like her father. You bounce your knee, not sure what to do with yourself while you wait, then stop. You don't want to piss her off.

"You don't have to watch the whole thing," you say finally, your face warming. "There's a lot of videos, and they get pretty long, but . . . it's wild, right? It has to be the Contaminant."

She hands the phone back, shaking her head slowly. "You're fucking with me. You made this with a video editor or something."

"No, swear to God," you say desperately. "The Contaminant messes with people on a genetic level, right? That's what makes it so dangerous, especially long-term. So could it cause something like this?"

"If you're worried about the water, you should go to a doctor." Simone raises a brow. "The way you're talking, maybe you should anyway."

"The doctors don't know much more than we do. You know that. You live . . ." You stop yourself. "I just thought maybe, since your dad works at the lab . . ."

Simone's expression softens. "He's trying to help. That's the only reason he's still there. He and some of the other scientists knew about the Contaminant long before the rest of the world did, but it was nearly impossible for them to get the story out. You can't just show there's pollution in the river—you have to prove it's hurting people."

"But it is." You think of the houses on your street that have been abandoned, the neighbors you've watched grow sick, the protests that gather outside City Hall every Sunday, smaller and smaller as people move away or pass away or simply give up.

Simone looks at you knowingly. "You have to prove it's hurting people they care about."

You sigh. Right.

"It's not even just indifference," she goes on. "It's worse than that. It's like they see this as a good thing." She laughs a little hollowly. "I'm sure they wouldn't think so if they'd realized they were arming Black kids with these kinds of abilities, though. That might get them to stop."

"So you're saying you believe me?"

"I'm saying I want to."

You hesitate, then hold out your hand. Simone looks at it, then looks back up at you.

"Go on, take it," you say, your blood roaring in your ears. "I can prove this is real."

You're not entirely sure this is true. You know, from your experiments, that anything you touch will be lifted out of time with you. But you never tried it with another person. You don't know what will happen.

Simone slips her hand into yours.

It feels like time stops before you even do anything. Just holding her hand has the same effect on you—the rush of excitement, the race of your heart, the sensation that you're the only thing in the world that's real. You try to quell your nervousness enough to concentrate—and then you do it. You stop time.

You can see she feels something, because she gasps. But

it's hard for her to tell in her bedroom that anything has changed.

You have to take her outside. You have to show her the rain.

"Come on," you say, grinning a little. "And don't let go, or it won't work."

She lets you lead her out of the bedroom and down the hall. The first thing she notices is her dog climbing up the stairs, suspended in motion. Then her parents, cleaning the kitchen, arranged like dolls in a house.

"Holy shit," she whispers. Something about the utter lack of sound must compel her to be quiet herself.

"And here you were calling me a liar."

"I never said all that."

You both fall into silence as you make your way through the warmly lit entryway. You can feel Simone's eyes on the back of your neck.

"How come it took this for you to talk to me, Jordan?" she asks softly.

Your face warms. You unlock the front door without turning around.

"We talk," you hedge.

"Not like this. Not about anything real. I can tell you're shy, though, so I tried to leave you alone."

You step onto the front porch. It's chilly outside, and neither of you stopped to grab your coats. You press closer together. The frozen raindrops shimmer before you like fallen stars.

"I just . . . didn't want to force it," you say finally. "There's no reason the two Black girls have to be friends." You laugh a little nervously.

"Well, you seem like you could use a friend." She hesitates. "I didn't mean it like—"

"No," you say. "You're right. I could."

You look up at her, and she's smiling again. Enjoying the perfect stillness of the moment. She leans in and kisses you. Lips soft and sticky-sweet with gloss, the smell of lavender soap on her skin.

Lightning shoots through you. You're so startled you lose your concentration. Time starts back up again, the sudden patter of the rain almost masking her soft laughter. She breaks away.

You can't help a grin of your own. "What was that for?" you ask.

"You trusted me with your secret. I guess I can trust you with mine." She lets go of your hand and nods for you to follow her back inside. "Come on. If you really have questions, you're better off asking my dad himself."

You drive back home through the dark, headlights brown-yellow against the black of the road. You're still buzzing with excitement. You learned from Dr. Mitchell that you're not the only one. He's had several people in the neighborhood reach out to him. There's a ten-year-old Black boy who can move small objects with his mind. A twenty-two-year-old Black woman who can start a fire with a thought. For every thousand people who get sick from the Contaminant, there seems to be one, like you, who gets stronger.

Dr. Mitchell promised not to tell anyone at his job about you without your permission. You know you'll have to tell your parents, though. Your mother was upset enough with your holey jeans. You have no idea how she'll handle this. But you're going to have to make some decisions soon, decisions that might affect your whole family. Do you want to be the first to go public with your powers? Like Simone said, that might be what it takes to get the lab to stop poisoning the neighborhood. But you've seen what happens to people the government decides are dangerous. When you take a risk like that, you have to be ready.

But you have a feeling you'll get there.

As you pull into the driveway, tires crunching over the gravel, your mind drifts back to Simone's knowing smile as you thanked her father and said goodbye. Your kiss is still a delicious secret between the two of you, one you're not ready to share with anyone else. At least not until you've had a chance to savor it yourself first.

There's no hurry, after all. You have all the time in the world.

THE WITCH'S SKIN

By Karen Strong

Another Boo Hag had arrived on Samara Island. The witch only came at night, shedding a stolen skin and shape-shifting into any form she pleased. It was then the witch would select a victim. If you were the unlucky chosen, the Boo Hag would sit on your chest and ride you, stealing your spirit.

But only if you were a man.

It was a fatal theft. Without spirit, the body was only a shell, and the soul withered. Before the sun rose in the sky, the witch's victims were dead.

Now all the houses on Samara Island looked the same. Windows and doors were painted indigo blue to repel the Boo Hag, and the women sought out herbs and root rituals to protect their husbands and sons.

In the bright light of morning, Nalah Everlasting crushed berries in a bowl. After gathering Spanish moss and pine needles to build smoke and keep the mosquitoes away, she had gone into the woods to find a fire beauty, a red-tinged fern with small cream-colored berries. Island folks knew touching a fire beauty's leaves could cause high fever, but the potent juice from the berries did its damage differently. One drop could burn skin down to the bone.

When she finished crushing the berries, Nalah carefully poured the juice into a mason jar and sealed it tight. It was a good defense against the Boo Hag, who couldn't survive long without a stolen skin.

"I done told you to stop that," a voice said behind her.

Nalah flinched and turned to see her mother. She hadn't heard her footsteps, but she never did. It was always as if Tena Everlasting glided on air.

"This is my last one," Nalah said. "Lucy Resby made a special request. To protect her husband."

"If the Hag wants John Resby, she'll take him. Nothing can stop that."

Nalah kept quiet. She knew the Resbys of Shell Bluff had little respect for the Everlastings. The Resbys were members of the ruling Council, descendants of scientists who had come from the Mainland before the Cataclysm. The Council had always looked down on the old ways of the indigenous families of Belle Hammock, dismissing their beliefs as superstition. But now the Council's opinion had changed on that matter.

Seventeen years ago, a Boo Hag had been killed on Carlitta Beach in Belle Hammock, the first in over a century. The Elders often told the story of the witch's demise. Nalah had only been a baby when it happened. In her reign of terror, the witch had taken fourteen spirits. The Defense Guild had found the Boo Hag without a skin, shrunken and withered from the sun. After parading the body on the main road, the Council had burned the witch in a tar cauldron. The smoke should have been an explosion of color, but it never changed. The Elders thought it was very rare, but it only solidified how much the world had changed since the Cataclysm and the appearance of the Veil, an opaque mist that surrounded the island.

Now another Boo Hag had arrived to steal the spirits of men.

On her nights with Malik Sewell, Nalah had never once feared for his life. As the ocean breeze rustled through the palmettos, Nalah and Malik would lie in his boat skin to skin and look at the stars, the mortal danger of the Boo Hag far from both of their minds. It had been a fatal mistake.

She had been a foolish girl, and Nalah vowed never to be one again. It was why she had ventured into the woods to find the fire beauty. She would do her part to protect every wife and mother on Samara Island from the Boo Hag. She would protect them from the heartbreak and loss she knew too well.

Nalah put Lucy Resby's mason jar in her traveling bag. Keenly aware of how her mother watched her, she stiffened and then took a deep breath to calm her nerves.

"After I take this to Shell Bluff, I'm going to see Malik," she said.

Her mother frowned. "You need to let that be. You can't bring him back. What's done is done."

Nalah rubbed her belly and the baby gave a strong kick. "It's not done. Not yet."

Nalah shielded her eyes from the brightness and adjusted her head wrap that proudly displayed her favorite colors, fresh green and bright red. She closed her eyes and tilted her head to let the sun's rays sink into her skin. She was one of the darkest girls on the island, her blue-black hue a trait of the Everlasting bloodline. Right before she was born, her father had sailed off with the Nautical Guild to investigate the Veil, but he had never returned. Island folks told her that she was the spitting image of him, so her face was the only physical memory.

Two ibis birds screeched overhead as Nalah made her way down the main road to Behaven Cemetery. A sleek rover-car slowly passed her, and Nalah scowled at the dust in its wake. It was powered by solar energy, like most things on the island. She couldn't tell by the heavily tinted windows who was in it, but she was sure it was someone from a Council family. Nalah had only been in one once, the frigid air raising gooseflesh all over her skin.

Nalah arrived at the cemetery's iron gates and bowed her head to say grace to the island spirits.

"My name is Nalah Everlasting, daughter of Yem. I mean no disrespect. I'm here to see my love, Malik Sewell."

She waited for a sign. A few moments later, a black cat

appeared from behind one of the tombstones. The luckiest of omens. Nalah smiled and opened the gate.

Walking down the path to Malik's grave, she passed many of the Elders with their unique tombstones. Many were marked with plates, old clocks, or other special objects for blood kin to easily locate them.

Malik's grave was marked by an obelisk. Nalah would have chosen differently, but she hadn't been Malik's wife. Without that official title, she had no claim to his burial rites. She touched the engraved symbols of his Council family crest and traced his name lovingly as the tears fell.

As she wiped her eyes, she glanced around the cemetery to see if she was the only living person among the spirits. When she confirmed that she was, she flipped over a large rock near Malik's grave. Underneath it was a shallow hole, and Nalah retrieved a cloth bag. She unknotted the twine and took a sniff. The strong odor confirmed the winnow's reed and sapelo pepper had grown in potency. Three days ago, she had ground the pepper to a fine powder in the cemetery. Her eyes had watered as the seeds released their essence into the air. The black seeds of the winnow's reed had been harder to grind, the tough shell difficult to crack. Nalah had covered her exertion with mournful cries so that if anyone had heard and came looking, they would only see a young girl crying over a grave.

Nalah would dust the shed skin of the Boo Hag with this spice mix. The sapelo pepper would do the job quickly enough, but Nalah knew the witch was strong. Nalah was too heavy with child and would be no match. It was the reason she had added the winnow's reed. It was a known soothing agent and would slow down the pepper's properties. Enough time for Nalah to escape.

No longer a foolish girl, Nalah had been vigilant and mindful in this preparation. It was a dangerous task with little room for mistakes, but she had no choice but to proceed.

Six months ago, a Boo Hag had arrived on Samara Island. In her reign of terror, the witch had taken eight spirits. Malik Sewell had been one of them.

Nalah lay down in front of his grave. The baby kicked again, and she shed more tears. Malik's body now decayed in the ground, his spirit stolen, his soul perished. The pain of her loss was always present, sunken deep into her bones. Malik was gone, but she had made a vow, and the time had come.

She was going to kill the Boo Hag tonight.

Malik Sewell had been born in the new world but learned the old ways. He could operate the material printer in the underground compound, but he could also weave a net and catch the biggest croakers.

Despite living on opposite sides of Samara Island, Malik hadn't been a stranger to Nalah. She would see him at school and at the weekly market. She watched from afar, curious about the scrawny, light-skinned boy who would come to Carlitta Beach to learn the casting net technique from the Belle Hammock fishermen.

Unlike the other Shell Bluff children, Malik didn't look down on her. Nalah had told him that she welcomed the new ways of technology, but she also wanted to honor the old ways that had been practiced on the island for centuries.

Malik became a friend and confidant. As they grew up together, it became a tradition to go out on his boat in the darkness, snake down the Turpentine River, and venture out into the ocean. They would watch the moonrise and meteors streak across the sky, all within safe distance of the Veil, the starlight making it shimmer like a pearlescent mirror.

Nalah couldn't remember when their friendship had turned into something more. The feelings had been so gradual but also inevitable.

One night, they lay in Malik's boat and he pointed to a moving object that they both knew was a satellite. A relic created before the Cataclysm.

"In the archives, I read they built these ships on the Mainland. Huge ships that ran on fuel and flew up into the atmosphere and into space," he said.

Nalah had also read those same archives. It had been one of the many marvels of the Mainland. But that was before the war known as the Cataclysm. Before the mushroom cloud had appeared in the sky almost two centuries ago. In the aftermath, the scientists from the Mainland created twelve guilds and forged a new beginning on Samara Island. As years passed, the scientists melded with the island lineages, and a different world emerged. Three powerful families from Shell Bluff created the Council, along with new sacred laws.

Nalah stared at the Veil, watching it undulate and pulse as if alive with its own spirit. The Elders had told the story of its appearance. Many years after the Cataclysm, the mysterious mist had surrounded the island. The Elemental Guild had determined the Veil wasn't harmful, but navigational drones could never find landmass beyond it. Nalah wondered if anything or anyone was left beyond its pale tendrils. She wondered if her father had ventured past the thick mist, or if he was forever lost, unable to return. The Council no longer sent scouting parties into the Veil, claiming the excursions were too dangerous.

"Do you think the Mainland still exists?" Nalah asked.

"I don't know," Malik said. "But you shouldn't worry about what lies beyond the Veil. All that matters is that we're together."

Malik took her hand and placed it over his heart. Nalah felt it beat rapidly beneath her fingers, making her own pulse quicken. He slowly put his hand over her heart, which was soft and warm. Their heartbeats synced into a frantic rhythm. Nalah's face flushed as Malik drew closer. She could see him in the moon's glow, the boy she had known for most of her life.

Nalah parted her lips as Malik kissed her gently. He slowly pulled away and watched for her reaction. She drew him back close. He kissed her again, deeper this time, and her stomach fluttered like a thousand butterflies had taken flight. Malik whispered her name, his voice velvet in her ear. The third kiss sparked a tingle that moved down her neck to her torso and low below her navel. She never wanted to stop kissing him. She never wanted to stop feeling the light he brought into her.

Malik Sewell was her sun.

Although Nalah and Malik were fully in love and had claimed each other, they still had to get their union blessed. It was one of Samara Island's sacred laws. All unions had to be approved by the Council.

They had stood in front of Sula Church. Nalah wore a radiant yellow dress and strapped boots. Her mother had oiled and braided her hair, and it shimmered in the sun. Malik was somber in all black, his hair cut low and edged with his Council family crest. His high-collared tunic hid the birthmark that reminded Nalah of a tiny fiddler crab.

Although her skin was still chilled from the icy air of the rover-car, Nalah didn't rub her arms for warmth. Instead she grabbed and squeezed Malik's hand.

When they entered the sanctuary of the church, three men sat at the Judgment Table. One representative from each Council family. John Resby, the High Elder, sat in the middle, and the bulge of his belly strained against his purple tunic. Silas Sewell and William Barnette sat on either side of him, both in red tunics.

"Malik Sewell, you asked for an assembly," Mr. Resby stated. "What is the request?"

"I want . . ." Malik's voice cracked and he paused. "I want a union blessing."

"With this girl?" Mr. Resby's light-skinned face turned red with irritation.

"Who are her people?" Mr. Barnette asked.

"She's the daughter of Yem Everlasting," Mr. Sewell said. "He was in the Nautical Guild. Sailed with the last scouting party into the Veil."

Nalah felt a light flutter in her stomach. Almost like the flip of butterflies when Malik kissed her, but this was something more. The Belle Hammock midwife had called it the quickening. The old woman had also asked why Nalah hadn't prevented the pregnancy in the first place. That morning, she had tried to choose a respectable dress, but she knew no clothing could disguise the baby growing inside her.

"How old are you?" Mr. Barnette asked her.

"I was born in 167," Nalah answered.

"You're seventeen years old," Mr. Sewell said. "Just a year younger than my nephew here. Neither of you has even joined a Guild yet. What is the rush?"

"I love her," Malik said.

"Did you trap this boy?" Mr. Resby glared at Nalah's too-tight dress, and she moved her hands over her belly, protecting the baby from his hostile gaze. He was one of the fairest men on the island, a trait of the Mainland scientist bloodline.

"No," Nalah said. "Never."

"I willingly claim the child she carries," Malik said.

"You have violated sacred law." Mr. Resby pointed angrily at Nalah. "We can't have bastards on this island."

Nalah wanted to laugh. Since its inception, the Council

had forbidden women to hold ruling seats. They had even removed their membership from several of the Guilds, deeming women unqualified. Of course they would only see her at fault. Only see her as the sole violator. She was more than sure the laws that these men, their fathers, and their fathers' fathers had constructed were far from sacred.

Malik clenched his jaw. "Since the child is already claimed, it's already a Sewell and not a bastard. By sacred law."

The men at the table gathered and murmured amongst themselves. After a few moments, they turned to face them. Both Mr. Barnette and Mr. Resby glared at Nalah.

"You have left us with no other option, nephew," Mr. Sewell said. "The Council blesses this union."

Malik swooped Nalah up in his arms and swung her around.

"Mind yourself, boy," Mr. Resby warned.

Nalah giggled as he put her back down and she straightened out her dress. They bowed their heads as a sign of respect.

Now that their union was officially blessed, Nalah could come back to Sula Church as a bride. She wouldn't be able to wear her favorite bright colors in the formal ceremony, but she could still honor the old ways by wearing a nubie charm around her ankle.

When they had made it to the church door, Nalah hesitated and touched the wood, which was cast iron warm. She turned back to the Judgment Table, where the men were still seated.

"All of you will be in my prayers tonight," Nalah stated. "Don't let the Hag ride you."

Nalah never returned to Sula Church as a bride.

After the Boo Hag had stolen Malik's spirit and killed him, Nalah walked the roads of the island north of the Old Mansion ruins all the way south to the Samara Lighthouse. Days, then weeks and months, passed. All through a dark haze, Nalah felt the loss of her love. She would lay her head in her mother's lap and wail until her mother stopped indulging her.

"You need to stop with this mess."

"Don't you miss Daddy?" Nalah wept. "Don't you wonder what happened to him?"

Nalah always wondered why she had never seen her mother cry. Maybe she had shed all her tears when Nalah was a baby.

"Crying won't change nothing," her mother said. "What's done is done."

Nalah tried her best to recover from the intense grief but found that she couldn't. The Sewell family in Shell Bluff paid little attention to her although she carried their blood kin, their disdain for her Everlasting lineage now apparent since Malik's death. She was also ignored by the Elders in Belle Hammock, since she'd disregarded their warnings about getting involved with a Council boy. She spent her days as she did her nights, mourning Malik and the reality of her life. All the while, the Boo Hag continued her reign of terror, stealing the spirits of men.

Nalah was at her lowest point when she felt the first kick of her baby, a reminder that even though Malik was gone, a part of him was still with her. The sadness slowly began to lighten.

Four months after Malik's death, Nalah stood in the kitchen late at night, drinking deep sips of well water. She stared out into the darkness and spotted her mother venturing into the woods without a solar lantern. Nalah hadn't heard her leave the house. She put down her drink and decided to follow her.

It was difficult following her mother in the dim starlight. She had ventured past the marsh and moved deeper inland to the part of the woods where island folks warned of the jack-o'-lantern. Following this ball of light could get you hopelessly lost in the wilderness surrounding Belle Hammock. Nalah had never seen this light, but now she was wary.

She tentatively followed until her mother stopped in an open area covered with resurrection ferns. Nalah hid behind a live oak, and its Spanish moss grazed her shoulders.

Her mother stripped naked and heat rose up from the ground, the smell of sulfur heavy in the air. Sweat appeared on Nalah's forehead. Her mother raised her arms and chanted in an ancient tongue. Suddenly, her skin split open down her spine, revealing red tendons and blue veins. As her mother stepped out of her skin, a translucent slime dribbled down her arms and lingered on the tip of her fingers like molasses.

The baby violently kicked in Nalah's belly, and she covered her mouth to stifle a cry. The Boo Hag sniffed the air, and Nalah wondered if she smelled her presence. But then the witch quickly wrapped up Tena Everlasting's skin and hid it in the ferns. She changed form into a large buzzard and took flight. The wind of her movement rustled the nearby cypress trees. A feral cry screeched above Nalah, and she shuddered.

The witch had been wearing Tena Everlasting's skin. A new Boo Hag hadn't arrived on Samara Island: the witch had been here all along. It had been her mother that the Defense Guild had found on Carlitta Beach, shrunken and unrecognizable. It had been Tena Everlasting who had burned in the tar cauldron.

Nalah's mother had been dead for seventeen years.

Nalah slid down the live oak's trunk to the ground. Her vision blurred with black spots. Her tears burned hot with anger. The Boo Hag had brought terror to the island. The witch had even taken what Nalah had never known to miss. The Boo Hag had killed her mother and stolen her skin.

The baby kicked again, and Nalah thought of Malik. The Boo Hag had ripped him from her life. The father of her child. Her love. Her sun. The witch had created a darkness of loss in her heart.

Nalah rose from the ground, hatred running thick through her veins. She knew what she must do. She made a vow, one she intended to keep. Even if it was the last thing she ever did.

Nalah would kill the Boo Hag, the witch who had taken everything.

In Behaven Cemetery, Nalah lay still in front of Malik's grave. The day was fading, and soon the time would come to fulfill her vow and kill the witch. She packed the spice mix of sapelo pepper and winnow's reed and put it in her traveling bag. Nalah would wait until dusk-dark, when the Boo Hag would venture out for her next victim.

When night approached, Nalah walked down the main road. When she heard the chilling cry of the buzzard overhead, she traveled through the woods to the same spot where she had first followed the Boo Hag three nights ago.

Nalah sat on the ground among the resurrection ferns with her mother's skin. She had dusted it with the spice mix and shook the skin in the bag like she was getting ready for a fish fry. Right now, the Boo Hag was on the prowl, selecting a victim to ride, taking an unlucky spirit for her own. One of the most recent victims was William Barnette, one of the Elders who had begrudgingly given her and Malik the Council's union blessing at Sula Church. So far, all the men had been from the Council families of Shell Bluff.

Bitterness seeped into the back of Nalah's throat, and the familiar heat of anger rose up her arms and into her face. The Boo Hag had stolen Malik's spirit. She had killed her mother. Nalah had been living a lie all of her life. This morning, she had wanted to throw the fire beauty juice at the Boo Hag. She had wanted the witch's skin to burn. It had taken Nalah's total strength to keep her from destroying the witch, but she wasn't a foolish girl anymore. The Boo Hag would have killed her, stolen her skin, and taken her baby. Then the witch's charade would have started all over again.

After falling asleep among the resurrection ferns, Nalah quickly jerked up when she heard the rustle of wind and heavy footsteps. The Boo Hag appeared and shimmered in the moonlight. Slimed with blood, her muscles and blue veins bulged full of spirit. The witch's eyes were wide sockets of blackness. The Boo Hag was in her true form, no longer wearing Tena Everlasting's skin.

"You dare cross my path, girl?" the witch hissed.

"I found this." Nalah raised the bag that contained her mother's skin.

"Mighty fine prize. You bold to be holding that." The Boo Hag crooked her neck, and blood dripped down her chin. "Now, you weren't fool enough to meddle with that skin? No need for all of us to be dead on this night."

"I'm no fool. I can't run from you," Nalah said. "Look at me."

"You bound to give that baby up any day now. That's true enough," the witch said. "Besides, you know I have no quarrel with you."

"You stole my mama's skin!" Nalah blurted out in anger. "You left her on Carlitta Beach. You let them parade her down the roads like a dead dog. You let them burn her."

"Your mama was weak," the witch spat. "I found her crying about your daddy. She begged me to take her life."

Nalah took a breath. "You lie."

"I didn't even know she had a baby until I found you," the witch said. "That's when I decided to hold off on my ways and love you."

"How could you love me when you killed Malik?" Nalah cried.

"You think I was gonna let him take you away from me? You're mine, and your child is mine." The witch raised her hands, and the trees whipped in the wind.

"I'm not yours," Nalah said. "I was never yours."

Small pinpricks of light appeared in the black, empty sockets of the witch's eyes. "I don't have time to play with you, girl. Time's a-wasting."

If Nalah kept the witch out of her skin until morning, the witch would burn. But she also knew the Boo Hag would kill her before that happened.

"Who did you take tonight?" Nalah asked.

"Why do you care? I do a favor every time I take a man's breath." The Boo Hag pumped her chest, and a splatter of blood hit the ground. "I done took care of John Resby. His fancy wife, Lucy, will find him dead soon."

The night sky continued to lighten. Morning was coming, but not fast enough.

"Why did you come here?" Nalah asked. "Why do you terrorize this island?"

"I ain't the one you should fear. Greater monsters roaming here," the witch said. "I think the time has come for you to know the truth."

Nalah was caught off guard by the Boo Hag's statement. She knew they were clever, and she didn't know what angle the witch was playing.

"What are you talking about?"

"The Veil. It's a lie. The Council men created that mist."

"That's not true," Nalah said. "The guilds are studying it and trying to find answers."

"You sure about that, girl? No skin off my back if you don't believe me." The witch chuckled.

"There was a war on the Mainland. The Cataclysm . . ." Nalah faltered, now unsure of the Elder stories and what she had read in the archives. Why would the Council want to hide from the Mainland? It had now been almost two centuries since the Cataclysm. Could Samara Island be that easily forgotten?

The Boo Hag moved closer, and the cloying smell of sulfur made Nalah cough.

"The men on this island are the reason I came here," the witch said. "They want to be kings and make up their own rules. Even your Malik. He knew about the Veil."

"I don't believe you," Nalah said.

"I can see right now we ain't gonna be the same no more," the Boo Hag said. "You go on into that mist. You and the baby. Better life waiting for you there."

Nalah looked above the witch's head. The night was continuing to fade. The Boo Hag's time was almost up.

"You're trying to trick me," Nalah said.

"Give me that skin, girl. Go on into the mist. Leave me here to feast on the men. Take your baby and leave."

Spirals of pink appeared in the sky, and a bird chirped a short staccato note. The Boo Hag may have been telling the truth. The Council had only grown more restrictive. With the technology left by the Mainland scientists, the Council had the means to create the Veil. What better way to claim power? What better way to control than with fear?

The Boo Hag had taken the spirits of men who had shrouded

Samara Island from the outside world. Men who had created the fallacy of the Veil. If this was the truth, maybe these men deserved their fate. Maybe even Malik. But her mother didn't deserve her fate. The witch had killed Tena Everlasting for her skin. The Boo Hag had given Nalah seventeen years of lies. Nalah hadn't forgotten. She had made a vow. One she intended to keep.

She threw the bag in front of the witch, and the Boo Hag scrambled onto her arms and legs, crouching down like a crab. Then the witch shrunk to the size of a small cat and scuttled inside the bag. Nalah watched as the witch shimmied out and rose tall, wearing her mother's skin.

The Boo Hag stretched her limbs. "What's done is done. You grown now. I told you about the Veil. Now you should leave."

Nalah stared at the witch. "You could be lying to me."

"I ain't lying." The witch pointed a finger at her. "But heed this: I'm going back to the house. If you return, you will regret it."

The Boo Hag slowly walked out of the clearing. The blood and gore disappeared from the resurrection ferns. The only evidence left was the bag that had held her mother's skin.

Nalah stood still for several moments. Soon the winnow's reed's soothing properties would wear off, and the sapelo pepper would burn the witch from the inside out. Nalah needed to get far away from this place in case the Boo Hag was stronger than she thought. She knew that if the witch caught her she would be as good as dead.

She rushed out of the woods to the dirt path that led to the Turpentine River. A path she knew well from all of her nights before, when she had followed Malik to his boat. When she reached the landing, it was still there, bobbing in the water. She climbed in, took the oars, and navigated down the river.

Noises soon traveled through the trees, and Nalah heard an agonized scream. She turned and saw several sparks shoot up in the sky. An explosion of color. Fresh green, bright red, and radiant yellow. The sapelo pepper had made its mark on the witch's skin. The Boo Hag was burning.

Nalah ventured to the mouth of the river and into the ocean. She kept rowing until she made it to the edge of the Veil. The mist curled around her, silvery and mysterious.

Lying down in Malik's boat, Nalah could no longer see the sky, only the pearly whiteness of the Veil. It wasn't too late to turn around. The Boo Hag was dead. Nalah could return home. But now she no longer had any family. Malik was gone. Both of the island communities had shunned her. What kind of life would she have under the Council's oppressive rule?

She placed one hand over her heart. If the witch was right, Nalah and her baby were going to a better place. It could be the truth or a lie. But it no longer mattered. There was nothing left for them on Samara Island.

Nalah took a deep breath, closed her eyes, and waited for what came next.

SEQUENCE

By J. Marcelle Corrie

A.

I didn't know how anyone could be this perfect.

Margot stood near the pool surrounded by all of her friends, or really anyone who wanted to be like her. As usual, she had a group of people around her, attracted by her infectious smile and the way she made people feel. As if they'd always find a friend in her, one who wouldn't judge or blame. Someone who'd remain by their side.

Just watching her from across the dome made me want to be closer to her. The way I had always imagined.

"Hello? Eden?"

Lily waved her hand in my face, her purple cuff clanking against her bracelets. Her button nose was scrunched up in that way that made her look too cute to be that upset with me. It was hard to take her that seriously because of it.

"Are you even listening to me?" She crossed her arms,

waiting for me to convince her that I heard every word she just said. But truth was that I didn't. I was too distracted by the way Margot's hair floated in the air, the nape of her neck exposed every few seconds.

"Sorry, I was just thinking about . . . something."

"Daydreaming as usual, huh?" Forrest tapped her finger against her cuff. She wasn't even looking at me as her cuff beeped, alerting her that her message was sent. "It's fine, you didn't miss much."

Lily groaned. "Do I have to start over again?"

"I think Eden can keep up." A hologram popped up from Forrest's cuff. Another advertisement to upgrade Society's system software. She deleted it. "Your stories don't require that much thought to put together."

Lily glared at Forrest, who just continued to scroll through her messages.

"Anyway, have you tried it?" Lily asked.

"Tried what?"

"Sequence, Eden." Lily rolled her eyes. "You really weren't listening, were you? Too busy staring at Travis?"

I couldn't even begin to understand what that meant until I followed Lily's gaze to the pool house. Margot was still there with her friends, but a group of guys circled them now, Travis at the center, preparing to do something obnoxious, I was sure. He pulled up the hem of his shirt to show off a six-pack he claimed to have. I turned away before he started flexing his muscles. I still didn't understand how someone so basic could gain that much attention.

"You know I don't like that guy."

"Whatever you say, Eden." She smirked. "But I see the way you're looking at him, and looks don't lie, girl."

I glanced over my shoulder again. Boy, was she wrong about that. Not that she'd ever believe me. In her head, Travis would always be my match, for a reason she'd never explained. She just always "had a feeling," whatever that meant.

And even if I told her I liked Margot (and she actually believed it), the entire district would find out before I got the chance to tell Margot. Not the way I'd want that to go. Lily's mouth was just too big to keep that kind of secret. And Forrest, well, I'm not sure she'd even care.

"Like I was saying, everything played out the way Sequence said it would. It was like one hundred percent accurate."

Forrest glanced up from her messages. "How can a program predict how your life will play out that accurately?"

"It just does, Forrest. It's technology." Lily made a face at her. "That's like asking me to explain how our holograms work. Do I look like a scientist to you?"

Forrest looked over her dark triangular shades, giving Lily's purple ensemble and her matching purple cuff a once-over. She pushed her shades back up. "Do you really want me to answer that question?"

"It was rhetorical, Forrest." Lily stroked her long braided ponytail, her brown skin shimmering in the light. "Anyway, I asked if I should stay home and study, but my Sequence showed me that even if I studied for that test tomorrow, I'd still get the same grade." She shrugged her shoulders.

"So you wasted your credits on a question like that?"

"I didn't waste my credits. I needed to know how to better spend my time."

Forrest grabbed her cup from the table beside us. "But Sequence is just a glorified Magic Eight Ball." After taking a sip, she placed her cup on one of the servers' trays as they strolled by. She nodded at them before they collected more abandoned glasses. "I mean, why can't people just trust their judgment rather than rely on some machine? It can't be that accurate."

"Well, maybe some people want another opinion, or maybe they want to stay in line with the life Society projected for them, so they don't get in trouble. It's not like everyone has everything figured out," Lily said. "And my Sequence even showed us having this conversation, so I'd say that's pretty accurate. Just look."

Lily held her arm in front of us as a hologram materialized. A few kids looked over at the bright light shining from her cuff until they lost interest. I stepped beside her so I could see everything.

After a few seconds, a home screen appeared in front of us, the word SEQUENCE at the top. Through the hologram was the city, streaks of purple and blue lights wrapped around the buildings in the distance. Our glass dome was nestled in the mountains and surrounded by nothing but trees, but the darkness right outside the dome helped us see the hologram better.

Lily tapped her cuff, the screen morphing into two videos: one labeled "A" and the other labeled "B." They both started to play at the same time.

"We're even wearing the exact same clothes," she said, pointing to video B. Sure enough, there we were, huddled together while everyone else mingled around us, separating and morphing into different groups. Servers walked by with trays full of hors d'oeuvres and drinks while people danced near the pool. Video A showed Lily at her desk, her books open, her notebook empty, and her attention all on her hologram feed, scrolling through pictures and videos posted from this very party.

No wonder she decided to come here instead.

Forrest narrowed her eyes. "So your Sequence told you that you would've just looked through your feed instead of actually studying."

"Well, at the end of each Sequence, it showed that I'd get a B on the test either way," Lily said. "So there was no point in staying home to study."

"We could've just told you that, Lily." Forrest swiped two shrimp puffs as a server glided by. She ate one, sliding the toothpick from between her lips. "And Sequence isn't one hundred percent accurate." Forrest pointed to her ear in the frame with her toothpick. "Those are studs. I'm wearing hoops."

I looked at the video more closely. It did show her wearing studs.

"And there's someone in the pool in your video and no one's—"

We heard a splash behind us. Travis laughed from the side of the pool as his friend's head surfaced, bobbing up and down in the water. After a few seconds, Travis took off his shirt and jumped in, splashing everyone around them.

Forrest turned back around. "Your Sequence still only shows one person in the pool."

Lily closed her hologram. "Really, Forrest? That's not even the point."

Forrest just shrugged, chewing on the second shrimp puff.

"The point is Sequence knows how everything will turn out. People use it to choose which college they'll go to, what to study, where to move. It's helped so many people choose the best possible outcome for their lives." Lily looked around for a moment. Then she leaned in. "Simi's mom used Sequence to decide if she should get a divorce."

I stepped back. "We really didn't need to know that."

"Oh, please. Everyone in the district knows this, and they're still together anyway. Otherwise Simi wouldn't be throwing this party." Lily shrugged. "But still, wouldn't you want to try it if you had to make a tough decision?"

Forrest looked at me. That question wasn't for her, I guess.

I glanced over my shoulder at the pool house. Margot was still with her friends, sitting on a lawn chair. Travis sat beside her, a towel draped over his shoulders and his arm draped over her shoulder. I turned back to Lily and shrugged. "If I had a tough choice to make, I guess I would."

Lily jumped up and down, her blond ponytail swinging from side to side. She squealed, her hazel eyes bright. "Tell me! What would you ask Sequence?"

I looked at her as if I'd been caught in a lie. "I—I don't know—"

"What would Eden have to ask Sequence that she doesn't already know?" Forrest clasped my shoulder and squeezed it. "Honestly, you've had your life figured out since the day I met you, and you still haven't veered in any other direction. You're pretty predictable."

"So I'm boring is what you're saying," I said.

Forrest opened her mouth to say something, but decided to shove more hors d'oeuvres down her throat instead. "Not boring, just predictable," she said with her mouth full.

"I'm sure there's a question everyone would like to ask." Lily pointed at Forrest's head. "Maybe I'll ask Sequence if you'd lighten up once we loosened those bantu knots of yours."

"Respect the knots, okay?" Forrest checked her white lipstick in her mirror, then patted her knots to make sure none had unraveled. They were all still in place, as was the rest of her white outfit. She unzipped her jacket. "I'm going to get another drink." She gazed around for a server. "I wonder if your Sequence predicted me making my exit." Forrest strolled away, giving us a twirl before heading inside.

Once she was out of earshot, Lily turned to me. "Joke's on her, because it actually did." She laughed before she looked at her messages.

I stole a quick glimpse of Margot and Travis still sitting together. He moved closer to her, their legs touching, his lips against her ear. Lily cleared her throat.

"Maybe you can ask Sequence if Travis likes you." She arched her eyebrow and pursed her lips.

Still wrong, but she wasn't going to let it go. Because I'd never shown interest in a guy before. So she'd latch on to any prospects at this point.

"Maybe he'll take you out on a date, or you'll head to university together," she said, looking up at the stars above the dome, "or maybe you'll get married, and have kids . . ."

"Lily, that's not—"

She gasped. "You'd make the most gorgeous babies . . . then I'll be an auntie!" Lily went on as I looked at my empty cup on the table, trying to focus on something other than what was going on across the pool. But I couldn't help it.

I could tell Travis laughed at everything she said, in an attempt to flirt with her. Margot, as gracious as she was, would return everything he said with a warm smile, her dark eyes engaged, despite the corny story I'm sure he was sharing. She started to look around, probably for a way out of the conversation, until her eyes landed on me. I looked away.

"Are you zoning out again?"

"I'll be right back." Before she could protest, I slipped past Lily and jogged toward the back door. There were more people huddled inside, holding drinks and plates of food, and playing simulation games in the den. I circled the kitchen island, trying to figure out what to do next, when I saw my reflection in the surface of the oven, my eyeliner smudged and my lipstick smeared around my lips.

This was exactly why Lily shouldn't do my makeup.

I grabbed a tissue from my bag, rubbing it against my face. Did Margot see this mess? Why didn't Lily or Forrest tell me I looked like this?

When the makeup wasn't coming off, I walked around to find the bathroom. Of course there was a line, so I washed my face over the kitchen sink. After rubbing my face for what seemed like forever, I looked even more like a mess.

"Are you okay?"

I looked over my shoulder to see Margot gazing at me. She narrowed her eyes at me as I peered over to check my reflection again. I froze.

After what felt like a lifetime, I finally squeaked out a reply. "Uh, yeah. I'm fine." I turned away, looking for another way out. *I'm blowing this. I'm really blowing this.*

"Are you sure?"

I nodded. "Yup, I'm sure." I headed toward the sliding glass doors to escape, but Margot stood in the way. I kept my eyes on the floor. I didn't want her to see this disaster of a face up close.

"I have makeup wipes if you need them." She dug her hand inside her clutch and pulled out a packet. She opened the lid. "Take as many as you need."

At first I hesitated, wondering if she thought I was as pathetic as I looked. I didn't want her to see me this way. She was supposed to see me at my best, when I was able to muster up enough confidence to tell her that I liked her. Instead I just took a sheet, wiping the makeup off my face.

Margot smiled. "Don't worry. You still look cute, Eden."

I almost froze again. Margot shut the lid, shoving the wipes back into her clutch. "See you around?"

"Uh, yeah." My mind raced, trying to figure out what that meant. Maybe she was saying that just to be nice. Maybe she really meant it? "Wait!" I blurted, cursing myself for the loud outburst.

She just looked at me, waiting for me to continue.

Crap. I had to say something.

"Um, I . . . I think . . ." I gazed over at the pool through the sliding glass doors. Travis was still standing there, but this time with his friends. Probably telling them he had Margot in the bag. "Travis seems really into you."

I immediately shut my eyes and sighed. That was literally the worst thing I could've said.

Margot just crossed her arms and smirked. Her cuff was gold, fitting seamlessly with her black dress. "A few people told me that. But he's not really my type." She pushed the door open. "Thanks for the heads-up, though."

As soon as she shut the door, I cursed under my breath. This was the way she was going to remember me.

I blew it.

My cuff lit up, a message from Lily waiting for me. After I pressed the key, a photo of her with Travis in the background popped up.

Lily: Someone's waiting to meet you . . .

I clutched my cuff and took a deep breath. She'd been

waiting to play matchmaker all day. After smoothing out my shirt and checking my reflection in the oven one last time, I stepped back outside to see Lily waving me over as if she were directing air traffic. I glanced over at Travis beside her.

This was going to be a long night of playing pretend.

Sequence headquarters was a lot smaller than I thought it'd be.

It was definitely sleek, spotless, impeccable; I could even see my reflection in the white marble walls. The curved sculpture at the center of the room mirrored the curves and bends in the furniture. Other than the receptionist, the waiting room was empty. According to her I came in at a quiet time.

After looking through their brochure for the seventh time, I wondered if I shouldn't have kept this from Lily and Forrest. This was the type of procedure I'd share with someone in case I needed support or if I was having second thoughts. Someone who'd know what to do if anything went wrong.

Maybe I shouldn't be here.

Did I really need this? My parents had my life planned since the moment I was born. I was meant to follow the footsteps of my mother—graduate from her alma mater, become an accountant, have two kids, grow old with my future husband beside me. That's the life that was assigned to me, and my parents made sure I always stayed on track. To maintain Society's orders.

But what if I wanted something different? What if I veered

from the path that was assigned to me? What would Society do to someone like me?

"Eden?"

I looked up. My assigned specialist, Dr. Nadeen, stood in front of a narrow hallway. She lifted her arm in the direction of the hall, her white cuff matching her lab coat. "Ready for round two?"

The specialist led me into a bright room, gesturing toward the chair at the center. Her assistant sat on a stool next to the equipment, a welcoming smile on her face.

I eased down, careful not to step on the wires gathered around the base of the chair, leading into a hole in the back wall. When I was settled, the assistant measured my pulse.

"How are you feeling, Eden?" Dr. Nadeen asked from the other side of the room. She was facing the wall, tapping at the surface where a hologram had appeared. All I could see was the angular pattern on the back of her shaved head.

The assistant placed small, circular pads on my temples and my arms, connecting them to wires. I gripped the armrest, my nails digging into the fabric. "I feel fine."

Dr. Nadeen closed the hologram and turned toward me. "Would you like me to go through the process for you again?"

I glanced at her, afraid to move my head in case the wires were to snap. I barely heard her voice above the thoughts tangled in my head. And hearing the process again would only put my nerves more on edge.

"No, I think I'm ready."

Dr. Nadeen nodded. "If you feel uncomfortable at any point, just let me know."

After plugging wires into my cuff, the assistant gave Dr. Nadeen a cue. The lights shut off, the room so dark I couldn't see my hands on the armrests in front of me.

A few seconds later, an icon appeared, a voice welcoming me to Sequence. I stared at the icon as it flashed across the screen, processing my information.

My name appeared. Then the question I wanted Sequence to answer:

Should I tell Margot that I like her?

I shut my eyes, scared to see how my life would play out—this time if I followed through. This time if I told Margot how I really felt about her.

How would she react when I told her? What if everyone else found out? Was I really ready to tell everyone? Was I ready for the reactions that'd be hurled at me? From Margot, from Forrest or Lily, from everyone who expected different of me?

Was I overthinking this?

When I heard the sound of glasses clinking, people chatting, and music pumping, I opened my eyes, my life playing out in front of me.

B.

I opened the sliding glass door and stepped into Simi's backyard. The city shined brightly in the distance as party guests huddled in circles, safely enclosed in the private terrarium. Servers walked past me with trays full of hors d'oeuvres, and I saw Lily waving at me. Forrest stood beside her, smirking in her bright white lipstick.

"Where've you been? We've been looking all over for you!" Lily nudged her head over at the pool house, where Travis stood talking to Margot. "It's almost time for you to make your move," she whispered. Forrest just shook her head and rolled her eyes, scrolling through messages from her white cuff.

I cleared my throat. "I just had to freshen up."

"Sure you did." Lily winked at me. "Anyway, I was just showing Forrest something. You have to see it!"

"You mean that program that predicts how your future will turn out based on the decisions you make?" An advertisement popped up in the air from Forrest's cuff. She deleted it before checking if her studs were still in her ears. It was a habit of hers, since she was prone to losing them. "It's just a glorified Magic Eight Ball."

"It is not, Forrest." Lily flipped her braided ponytail over her shoulder. "Do you always have to be a cynic?"

Forrest glanced at her before getting back to her messages. "I'll treat that as a rhetorical question."

"Wait, what did you show Forrest?" I asked, interrupting their usual banter. Once she realized I was still standing there, Lily stopped and turned to me, her scowl instantly morphing into a smile.

"I was showing her my Sequence!"

Forrest nodded, adjusting the zipper on her jacket. "Yeah, watching Lily's life decisions play out has been super eye-opening."

"People have used Sequence when they've had to make life-changing decisions, Forrest."

"You mean like your life-changing decision of whether to study or go to this party?"

Lily rolled her eyes. "Anyway, would *you* try Sequence, Eden?"

"Why would Eden waste her credits on crap like that?" Forrest interrupted.

They went back and forth while I watched everyone around us, the crowd dancing at the far end of the dome, the groups gathered around the empty pool and the pool house. My eyes landed on Margot as she continued to talk to Travis. They had moved to an area away from their lingering friends to talk. Their conversation couldn't have been anything good, considering how obnoxious Travis could be. Margot was the type who'd see right through his act.

Lily stepped into my line of vision. "Hello? Eden? Are you even paying attention to me?"

"Sorry, what?"

She crossed her arms over her purple blazer, a smug smirk at the edge of her lips. "Too busy looking at Travis, huh?"

I exhaled. "Sure, Lily." I glanced across the pool again, my eyes on Margot. "I'll be right back. I need to talk to Margot."

"Margot?" Lily narrowed her eyes. "Why?"

I hesitated for a moment while Forrest and Lily watched me. I shrugged, hoping I could play it off. "I just have to ask her a question. I'll tell you later."

Before either one of them could respond, I strolled around the pool, slipping past others just to get near the pool house. My heart started to pound out of my chest the closer I got to Margot. I still didn't know exactly what I wanted to say. But I knew I wasn't going to leave until I told her how I felt about her.

I stepped from behind Travis, who was bragging about how many credits he had. Margot didn't look impressed, but she did look grateful that my presence interrupted him.

"Hey, Margot." I glanced at Travis for a second. "Travis."

He narrowed his eyes at me. "Hey . . . who are you?"

"Eden." I looked back over at Margot, a piece of her hair hanging in front of her face. She pushed her long hair over her shoulder, the Z pattern of her strands more noticeable in the light. Her gold necklace shined, matching her metallic gold cuff. She pulled at the sleeves of her black turtleneck and adjusted the band of her tight skirt. "Can I talk to you for a second?"

Margot nodded, looking as if I'd saved her from a lifetime of boredom. She followed me behind the pool house, where we had a full view of the city and the cluster of trees on the mountains beside us. There were other terrariums in the mountains around us, some dark, some illuminated. We gazed at the purple lights circling the city, when Margot nudged me.

"Thanks for saving me. I wasn't sure how I was going to get out of there."

I smiled. "Anytime. He can be a little—"

"Annoying, overbearing, and arrogant?" she said. "I don't understand how so many girls like him."

I shrugged, gazing down at the dome beneath us. "Me neither."

The music seemed to get louder, filling the silence between us as we looked beyond the glass. After a few moments, Margot leaned her back against the glass and crossed her arms. "So since when do you go out, Eden?"

"What do you mean?"

"Well, the Eden I know wouldn't be wasting her time here, having to endure meaningless small talk while going through the motions of trying to impress everyone." Her gold cuff lit up, but she ignored it. "I'm just shocked to see you here."

I looked at her dark-brown eyes. "I go out sometimes."

"Since when?"

"Since now." I smiled. "Things change."

"I guess so." She glanced back out into the distance. "So what did you want to talk about?"

My heart started to pound again as I bit my bottom lip. I heard a splash behind us, followed by some yelling and laughing. Margot didn't seem distracted by it, her focus set on me while she waited for an answer.

I still didn't know how I was going to tell her. I still didn't know what she'd think of me after I told her. But all I wanted to do was tell her how I felt.

I exhaled. "I really like you."

Her eyes shifted to me. I could tell she wasn't expecting me to say that. "What do you mean?"

I clasped my hands together, looking out at the trees around us as if they'd give me strength. "That I . . . really like you."

"Oh." Margot looked down at her cuff as it blinked. The music seemed to echo everywhere. "I don't know what to say—"

"I'm not looking for an answer about whether you'd . . . want to go out with me or anything," I said. "I just wanted to tell you—"

"I understand." Margot nodded, taking a step back. She clutched her arm.

My heart started to sink. Maybe I shouldn't have said anything.

Margot glanced at her cuff. She didn't say a word.

I definitely shouldn't have said anything.

She scratched the back of her head, the silence between us growing with every second until she spoke up again. "Sorry, I just . . . didn't see this coming in my Sequence . . . So I don't know what to say."

I looked down at the grass. As far as I knew, this was over. "So you've tried Sequence, too?"

"To stay in accordance with Society's life plan for me."

She shrugged. "That's what the elders in my family tell me, anyway."

"Me too." Even though this exchange wasn't going the way I'd hoped, I still managed to give her a smile. As low as I was starting to feel.

She held up her gold cuff, waiting for me to do the same. "So you'll call me?"

"What?" I gazed up at her. She just chuckled.

"Will you call me? I need your information." She pointed to her cuff. "You know . . . so we can get together."

I didn't believe what I was hearing until she waved her arm to get my attention. I lifted my arm, my heart pounding out of my chest. A band of green light shined around my black cuff once our information synced. "I'll call you."

Margot leaned over and kissed me on the cheek. My entire face grew warm as she strolled back to her circle.

"Can't wait."

Even after the assistant peeled those pads off my skin, it still felt like they were all over my body.

I rubbed my arms as I stood in the train station, waiting for my train to arrive. My cuff lit up, the message I'd been waiting for sitting in my inbox. Before I left, Dr. Nadeen told me I'd receive a copy of my Sequence by the time I got home, but I didn't think it'd be this fast, considering I just left the office five minutes ago.

My cuff lit up again. This time a message from Lily.

Lily: Are you still coming to Simi's party tonight?
I have to tell you about Sequence!

I gazed at the message, thinking of what to send back.

Eden: Will Margot be there?

The train pulled up as I hid my hologram, my cuff lighting up when I received another message from Lily.

Lily: I think so. Why?

When the train doors opened, I stood aside, letting everyone file out. I grabbed a seat in the corner of the car after the doors closed, the automated voice stating the next station. Seconds later, the train glided over the glowing blue tracks, leaving the brightness of the city, into the lush mountainside.

My last Sequence ran through my head over and over again.

I sent a message back.

Eden: I just need to talk to her.

Eden: That's all.

A NOTE FROM THE EDITOR

It's not every day you get to work with such an incredible group of authors on such an incredible book. What I love about this collection of stories is that, while all are fictional, some are pulled from and inspired by real life events, settings, and cultures. For instance, Dhonielle Clayton's story is steeped in Southern folk magic, and Karen Strong's is based around the Gullah/Geechee myth of a Boo Hag—an evil haint who goes around stealing a victim's life breath. And, the setting is inspired by the Georgia Sea Islands, specifically Sapelo Island, which is significant because Karen is Georgia born and raised *and* it's a community that has kept so much of its culture; nearly all of Sapelo's residents are direct descendants of enslaved West Africans.

Then there's Elizabeth Acevedo's tale, set on the eve of the first major slave revolt in the Americas in 1522. Was actual magic used? That's up to Elizabeth's interpretation. But there *was* a revolt in Santo Domingo, where enslaved people led an uprising on the sugar plantation of Admiral Don Diego Colón, son of Christopher Columbus. Many of them escaped to the mountains, where they formed independent communities.

It was such fun to work with these authors, to learn about what inspires them. Rebecca Roanhorse was influenced by the lives of African Americans in New Mexico and the West. The first element of her story comes from the legendary Mary Fields, also known as Stagecoach Mary: a pioneering mail carrier and notorious brawler, who took absolutely no bull from anyone. The second element draws from what is presently known about the all-Black settlement of Blackdom Township, Roswell, New Mexico. Marion Boyer, who fled the Ku Klux Klan, founded Blackdom in the early 1900s. The small utopian town supported a church, a newspaper, and many local businesses before finally disappearing into the history books.

There's something here for everyone. Whether it be Ibi Zoboi's story, inspired by soucouyants from Caribbean lore; Danny Lore's piece, which reimagines the Greek myth of Athena and Arachne; mine, inspired by a lifelong fascination with vampires; or the story by Charlotte Nicole Davis, who pulls ideas and insight from the Flint water crisis.

We hope these stories have inspired you!

—*Patrice Caldwell*

ABOUT THE CONTRIBUTORS

ELIZABETH ACEVEDO is a *New York Times* bestselling author. She is the winner of a National Book Award, Printz Award, *Boston Globe–Horn Book* Award, Pura Belpré Award, Walter Award, and *Los Angeles Times* Book Prize, amongst other accolades. Her books include *Beastgirl & Other Origin Myths* (YesYes, 2016), *The Poet X* (HarperCollins, 2018), *With the Fire on High* (HarperCollins, 2019), and *Clap When You Land* (HarperCollins, 2020).

Acevedo holds a BA in performing arts from the George Washington University and an MFA in creative writing from the University of Maryland. She is a National Poetry Slam Champion, and resides in Washington, DC, with her love. She can be reached on social media platforms @AcevedoWrites.

AMERIE is a Grammy-nominated singer-songwriter, producer, and writer of fiction, as well as the editor of the *New York Times* bestselling anthology *Because You Love to Hate Me*. The daughter of a

Korean artist and an American military officer, she was born in Massachusetts, was raised all over the world, and graduated from Georgetown University with a bachelor's in English. She lives mostly in her imagination, but also on Earth with her husband, her son, her parents and sister, and about seven billion other people.

PATRICE CALDWELL is a graduate of Wellesley College and the founder of People of Color in Publishing—a grassroots organization dedicated to supporting, empowering, and uplifting racially and ethnically marginalized members of the book publishing industry. Born and raised in Texas, Patrice was a children's book editor before becoming a literary agent.

She's been named to *Forbes*'s "30 Under 30" list, a *Publishers Weekly* Star Watch Honoree, and featured on Bustle's inaugural "Lit List" as one of ten women changing the book world. Visit her online at patricecaldwell.com, Twitter: @whimsicallyours, Instagram: @whimsicalaquarian.

DHONIELLE CLAYTON is the *New York Times* bestselling author of the Belles series, and the coauthor of the Tiny Pretty Things series and *The Rumor Game*. Her short stories have been included in the following anthologies: *The Radical Element: 12 Stories of Daredevils, Debutantes & Other Dauntless Girls* edited by Jessica Spotswood; *Unbroken: 13 Stories Starring Disabled Teens* edited by Marieke Nijkamp;

Meet Cute: Some People Are Destined to Meet; *Black Enough: Stories of Being Young & Black in America* edited by Ibi Zoboi; *Foreshadow* edited by Nova Ren Suma and Emily X.R. Pan; and *Vampires Never Get Old* edited by Zoraida Córdova and Natalie C. Parker.

She hails from the Washington, DC, suburbs on the Maryland side. Dhonielle earned an MA in children's literature from Hollins University and an MFA in writing for children at the New School. Dhonielle taught secondary school for several years and is a former elementary and middle school librarian. She is COO of the nonprofit We Need Diverse Books and cofounder of CAKE Literary, a creative kitchen whipping up decadent—and decidedly diverse— literary confections for middle grade, young adult, and women's fiction readers. Dhonielle is an avid traveler, and always on the hunt for magic and mischief. You can find her lurking online @brownbookworm on the Twitterverse and Instagram.

Photo Credit: Andrea Kwamya

After years of working in apparel and home furnishings, **J. MARCELLE CORRIE** is now a marketing professional in publishing. She writes young adult science fiction featuring people of her community and beyond. When she isn't writing or working, you can find her at bookish events across New York City. Visit her website at jmarcellecorrie.com and follow her on Twitter and Instagram @jmarcellecorrie.

SOMAIYA DAUD was born in a Midwestern city and spent a large part of her childhood and adolescence moving around. Like most writers, she started when she was young and never really stopped. Her love of all things books propelled her to get a degree in English literature (specializing in the medieval and early modern), and while she worked on her master's degree she doubled as a bookseller at Politics and Prose in Washington, DC, in their children's department. Determined to remain in school for as long as possible, she packed her bags in 2014 and moved to the West Coast to pursue a doctoral degree in English literature. Now she's writing a dissertation on Victorians, race, and theories of translation and world literature. Her debut novel, *Mirage*, was shortlisted for the Children's Africana Book Award and received starred reviews from *Booklist* and *School Library Journal*. You can find her on Twitter @SomaiyaDaud.

CHARLOTTE NICOLE DAVIS is the author of *The Good Luck Girls*, a young adult fantasy novel released in fall 2019 with Tor Teen. A graduate of the New School's writing for children MFA program, Charlotte loves comic book movies and books with maps in the front. She currently lives in Brooklyn with a cat with a crooked tail. Twitter: @cndwrites; Instagram: @cndwrites.

Photo Credit: Ismael Vásquez Bernabé

ALAYA DAWN JOHNSON is the author of seven novels for adults and young adults. Her most recent novel for adults, *Trouble the Saints*, was released in spring 2020 from Tor books. Her young adult novel *The Summer Prince* was longlisted for the National Book Award for Young People's Literature, while her novel *Love Is the Drug* won the Nebula Award for Middle Grade/Young Adult fiction. Her short stories have appeared in many magazines and anthologies, including *Best American Science Fiction and Fantasy 2015*, *Feral Youth*, *Three Sides of a Heart*, and *Zombies vs. Unicorns*. She has won two Nebula awards, the Cybils Award, and been nominated for the Indies Choice Award and Locus Award. She lives in Mexico City, where she has recently completed her master's degree in Mesoamerican studies at the Universidad Nacional Autónoma de México.

JUSTINA IRELAND is the author of *Dread Nation*, a *New York Times* bestseller and an ALA Best Fiction for Young Adults Top Ten selection. Her other books for children and teens include *Vengeance Bound*, *Promise of Shadows*, and the Star Wars novel *Lando's Luck*. She enjoys dark chocolate and dark humor and is not too proud to admit that she's still afraid of the dark. She lives with her husband, kid, dog, and cats in Maryland. You can visit her online at justinaireland.com.

DANNY LORE is a queer Black writer/ editor raised in Harlem and currently based in the Bronx. They've worked in comic and gaming shops since the beginning of time. They've had their short fiction published by FIYAH, Podcastle, Fireside, Nightlight, EFNIKS.com, and more. Their comics work includes *Queen of Bad Dreams* for Vault Comics, *Quarter Killer* for Comixology, and *James Bond* for Dynamite Comics in December 2019. They have short comics in *Dead Beats* and *The Good Fight*. They edited *The Good Fight* anthology and *The Wilds* (Black Mask comics). They live with their amazing wife and doubly amazing cat.

LEATRICE "ELLE" MᶜKINNEY, writing as L.L. McKinney, is a poet and active member of the kidlit community. She's an advocate for equality and inclusion in publishing and the creator of the hashtag #WhatWoCWritersHear. Elle's also a gamer, Blerd, and adamant Hei Hei stan. She spends her free time plagued by her cat—Sir Chester Fluffmire Boopsnoot Purrington Wigglebottom Flooferson III, Esquire, Baron o' Butterscotch, or #SirChester for short. The critically acclaimed *A Blade So Black* is her debut novel, and *A Dream So Dark* is its sequel. Find her on Twitter @ElleOnWords, Instagram @ll_mckinney, and Facebook at ElleOnWords. Learn more about her by visiting her website, llmckinney.com.

DANIELLE PAIGE is the *New York Times* bestselling author of the Dorothy Must Die series, the Stealing Snow series, and the graphic novel *Mera: Tidebreaker.* In addition to writing young adult books, she works in the television industry, where she's received a Writers Guild of America Award and was nominated for several Daytime Emmys. She is a graduate of Columbia University and currently lives in New York City.

REBECCA ROANHORSE is a Nebula and Hugo Award—winning speculative fiction writer and the recipient of the 2018 Campbell Award for Best New Writer. Her short fiction has also been a finalist for the Sturgeon, Locus, and World Fantasy Awards. She is the author of the Sixth World series, which includes *Trail of Lightning* (selected as an Amazon, Barnes & Noble, *Library Journal*, and NPR best book of 2018, and a Nebula, Hugo, and Locus Award finalist) and *Storm of Locusts.* Her middle grade novel, *Race to the Sun*, is part of the Rick Riordan Presents imprint. She also penned *Resistance Reborn* as part of the Journey to Star Wars: The Rise of Skywalker series.

Her short fiction can be found in *Apex Magazine, New Suns, The Mythic Dream, Hungry Hearts*, and various other anthologies. Her nonfiction can be found in *Uncanny Magazine, Strange Horizons*, and *How I Resist: Activism and Hope for a New Generation* (Macmillan). She lives in northern New Mexico with her husband, daughter, and pups. Find more at rebeccaroanhorse.com and on Twitter @RoanhorseBex.

KAREN STRONG is the author of *Just South of Home*. A graduate of the University of Georgia, Karen is a STEM advocate and worked in the information technology industry for several years as a software engineer, systems analyst, and technical writer. She now spends her early mornings writing fiction. You can visit her online at karen-strong.com.

ASHLEY WOODFOLK has loved reading and writing for as long as she can remember. She graduated from Rutgers University with a bachelor of arts in English and works in children's book publishing. She writes from a sunny Brooklyn apartment, where she lives with her cute husband and her cuter dog. Ashley is the author of *The Beauty That Remains* and *When You Were Everything*.

IBI ZOBOI is the *New York Times* bestselling author of two novels for young adults, *Pride* and *American Street*, a finalist for the National Book Award; as well as *My Life as an Ice Cream Sandwich*, her middle grade debut, and a forthcoming biography for young readers about science fiction pioneer Octavia Butler. She also edited the anthology *Black Enough: Stories of Being Young & Black in America*. Ibi holds an MFA from the Vermont College of Fine Arts. Born in Haiti and raised in New York City, she now lives with her family in New Jersey.

ACKNOWLEDGMENTS

I often talk about how *A Phoenix First Must Burn* is, in so many ways, a book of my heart. Putting this anthology together was a dream fulfilled; I am so grateful that it exists. I couldn't have done it alone as it wouldn't have been possible without the love and support of so many people.

First and foremost, many thanks to my family. Especially to my parents, who ensured that young me had stories about people who looked like me, who taught me to love myself, my skin, and my body. Who time and time again pushed me to believe in myself, to actualize my dreams. Daddy, thank you for saying that I didn't have discipline but that I did have talent I shouldn't waste and, if I wanted my dreams to come true, I'd have to set aside the time to ensure they did. That conversation changed everything. Special love to Granny and Papa and Uncle Kokayi for always asking about my writing. And, of course, love and gratitude to my siblings: Kamau, Zakiya, Aissatou, and Kaira. You're the ones I do this for.

Thank you so much, Pete Knapp and Kendra Levin. Pete, you believed in me at a critical time. Thank you for putting your all into developing and selling this project, for cheering me on at every stage. Kendra, your editorial guidance was invaluable. To be an editor working with another editor in the way that I did was a remarkable experience. You taught me so much, and without you these stories wouldn't shine as brightly as they do. Thank you to Sara Megibow for taking me under your wing. I really appreciate you looking out for me and this project in the ways you have. Same to Aneeka Kalia and Dana Leydig. Aneeka, you worked on this project from the beginning and when you and Dana became team editorial, I knew this book would be in the best of hands. Thank you.

Thank you to my cover goddesses, Samira Iravani and Ashe Samuels. Thank you to Ken Wright, Vanessa DeJesús, Felicity Vallence, Christina Colangelo, Caitlin Whalen, Brianna Lockhart, Venessa Carson, Kim Ryan, the copyediting team—Marinda Valenti, Krista Ahlberg, Janet Pascal, and Abigail Powers, I cannot thank you enough!—and everyone else at Viking Children's Books and Penguin Teen who championed this book.

To the contributors without whom this book would've never existed, thank you for trusting in me and for writing some of the best, boldest, and bravest stories I've ever read. Special thanks to Dhonielle Clayton and Ibi Zoboi for all the advice on putting the anthology together. And to Dahlia Adler and Elsie Chapman, who also talked to me about their own experiences editing anthologies.

To my friends who supported me in so many ways, thank you for always believing in me—especially Arvin Ahmadi, who cheered me on as I wrote my own story on a steady diet of the best chocolate croissants Paris had to offer. Cristina

Arreola, thank you for your support and hosting the cover reveal; Akshaya Raman, who got all my late night/early morning panic texts; Adam Silvera for having such a great eye re: all things cover related (phoenix books for life); and my #LiteralBlackFriends, who are always there to cheer me up, encourage me, bandage me (literally) when I've fallen, and share bad recorder covers of songs (I'll never get the *Jurassic Park* one out of my head . . . thanks).

And, finally, to the bloggers, the bookstagrammers, booktubers, librarians, booksellers, and teachers who have been cheering and posting about this book from the beginning, thank you. Last but never least, to all the readers—thank you for the love, for ensuring with your support that stories like these continue to exist in the world. I hope you've enjoyed these stories of my heart.

START A CONVERSATION!

Turn the page
for a list of questions for discussion.

DISCUSSION QUESTIONS

1. How does each protagonist grow into showing their personal power? Consider the ways power manifests externally and internally.

2. How does each story confirm or conflict with your ideas of Black girlhood?

3. Think about adventure stories you have read. They often follow a cycle wherein a central figure experiences tests and trials they must overcome in order to reveal hidden talents or strengths. Which of the tales would you consider to be an adventure? What hidden talents or strengths are revealed throughout the course of each story?

4. Which stories capture elements of spiritualism that resemble those of the African diaspora such as Santeria, candomblé, or voodoo?

5. What conflicts does each of the protagonists face, and how do the conflicts shape them? Consider internal and external conflicts.

6. Many science fiction and fantasy stories comment on societal ills that exist in the real world, such as racism or sexism. Which of the stories do you consider to be a social commentary? How? Why?

7. What elements of mythology or folklore belonging to the people of the African diaspora can you find in the stories? Consider fantastical and supernatural beasts you may be familiar with from other stories, such as mermaids and vampires. Which elements and entities are the same? Which are different?

8. What types of deities are present in these stories? What powers do they have? How can you connect them to religious philosophies of the past or present? How do they affect the characters in each story?

9. What role does environment or setting have in shaping the events and characters of each tale? How does changing time or geographic location affect your ability to interpret the events of each story?

10. Examine family relationships in any of the stories. What conflicts and connections exist between each protagonist and their family and/or friends? What barriers exist between them?

11. What is the role of fate or free will in each story? Which of the forces is stronger?

12. Each of the tales captures moments of resistance and hope. Which are more transformative: moments when resistance is required, or those when we are called to maintain a hopeful position?

These discussion questions were written by Julia E. Torres. Julia is a veteran language arts teacher librarian in Denver, Colorado. Julia facilitates teacher development workshops rooted in the areas of anti-racist education, equity, and access in literacy and librarianship, and education as a practice of liberation. Julia works with students and teachers locally and around the country with the goal of empowering them to use literacy to fuel resistance and positive social transformation. Julia also serves on several local and national boards and committees promoting educational equity and progressivism. She is the current NCTE Secondary Representative-at-Large, a Book Love Foundation board member, and Educator Collaborative Book Ambassador.

Look for Patrice Caldwell's
paranormal romance anthology

ETERNALLY YOURS